BUILDING BRIDGES

BRIDGES BROTHERS, BOOK 1

LIA FAIRCHILD

ALSO BY LIA FAIRCHILD

Compulsive

Liar

In Search of Lucy

Circle in the Sand

Vigil-Annie

Emma vs. the Tech Guy

Special Delivery

Home for Christmas

High Maintenance

LOGAN

Nothing like waking up to the smell of bacon and sweaty socks on a Saturday morning. Ryder is lying next to me—head at the foot of the bed, feet under my nose—on top of the covers. He looks small in a pair of gray sweat pants and one of my old T-shirts. I lie there a moment, grateful for a good-night's sleep. Another one where I don't remember the nightmares. I'm only left with the clues: rapid heartbeat, sweaty forehead, lurking sense of fear.

I turn on my side and face my thirteen-year-old half-brother, pondering how my life went from sleeping across from guys who had my back under the most harrowing of circumstances to playing manny to the family I once left behind.

This is not the first time Ryder has snuck into my

bed at some point during the night. He might be a dare devil during the day but sleeping is a different story; I guess we have that in common. His nightmares are different from mine, though—and the person he used to climb in with at night is never going to be there for him again.

I suppose it happens more than it should for a kid his age, but this isn't a normal situation. It's pretty screwed up.

I shove his socked feet a few inches away from my smell zone. I won't admit it to the little runt, but I don't mind him here so much. Especially because I'm fighting my own demons, so I get needing the company of family. And, I know this guy better than I know any of my three brothers. I don't give a damn that we had different mothers. I changed his disgusting diapers, pushed him around in one of those plastic cars while he pretended he was in the Indy 500. He's taken a hard hit from life and keeps it all bottled up inside.

Ryder's long eyelashes flutter and slowly open. He looks so much like my stepmother, Nina, I almost choke on the lump in my throat.

He squints at me with tight lips that say, Are you mad? Considering his own damn bed is literally on the other side of the wall, and I somehow got roped into moving back in to help the family, I should be. But instead, I smile back, and though I'm not sure what, I try to think of something to say—anything to take his mind from losing his mother and dealing with this craptastic family we've been left with. But like I said, I know what he's going through, and now it's like I'm living it all over again. But none of those other stoic losers are going to be there for Ryder...or each other for that matter. So it's up to me.

I inhale a deep breath and let it out. Putting words to feelings is not a strong suit among men in my family. Most of us are hovering at precision-level sarcasm or just plain denial.

Ryder flips over so his head is on the same end as mine. "Would you rather eat a bowl full of scabs or lick a dog's ass?"

"Dude! Too early." I rub my hand over my jaw and then through my hair.

After a few minutes of silence, I decide to investigate the reason behind his bed invasion. "Did you have a bad dream last night?"

He shakes his head and his face turns solemn.

"What is it then?"

"Is it true?" he asks, tucking his hands under the pillow and staring at me with wide, cobalt eyes.

My brows rise in response as I stall for time. His intense stare tells me I can't feign ignorance. I know what he's talking about. The rumors started last week. Given they'd waited almost three months after the death of my stepmother, Nina, and my aunt Sheri, I thought maybe they'd let it pass this time. And when I saw some bullshit post on Justice's social media page, I'd hoped it would fade away...like it did when my mom died.

"It's small town mentality," I whisper, giving the response I'm sure Nina would say if she were here. "And small-minded people." We don't exactly live in a small town, though. Ventura: the less attractive, step-sister to Santa Barbara.

Ryder lifts up on one elbow, shoots me squinty eyes, and then sits up all the way, facing forward. "So…it is true?"

I sit up next to him, my stiff body protesting. "What exactly did you hear, Ry?"

He turns his eyes to the ceiling as if he isn't able to say the words, but I have to know what is going through his mind if I'm going to help him. A moment later he speaks.

"We were doing a chem lab, and I heard Arianna at the table behind me." He draws in a deep breath and sighs it out.

During the pause I cut in. "She the one giving you the chubs?" I smirk and nod like it's all good to be sporting wood in the middle of class.

"No…shut up and listen." His lips pull into a tight line. "She was telling everyone in her group that our family is cursed. She heard her parents talking and saying how all the women in our family die or leave."

Shit. "It's just gossip, man. People get bored with their own pathetic lives." I get up from the bed, recover from a slight stumble, and grab the shirt that's on the chair in the corner. He watches me but doesn't say a word, which tells me I'm supposed to keep going. "Her mom's probably a drunken whore," I say under my breath.

His eyes go wide, and his spine spikes straight up. "Really?"

"No, forget I said that." With his brows knitted, I can tell he's thinking about whom he can share that tasty treat with because I had to shoot off my big mouth. "Hey!" I point a finger at him. "Don't repeat that or I'll kick your ass in front of all those weenie little middle schoolers." He shakes his head, and I come over to the side of the bed and sit. I try to ignore the ache but rub at my thigh reflexively. "Look, some people have nothing better to do than to make shit up to entertain themselves. Trust me."

I'd heard the same crap when my mom died of cancer when I was a couple years younger than Ryder. Like our family was cursed or something because we have this eerie habit of losing woman. It humiliated me for weeks until the next scandal took the spotlight. But when my dad remarried, Nina couldn't have done more for Mason and me. Now I don't give a crap what people say about my family. I already know what we are—falling apart.

I throw the shirt over my head and pull it down as I toss a quick glance at him to gauge his reaction.

He jumps off the bed and plants himself right in front of me, chin jutting up toward my face, a decidedly angry crease in the skin between his brows, which I'm not sure I've ever seen. I try not to focus on the fact that no kid should look this wrecked. "Mom and Aunt Sheri are dead...and your mom died, too." His eyes dart away for a moment as if the fuzzy picture he was trying to see comes into focus.

I wasn't sure if that was a question for me to answer, and I didn't know what to say.

We stare into each other's eyes for mere seconds before his glass over. I pull him into a hug. "It was an accident, Ry. A horrible, terrible car accident. That's the only reason." I feel him nodding into my chest. Or maybe the little turd burglar was rubbing the snot off his nose.

I grasp his shoulders and push him back so I can see his face. Steeling himself as he always does, he draws in a cleansing breath and stands taller. I palm the top of his light brown mop of hair. "Let's get some breakfast before those jack-asses eat all the bacon. It's Saturday breakfast," I say brightly.

Ryder heads for the door, but as he grabs the handle, he turns back to me with a slight grin. "Hey, what about Grandma Weezer?"

My lids fall closed a moment, and I drop my chin to my chest. He desperately wants this to not be true. Hell, for all I know, maybe it is true. Or maybe it's a horrible twist of fate or fucking karma because the fact is the Bridges men have never been worthy of the women in their lives. I know the reality I need to impart on my little bro—that life sucks. But that will have to wait until after bacon.

"Sorry, Ry. Grandma Weezer is my mom's mother. She's not on the Bridges' side." He doesn't need to know our dad's mom—Gramps's wife—took off when Dad and my Uncle Frank were teens.

"Oh, yeah," he says, and his shoulders slump as he walks out the door.

I follow Ryder out to the kitchen, expecting a boatload of brash Bridges to be fighting for a spot at the table as Gramps hunches over our old stove. The cold silence should have been a clue, but instead, the reality of the lifeless scene slaps me in the face. Ryder stops and I press up to his back and lay a hand on his shoulder. We both gaze into the almost empty kitchen where Gramps sits alone at the table, scooping the last bit of eggs from his plate. Just to the left of him sits a large bowl of scrambled eggs and a plate of crispy brown bacon. Clean, unused plates are neatly stacked next to the food, and sparkling clear juice glasses sit in a row on the other side.

"There's plenty," he grumbles with a nod.

The sound of the television in the other room floats into my ears and I knit my brows. Nina never allowed the TV to be on during Saturday breakfast. My chest tightens. I turn and glance to the doorway, catching a glimpse of two denim-clad legs stretched from the couch over to an ottoman. Most likely that's my uncle Frank, because sitting next to the ottoman with his knees drawn up to his chest is my cousin Colton. My uncle and cousins moved in a few weeks after Nina and my aunt Sheri passed, unable to cope on their own.

"Where is everyone?" Ryder says to Gramps.

Just like I helped raise Ryder, my granddad helped

raise me, especially after my own mother died. His eyes shoot right to mine with what feels like a warning. Keeping my gaze, he lifts a hand. "They're around. Just get yourself some food, Rebel Ryder." That is the nickname Gramps gave to Ryder because he's a crazy little shit.

I hand Ryder a plate, and he reaches out for it slowly. I can see realization dawn in his eyes. "This sucks! They promised."

I should have thought to prepare him for how different life would be without the two women who held us all together. Saturday breakfast had always been a constant in our house. Loud, chaotic, but full of love and laughter, the two families of Edward (my dad) and Frank (my uncle) Bridges gathered together to share food and our lives. Of course, we all had things that kept us away sometimes, and Uncle Frank's family couldn't always make it, but it was never like this. Three months. That's all it took for the Bridges men to prove they weren't shit without the women who raised us and kept us going.

Of course, I didn't assume everyone could make it, but this is ridiculous. And where the hell is our dad? I know he's not at work because Mason says he's still showing up late and cutting out early—leaving the eldest Bridges brother to pick up the slack. None of us has the balls to ask what the hell he's been doing lately, though.

My eyes catch the pink juice cup on the counter next

to the sink. It's full. A knot forms in my gut, and I take in a measured breath. "Gramps, where's Belle?"

As slim of a chance it is, I hope she's at the park with my dad. Sometimes he takes her there to give Uncle Frank a break. Raising two kids while you're unemployed, freeloading, and lazing on the couch with your hand down your pants must be freaking exhausting.

"I'm not running a damn day care, Logan."

I pull my lips tight, and before I can voice my annoyance, Gramps shoots me with, "She's in her box."

That statement alone could earn us a visit from Child Protective Services, but it's not as bad as it sounds. Belle took a couple of packing boxes when they moved in and made a little fort for herself to hide in. Her brother, Colton, is the only one she lets in there with her. Probably because she knows he won't talk much.

I turn back to look at Colton in the living room as Ryder fills his plate. At just eight years old, our fair-haired cousin has barely uttered a handful of words since he was told his mother was never coming home. He reserves most of his speaking for school, which he does to survive.

I watch as he appears to be watching television, but the look in his eyes tells me whatever's on the screen is not even registering.

"Get some of that juice, Rebel Ryder," I hear Gramps say.

I can't seem to tear my eyes from Colton. I know Ryder is hurting and he needs me, but Colton looks so lost and Uncle Frank is completely useless. Yes, he's got to be hurting like hell to have lost his wife, but we're all struggling here. And if I'm being honest, Frank was a has-been before Aunt Sheri died. Part of me wants to grab him and shake the sense back into him. Scream at him to be strong for Colton and Belle.

I turn and give Ryder a nod to make sure he's okay, and I see him sitting right next to Gramps even though the table is surrounded by empty chairs.

"I'll be right back," I say to them before heading out of the kitchen. I go the long way around so I can stop by the "bunk room" and check on Belle. That's the den we made up for Colton and Belle's bedroom.

The hardwood floor of their room is barely visible under the piles of toys, clothes, and trash. Two large boxes form a teepee shape in the back corner of the room. I don't want to get her riled up so I pass stealthily by just to make sure she's okay. I catch a glimpse of a tiny pink sneaker sticking out from her hiding spot, and a few incoherent words from her adorable voice echo from inside. For a moment, I try to imagine how my three-year-old cousin will turn out, the only female in a house full of stooges. Though I know it's ridiculous, I send a silent prayer that what people say about my family isn't true. For Belle's sake.

At the end of the hall, I turn and head back to the living room. I cross in front of Frank and Colton, stalling when I'm right in front of them, blocking the TV. Neither of them blinks or even looks at me. I continue on to Gramps's recliner chair and take a seat. I see now they are watching *Pawn Stars*, my granddad's favorite show, which means neither of them bothered to change the channel.

"Hey, Colt. You smell that bacon?"

No response.

When I glance up to Frank, he harrumphs as if I'm wasting my time. I ignore him and slide down from the chair to sit on the ground so Colton and I are eye level. I tap on his black Nikes.

"Buddy, are you hungry?"

His crystal blue eyes turn in my direction and grab hold of me. He's asking—no pleading—for something much more than food. I work to keep my expression calm and comforting, but I'm pissed that I feel so help-less, and I'm more pissed that Frank is wallowing in his own pain instead of helping his kids.

Colton's always been an incredibly smart boy, but pain and grief have given his face a look of maturity that saddens me. His eyes pull from me as if he senses I'm no use to him. I follow his gaze down into his lap where he's holding his mom's old smart phone. Obviously, it's been disabled, but Colton clings to it—has since the day we lost them—scrolls through her camera roll a dozen times a day looking at her selfies and images of her and the kids. Funny, there aren't too many of Frank in there.

My stomach grumbles so loud Colton looks up at me, and I see him fighting a smile. "This is your fault you know? I'm waiting for you to eat." I almost quote my stepmother's motto: *No one eats till all asses are in the seats,* but I think better of it. Instead, I stand and take a different approach. I reach my hand down and pull out my authoritative voice. "Let's go, Colton."

He glances to his dad who doesn't flinch and then looks back up at me. I don't waver, only pull my lips tighter before saying, "Now."

He gets up and I can't help but feel a little parental satisfaction. I put my hand on his shoulder and guide him back the way I came so we can get his sister. Before we reach the room, a loud crash and a piercing wail send my heart straight to my stomach.

2

LOGAN

The double doors of the hospital slide open, pulling me into the not-so-unfamiliar setting. When you grow up in a house of all the boys, especially ones as crazy and completely devoid of common sense as we were, you spend a lot of time in places like this. Man, those were some good times, though.

As I look for my uncle, I remind myself this is Belle we're talking about. I can't help but feel partially responsible for her being here. She's not even four yet, still just a baby, and we all let her down. When we raced into her bedroom, it was like she was a tiny leaf among giant redwoods, and we let her fall. Her ankle had already swollen up pretty damn good, but amazingly she was barely whimpering. My tough little cousin being raised by a bunch of loud, obnoxious oafs. I can see her future —all dressed up for her senior prom, probably with her dress unknowingly tucked into the back of her underwear, wobbling on some tacky, spiked pumps and swearing like a sailor.

I head to the intake desk, but before I reach it, I see Colton sitting outside a room down a short hallway. He's looking down at the phone in his hand. It's the way he self-soothes. I'd emailed my mom's brother in Kentucky who's a shrink, and he said for now, just let him do what makes him feel better.

I assume Uncle Frank is still in with Belle and the doctor, so I take a seat next to him and try to think of something to say. Selfishly, all I can think is, *Why is this shit up to me?* How have I become the Dr. Phil of our family? It's one of the reasons I left home in the first place. And it's not like I don't have my own issues to contend with.

I run my hands through my hair and rest my head back against the wall behind us, giving Colton a little more time to look at pictures of his mom and sister. *Hell, who am I kidding?* I'm stalling for time and scrambling for words that don't sound lame. I can't blame this on Frank; we all know he hasn't been in his right mind. But this can't happen again. Things are going to change even if I'm the only one who has to make that happen.

I turn toward Colton, ready to tell him everything is going to be fine when the door slides open and a young woman emerges. She catches my eye for a moment before shutting the door behind her. I jump up and inadvertently land right in her face. And, I might add, she's not in the least fazed by me invading her personal space.

"How's Belle?" I ask.

She raises a dark brow and tilts her head like I can read her mind.

Maybe I can because I answer her silent question. "I'm her cousin and I help take care of her."

For a moment, our gazes lock as if we are sizing each other up, but the power seems to be in her favor. Two wide, gray eyes take hold of mine as if they've just discovered something. Then her lids drop, and she moves aside.

"Belle's going to be fine. She's a sweetie." Though her words are endearing, her body language and expression are subdued. When I don't say anything, she narrows her eyes at me and brings a file to her chest before taking a few steps away. "The doctor will give you the details," she says over her shoulder.

Something in those narrowed eyes hits a chord with me and I call out, "Wait a sec."

She stops and turns, black shoulder-length hair falling forward, revealing streaks of purple painted on the ends. The contrast of her in this environment throws me, but I ask my question anyway. "Sorry, I just thought… Do we know each other?"

She steps closer, her lips pursed as she stares me down as if she's unsure of her answer. "You don't remember me?" she says finally.

I can't tell if she's messing with me, but there's something damn familiar about her. "I…don't know. Should I?"

I hear a vibrating sound she doesn't seem to notice at first. Then she averts her eyes and backs away. "I'm sorry… I've got to go."

She walks away, leaving me baffled and staring at her firm little backside, which clearly is not camouflaged by the teal green hospital pants I never realized were so sexy.

The door opens again, causing me to drag my eyes away from her ass. A stocky, elderly man makes his way out followed by Frank, who stands in the doorway. Colton jumps up and runs up to his dad. "Okay, Colton. Sissy's asking for you." He turns to usher Colton into the room, and I say, "Hey, what about me?"

"We're fine. It's just a hairline fracture. You can go."

I let out a half laugh and follow him into the room. I don't give a shit if he thinks I don't trust him even though it's partially true. But I'm not going home without seeing my Belly Bean. I gave her the nickname when she was born. Aunt Sheri sent me a bunch of pictures, and each one, she was wrapped in a pink or other light-colored blanket. It reminded me of those flavored jelly beans.

In the room, Belle is sitting up, wearing what looks like a black boot with straps.

"Hey, Belly Bean," I say and then eye Frank, questioningly.

"It's a walking cast," he says. "She has a hairline fracture that should heal quickly, but we'll need to carry her as much as possible until she gets used to walking on this thing." In barely a whisper, he mouths, "Pain in the ass," and shakes his head.

"Yay, you carry me." Belle reaches her arms out to me. "Woggan! L-Logan," she repeats, practicing the L sound she struggles with.

"We're not leaving just yet, baby," Frank says.

"Now I'm just like L-Logan." She points and then taps her boot.

I start to laugh at that, but before I can even process the implication of dealing with this boot in our family, I do a double take at Belle's hair. When I carried her to Frank's car and placed her in her car seat, her hair was a ratty mess that looked like a cow sucked on it. Now it's in this smooth braid thing that starts on one side of her head and curves around to the opposite side.

Belle points to her wrist and says, "I want Maui. She pulls at a colorful woven bracelet I haven't seen before.

"Maui?" I question, as I look at her and take her wrist in my hand.

"No! Maui," she says insistently.

I look down and run my fingers across the bracelet. It's pretty but there's something soothing about it. I close my eyes and do it again. Maybe it's some sort of healing thing. When Belle's whining pulls my attention from the bracelet, I look at Frank, who is now on his phone. It looks like he's texting.

"What is she talking about?" I ask him.

"I don't know," he says without looking up.

Colton is hugging his dad's leg as Frank texts like he's waiting at a bus stop or in line to buy coffee.

"Uncle Frank," I say louder. "What's with the hair and the bracelet?"

He looks up like he's just finally heard what I said. "It was that nurse."

"Nurse...Maui...I want Maui. She fixed my hair pretty."

Frank slips his phone into his pocket. "She's gone and we're going home soon. I'll buy you some ice cream."

That is Frank's answer to everything. Even after the damn funeral, he bought the kids ice cream.

Belle's eyes water, and she leans forward, resting her palms on the boot. "My ouwi hurts and I need Maui."

Something in her voice compels me to head for the door. I stop with my hand on the handle and look at Frank. "Why don't I just go get the nurse, and maybe she can figure out what Belle's talking about."

Frank begins to protest when I feel the door push against me and I step aside.

"Maui," Belle squeals.

The nurse I talked to before strolls in right past me as if I don't exist.

"I came to say goodbye to my little belle of the ball." She must be smiling because Belle is beaming as they look at each other.

The nurse stands with her hands on her hips, and I notice a tattoo of music notes on her right wrist. When I look up, I spot part of a tattoo right above her collar, disappearing down the back of her shirt. Between the hair, tattoos, and attitude, our nurse certainly doesn't look the part.

I sidle up next to her, and she moves closer to the bed. I get the feeling she's purposely ignoring Frank and me. If I wasn't so mesmerized by her presence, I might be annoyed.

"I'm going to pull the car around," Frank says. "I'll take Colt with me." He grabs his hand and leads him to the door. I give them a quick nod before turning my attention back to the nurse, who is now retying the bracelet on Belle's wrist.

"Now if this comes loose again," she tells her, finally glancing at me, "I'm sure your daddy or Logan will tie it back on for you."

Hearing my name catches me off guard, and I make a weird grunting noise. Now I know for sure I somehow know this woman.

"I have one more thing for you before you go," she says and reaches into her pocket. She pulls out a sheet of colorful stickers and hands it to Belle, telling her to pick one while she talks to me for a moment.

We move aside toward the door, and I can't help but smile, wondering what this mysterious girl wants from me and how she knows me. I'm not typically overly confident when it comes to women, but something about the look she just gave me feels very familiar. She's not exactly my type, but there is that pull of sexual tension. At least I think that's what it is.

But to my surprise, she leans in and with an intense

whisper says, "I think you're neglecting Belle, and I'm seriously considering calling in a report to CPS."

My suave smile fades and my mouth falls open. My heart rocks inside my chest like she has a gun pointed to it. All I can manage to say is, "What the hell?" which probably doesn't help our case much.

She leans back, giving me some much-needed space. My mind spins as her words echo in my head. I glance from her to Belle and back to her again. Is this chick insane? She doesn't know anything about us.

"Her hair was a knotted mess," she continues with one hand on her hip. "Have you not heard of a brush? And not only that, she has a cold sore in her mouth, too many scrapes and bruises for a little girl her age, and when I asked if she'd had breakfast today, she said no."

Holy shit! I can see how that looks bad to her. But neglect? I panic and consider running to get Uncle Frank, but he'd only make things worse.

As I internally struggle through the turmoil she's just whipped up in my gut, she crosses her arms over her chest. Talk about brutal beauty. It's like getting run over by a Porsche. I take a moment to regain my composure.

"Well, Logan?"

Watching her lips form my name, I draw in a sharp breath when recollection hits. "Wait a minute. I do know you. We went to high school together."

Though her head shakes from side to side, and her lips pull into a thin seam, I can see the confirmation in her eyes. It's clear to me those soft gray orbs have some stories to tell, and right now they're telling me I probably wasn't her favorite person.

"That's right," she says. "And it's about the only reason I'm standing here right now instead of on the phone."

Though she's rattled my cage, I firm my stance. "We're not neglecting her." My tone is sharp, stern, but then I soften and lower my voice. "Frank might not be father of the year," I say, knowing I'm being generous. "But he's not abusing her, no one is. She's a happy girl."

"She might be happy, but she's not being taken care of properly, I can tell that much. And that's called neglect."

"Please don't do this..." *Dammit.*

"You don't even remember my name, do you?"

"Sure I do. Your name is—"

"Her name is Maui," Belle says, still looking at the stickers.

I crack a slim smile of relief. "Mollie," I say and release a breath. It's a good thing I'm well-versed interpreting Belle, even if it took me longer this time.

A memory flashes through my mind. "Now I remember. You were my fake wife in that child development class senior year. Mollie...Fisher?"

She plays with a bracelet on her wrist similar to the one Belle is wearing, but it's sandwiched between two metal ones. "Yeah I was, until your skanky little cheerleader girlfriend told me we needed to switch partners."

I had no idea that happened. "I thought you switched because you thought I was a douche."

Her brows tick up. "Yeah well..."

I reach out and touch the middle bracelet on her wrist. Like Belle's, it's colorful and looks like someone had woven it by hand. "Did you make this?" I say softly. "It's pretty."

She lowers her arm so I'm forced to take my hand away. "Listen, I take my job very seriously, and my number one concern is that little girl."

"Good, so is mine."

"Just because we knew each other doesn't mean I won't do the right thing. I know your family's having a hard time, but that doesn't mean she has to suffer." Her wispy gray eyes, which are even more stunning now with the sunlight coming through the window high-lighting them, no longer appear angry. They're almost pleading with me, as if she wants me to convince her.

I put my hands in my pockets, bend my head down, and hook my gaze onto hers. "Mollie, I understand your position, and I think you're an incredible woman for what you do as a nurse and for how much you care. But I swear to you, we all love Belle. This was just one of those stupid accidents that happen." I sigh and shift from foot to foot. "We're doing the best—" Her eyes narrow and I correct. "I know we can do better, and I promise you we will. I swear to you we all love her so much, and we will take better care of her."

I watch her chest move up and down as I speak to her, and it looks as though she believes me. But I also want to make sure that she trusts me, so I pull out my phone, unlock the screen, and click on the contacts before handing it over to her. "Give me your number, and I'll text you so you can text me or call me anytime."

It feels like an eternity before she blinks and then reaches out for my phone. She keys in her number and hands it back. "I want to hear from you soon," she tells me with a pointed tone.

"Thank you." I grin, but she doesn't return it, and I'm okay with that because relief fills me. "Frank's probably out there with the car," I say, almost like a question.

She turns from me and takes her attention over to Belle. "Did you pick a sticker?"

Belle nods and says, "Can I have that one?"

Mollie takes the sticker and presses it to the back of Belle's hand, and she lets out a little giggle.

"What do you say, Belle?" I tell her.

"Thank you, Maui."

"Try to say, Mol-lee," I say.

"Mowl-ee."

"Better," Mollie says with what looks like a genuine smile. "And you're welcome. Now let's get you out of here in style. I'm going to go get a wheelchair for you."

Mollie looks at me one last time as she walks to the door, and this swirl of emotions mixes in my gut. I have no time to analyze what they are; I only know none of them is animosity. "Thank you, Mollie...for everything."

In the car, I send Mollie a quick text so she has my number. I don't turn on music like I normally do. I roll down the window and let the fall wind clear my head. Clouds drift over the sun, and I zone out and think about what I need to do. It's a quick conclusion. It's what I have to do because I'm the only one I trust at this point. It's not my place to tell Frank how to live his life, but if my father doesn't get through to him, then I guess it's up to me. I stare at the cars in front of me and try to think back to senior year of high school. That girl with the quiet confidence and the sweet smile I always wondered about but barely said two words to. It was so long ago, but now that I know it's her, she doesn't look all that different. She might have tattoos and black and purple hair, but that sweet girl is still in there.

My phone pings on the center console as I'm pulling up to the curb in front of our house. It's a text from Mollie. *Text me tomorrow.*

3

LOGAN

I spend most of the morning cleaning the house and the yard, but with only my two younger brothers to help and months' worth of crap to deal with, we haven't made a lot of progress. We're not at hoarders-in-a-trailer-park level, but we definitely need to make some changes. And ones that stick. Nina had everything so organized, making sure everyone did their part. Now, it's a national freakin' holiday if someone does the dishes without a fight or the trash in the kitchen isn't overflowing. Once again, I fight my feelings of regret and selfishness that just a few short years ago, I was fulfilling my destiny, on the road to something more than being a housekeeper and babysitter. It's a crappy attitude, but I'm only human.

As I walk down the hall and survey each room, a vision of Mollie floats through my brain. I'm seeing everything through her eyes, knowing instinctively what she would expect. I can't help but wonder if I'm doing all this only for Belle and our family, or if a part of me really is a selfish prick who wants to impress the hot nurse. *No, screw that.* I've never given a damn about impressing any woman. It was the look in her eyes that did me in. I can't see that disappointment again. It gutted me like I've never experienced. And she was right; I knew it the moment the words came from her perfectly plump lips.

I'd waited until late last night to tell Frank and my dad what had happened. Frank snarled and said, "She didn't report it because she doesn't have shit on us." Like we'd just pulled off a jewelry heist. I shouldn't have been surprised by his reaction. People say dealing with death changes you, but Aunt Sheri dying didn't change Frank. Unemployment did. A man needs to provide and take care of his family. It's in his nature. It's in my nature. And though I tell people I left home to escape my family and the business, a part of me knew I needed a bigger purpose—something that called to me and made me feel like a man. The Army did that for me, a hundred times over. And now, some might think I'm hiding out here, not willing to face the broken man I became. The one I'd been trying to build back up the last few years. I can live with that for now because my focus can't be on me any longer.

And as fate would have it, my phone pings with a missed call from Prescott Jennings, the only other living soul who was there that day, more evidence of my cowardice. I thought he'd given up on me. Last time he tried to reach out was almost a year ago.

I step into my dad's bedroom to check on Justice and Ryder, who are trying to match up socks from the mound that's been growing in a chair for the last two months. I see they've dumped them onto the floor and are sitting across from each other doing their normal razz-each-other-until-someone-cracks routine.

Ryder picks one up and sniffs it. "Are you sure these are clean?"

It's moments like these when I know he hasn't totally lost his innocence.

Justice looks up at me in the doorway. "I don't see why I have to be stuck here doing this crap." My other half-brother is sixteen and has been in complete denial of his mother's death. Probably because he's got no one to confide in, and he sure as hell won't talk to me. We butted heads right up until I left the house after high school to join the Army, and every stay I had back home. Mostly because I treated him like the tagalong he was. Now that I'm back, nothing has changed. So, we try to stay out of each other's way. A typical Sunday for him has been hanging out at one of his punky friend's houses. I can understand his attitude. What teenager wants to be around this depressing sinkhole? But I'm not giving him an out this time.

"All you two have done lately is jack around and that changes now."

"And who made you king of the shitheads?" Justice says, chucking a rolled-up sock at my head. "What about Dad?"

"Do you see Dad around here?" I say, unfazed by his attack.

"He's at the cemetery visiting Mom, dumb ass," Ryder chimes in.

"You're the dumb ass, dumb ass." Justice scoops up a pile of the socks and throws them at Ryder's face, essentially covering the matches that were spread out beside Ryder.

Ryder leans to the side and yells, "No wonder you're a sucky quarterback."

Justice leaps across the mound of socks, but Ryder jumps away just in time. He gets up and hides behind me.

Justice knows I'll kick his skinny little ass and have done it many times, so he freezes in front of me and glares.

I stretch my head back and look over my shoulder at Ryder. "Colton is cleaning his room. Why don't you go help him?" I make sure to be a barrier between the two as Ryder leaves the room.

I put my hand on Justice's shoulder and give him a look that tells him I'm not screwing around. He's almost as tall as me, and lanky, which is probably one of the reasons he has a great fear of getting hit on the field. This isn't your average quarterback prima-donna shit either. He's terrified. He's run away or out of bounds so many times, people have taken to yelling "Yeehaw" when he does it.

"Look, man, I need to tell you something and it's important. It's the reason I called a family meeting today." He rolls his eyes but I ignore him. I know that's the last thing he wants to be a part of. It was something we used to do before so now it's just a painful reminder. Which is why I'm worried the others will leave me hanging. I'm not sure what options I have left to redeem this family if they do, especially if I'm the only one who gives a shit. "I know it's a lot of pressure to put on you, but it's time to step up and start acting like a man. You need to stop fooling around and pulling this crap with Ryder all the time. You should be setting an example for him and your cousins. They need you too."

His glazed over eyes tell me I lost him a few sentences back. But then he executes his famous hair flip. "I know these talks." He sulks away so my hand falls from his shoulder. "Being a man means giving up football and working for Dad. You can forget it."

I understand how he feels, but at the same time, I've made my own sacrifices. Still, I know talking down to him will only have him shutting down. "No, that's not what I'm saying. It's just—"

The doorbell rings and Justice looks toward the bedroom door with wide eyes. "That's Turner!"

"What's he doing here?"

"He said he'd help me clean to get it done faster, and

then we can go throw some ball around." His words trail away with him.

"Dude, I told you family meeting at—" Pointless to continue, I stalk after him.

Before he grabs the door handle, he says, "Chill, I'll be back in time for your little tea party."

I clench my fists at my sides, not wanting to beat him down in front of his friend. I get the meeting means nothing to him, but if he knew why I called it, he'd understand. "You tell Turner to take his sorry ass back home," I say, voice a strained whisper, a fist pressed against the door, holding it closed.

"You know, we really don't have to listen to you. This isn't boot camp, Sarge. Just because you—"

My narrowed eyes halt him, but I contain my frustration, knowing he's goading me. I never expected a damn ticker tape parade coming home, but after what I'd been through...I thought maybe he'd cut me some slack. Instead, I'm always the one cutting him slack. Then an idea hits and I breathe in satisfaction because I know I've got him. "You don't have to listen to me?" I hold back a grin. "I guess I'm not the guy you want to help you get your driver's license."

He sighs and blinks slowly. "That's just wrong, dude."

I release my hold on the door, nod, and step back. Since I don't trust him, I wait to make sure he delivers the message to his friend. But when he opens the door, he simply stares. Then his brows rise in a way I know it's not Turner he's focused on. I pull the door wider and mirror the expression on Justice's face.

I'm stunned, not only because I'm so surprised she's here, but also because I almost didn't recognize her. Her hair is pulled back into a long ponytail, and it seems like she's wearing almost no makeup, yet her skin glows. And while her face and hair are unassuming, her body is almost intimidating. She's wearing tight jeans with a couple of layered tank tops that show off seriously toned arms.

When I finally realize I'm gawking and being rude, I open the door all the way and say, "Mollie. Come on in." I introduce her to my horny teenage brother and quickly tell him to go finish what he was doing. I know it should be obvious why she's here, but this is not a planned visit. I suppose that was her intention, which puts me on high alert and has my brain reeling. Horrific visions that have no chance of happening flash through my mind: Colton swinging from the chandelier like a monkey, Justice looking at "See Emma Watson Naked" sites on the Internet, Frank stumbling in drunk. Aside from the one about Colton, the rest are not entirely improbable of happening.

"I know you weren't expecting me," she says, reading my first, and hopefully only, thought.

"It's okay. I'm glad you're here." *Why did I say that?*

I shut the door and lead her a few steps away into the living room. I'm relieved this was the first room we cleaned today. I use the word "clean" loosely as I notice a Dodgers foam finger sticking half-way out of the closet along with a pile of jackets.

"Have a seat." I gesture to the couch so she's faced

away from the foam finger, which has been surgically transformed to give the middle finger.

She takes the seat, perches on the edge, and gazes around the room with those intense gray eyes I'm already itching to have directed at me. "You have a nice place."

"Compared to what?" I sit in Gramps's chair and cross my arms over my chest.

Her brows meet in the middle, and she cocks her head. "Well, compared to my place it's…homey."

"That's one way to put it." I'd always loved my home growing up so these comments don't make sense and have to be a defense mechanism. "Sorry, I—"

"You don't have to explain. I'm sure you feel scrutinized. I show up here unannounced."

I nod. "So, you know where I live."

She lets out a short but hearty laugh that shows she's comfortable in her own skin. And it catches me off guard, putting me at ease instead of making me feel like the idiot I am. "Yeah, that was obvious. How did you know where I live?"

She ignores my question and takes in a breath. "Look, I'm sure you probably think I popped in here to catch you off guard… "

"Isn't that why?"

"No. Well, maybe a little. But honestly, I just wanted to check on Belle, and see if there was anything I could do to help. I know I came on a little strong at the hospital, but I'm not the enemy, Logan."

Just like at the hospital, hearing her say my name

affects me in a way I can't comprehend. It feels so familiar and yet I know we barely knew each other in high school. But her statement is so compelling I don't have time to process all of my emotions and reactions to this girl. "No, you were right, and I'm glad you said something. So really, you already have helped."

"I'm glad." She pauses and I watch her, waiting. When she catches my gaze, her eyes dart away. "So…I thought I remembered you had an older brother."

"Mason." I nod.

"But that wasn't him."

"No, Justice is my half-brother. He and Ryder, actually." I lean forward and rest my elbows on my thighs, clasping my hands together. "My dad remarried a couple years after my mom died. Mason and I were young enough so it felt like four brothers growing up but old enough we got saddled with helping…a lot." Now I look away, suddenly feeling like I'm rambling for no reason. "But you probably don't care about that," I say, playfully.

Laughter comes from down the hallway, and her attention is drawn toward it. It's a heart-melting giggle I've grown accustomed to hearing but it hasn't lost its magic.

She turns back to me, our grins matched and our eyes connecting with shared appreciation. She seems so different from the person I barely remember, but at the same time, there's something familiar. Close.

She breaks the stare and stands. "I'm not sure what I expected to see when I came here, but something inside me just took over, and I ended up at your door. I should probably go."

"Wait." I stand and move up closer to her, catching a whiff of something enticing coming off her. It's flowery and kind of sweet, like standing in between an orange tree and a field of flowers as the wind blows. I have to restrain myself from leaning in to capture more of it. Most everyone around here smells like sweat or socks. Or sweaty socks. "I'm glad you came." An extremely *not* awkward pause happens between us. I don't know what she's thinking. And even though I want her out before Dad, Frank, and Mason show up, I find myself hating the idea of her leaving. "Do you want to see Belle?"

Her eyes light up. "I'd love to."

As I walk her back toward Gramps's room, my heart races, hoping nothing will make her feel uneasy about our family. I pause at the first door, where Ryder sits on the bed and Colton appears to be inside his closet. I glare at Ryder, who was supposed to be helping his cousin clean the room. "He's looking for the darts to these guns," Ryder says and holds up a black and red toy gun.

Colton pops his head out of the closet.

"Guys, this is Mollie. She's..." I look at her, and she curls her lips beneath her teeth. "A friend," I continue.

Both boys' eyes widen like she's a triple decker ice cream cone delivered right to their door. Colton scrambles out of the closet and races Ryder to Mollie's side. They haven't seen a woman in the house for quite some time. I actually get what they're feeling right now.

"Hey, fellas."

Ryder reaches out his hand just like I'd taught him. "I'm Ryder."

I keep my prideful grin inside so he doesn't think I'm making fun of him.

"It's so nice to meet you, Ryder."

When he releases her hand, she bends down next to Colton. "And of course I remember you."

Colton doesn't reply, but this is the most I've seen his little lips turn up in weeks.

"You're a brave big brother. Are you helping take care of your sister?"

He nods and Ryder rolls his eyes. "We both do."

Her attractive smile is infectious, but it's her voice that seems to touch me somewhere deep inside. Maybe it's her comforting nurse tone.

"I'm glad to hear that."

"Do you work out?" Ryder asks, his stare burning a hole in her biceps. "You've got strong muscles for a girl."

I cringe and shoot him the evil eye. We have more work to do on appropriate social behavior. "Sorry about that. My brother tends to say whatever he's thinking." I have no clue if all tween boys do that but I hope he's over it soon."

"It's totally fine, Ryder," she tells him without looking at me. "I do like to stay in shape. I work out and I do some kick-boxing."

She's not rail-thin, which is nice, but I wouldn't describe her as a big girl. She's simply toned and fit and yet somehow, she still pulls off feminine. Maybe it's her kind eyes or that incredible smell she's wearing that's now resting right on top of my upper lip. By the looks on these boys' faces, it's probably the smile that's so endearing it comes through her eyes. Those feathery gray irises come back to meet my wide brown ones, and then I know that's what it is. Definitely the eyes.

"Wow, that's awesome. Logan does all that combat stuff, too…well, he used to, right, Logan?"

I try not to react, and Mollie doesn't appear to give it a second thought.

"Logan tell her about—"

"Later, buddy, okay?" That's the last thing I want to tell her.

He ignores me but goes a different route. "Hey, Mollie, would you rather have to surgically remove a guy's penis or sew one back on?"

"Jeez, Ryder!" I touch her arm. "I'm sorry, Mollie." I shrug. "It's sort of a thing he does."

She laughs and seems to enjoy my embarrassment. Then she tells Ryder she's a nurse and doesn't do surgery.

"Come on," I say, gesturing down the hall. "Let's go see Belle." She waves at the boys, and we make our way to the very end of the hall where Gramps's room is. They're both sitting on the bed playing Pretty Pretty Princess, her favorite board game. I can see why any little girl would love it, but a part of me knows that one of the main reasons is because she gets a kick out of making all of us men wear jewelry. Gramps is wearing one earring, a bracelet, and the crown, which I'm sure

Belle is not happy about. She slips a plastic ring on her finger and then notices us in the doorway.

"Maui!" She starts to scoot toward the end of the bed but the combination of her boot and the board on an unsteady surface causes an earthquake-like tremor on the board.

Mollie notices and quickly steps in. "Don't get up, honey. Let me come watch your game." She sits on the edge of the bed next to Belle, who throws an arm around her neck and pulls Mollie's face an inch away from her own.

"Did you come to my house to pway with me?"

Mollie lays a gentle hand over Belle's and says, "Hi, sweetie pea. Just wanted to see you."

While Belle is grinning from ear to ear, Mollie glances over at me with me an awkward shrug that makes my heart stall for a second. I find myself a little jealous of Belle's proximity to her. She turns back to Belle, and they just look at each other for a moment. Mollie seems to have such a gentle, calming touch, I want to experience it personally. Again, a feeling of closeness comes over me, and I can't grasp what it means. It must be that special presence nurses seem to have. I always appreciated their jobs and I respect what they do, but when my whole world changed, I gained a whole new perspective on exactly how important they are. Personally, I couldn't have made it to where I am now without them. Yes, I do believe them to be angels and now one is in my house.

Mollie runs her hand down the length of Belle's soft,

dark curls. Amazingly, Belle seems to know what Mollie is thinking. "Logan brushed it because I don't have a mommy."

I see Mollie swallow, and her chest pulls in a gasp of air. "I know, sweetie. I'm sorry. You look very pretty, though."

Belle still doesn't release her death grip, so I decide to intervene. "Remember what I said about personal space, Belly Bean."

"She likes it. She's smiling."

"Finish your turn, squirt," Gramps says, finally providing some assistance. It's not that he doesn't care to help, but Gramps likes to let us all fall on our faces before he jumps in.

"Go ahead," Mollie says. "I'll watch you."

When Belle finally lets go and scoots back into her spot, Mollie presents her hand to Gramps. "Hello, Mr. Bridges. I'm Mollie."

"It's a pleasure to meet you, young lady. And please call me Bud." The crown starts to slip off his thinning white hair, but he pushes it back into place, knowing Belle wouldn't allow him to take it off. Then as he's moving his piece around the board, he eyes me and says, "It's about time Logan brought home a young woman for us to meet."

Mollie opens her mouth to speak but then looks at me instead, catching me staring at her in the process. I was so entranced by her lips that Gramps's words took a few extra seconds to reach me. I guess she figures I won't answer. She gestures from me to her and with way too much assertiveness says, "Oh, we're not… dating. We went to high school together."

Her words sound almost as sterile as her hospital, but the smirk playing at the corner of her mouth taunts me. "Actually…" I say, not taking my eyes off hers, "we were practically married."

Her reaction is slight, but I catch it before she hides it away and then she turns to Gramps. "But he blew it."

For an old guy, Gramps has all his faculties, and he's lived more and done more than anyone I know, so this routine doesn't faze him. "Way to go, Romeo. Guess you're kicking yourself now." He runs his thumb and index finger down the length of his silver mustache, half hiding his smirk.

"Thanks, Gramps." He gives me a nod as I continue. "Mollie's here to check on Belle. She's the nurse who helped her at the hospital."

"Maui gave me a braid and a bracelet." Belle holds up her wrist, showing the one Mollie gave her along with a plastic pink one from the game.

"Mol-lie," Gramps says, looking at Belle.

"Mau-lee."

We all hold in our laughter, and Gramps looks at Mollie. "I accused the little shyster of cheating with that bracelet." Then he taps Belle on the boot. "Forgive me, my love."

Belle is too fascinated with Mollie to notice what Gramps said. She fingers the bracelets on Mollie's wrist, only one of which is colorful like the one she gave Belle.

The others are black and silver beaded, which seem to fit her personality.

Mollie gently removes Belle's hand from her wrist and rises from the bed. She tugs at the hem of her shirt and smooths it out. "I have to go, but—"

"No, not yet," Belle whines. She reaches for Mollie, who takes her hand.

"How about if I come back another time and play your game with you?"

I cringe because Gramps has been on all of us for giving in to Belle's whining, but he doesn't say a word.

"Yay. L-Logan will play too."

She beams at Belle, but her eyes turn to me for a second, long enough to know the idea of seeing me again doesn't seem too terrible to her. When she turns back to them to say goodbye, I notice a tiny indention on her cheek when she smiles. It's not so pronounced that you'd notice it with just any grin. She'd have to let loose a big one for it to really be seen.

I walk her back to the door, and we stand in the foyer. She fiddles with her bracelets, turning her wrist face up. I spot the music notes I saw at the hospital and am dying to know what music she likes.

"Thanks for not making it hard on me for coming unannounced."

I wait for her eyes to meet mine. "Thanks for keeping an open mind about Belle...and me...I mean us. My family."

"To be honest, I haven't totally made up my mind. This wasn't some exam I expected you to pass or fail.

I'm vested now. I can't just turn away and hope for the best."

My chest tightens at the emotion in her voice. At the amazing, caring person she is. "I know that." I know she cares about Belle, but it's more than that. And I don't only mean me. I know now it's our whole family. She's pulling for us. I can feel it.

4

MOLLIE

I drive with the windows down the whole way home from Logan's house. The wind whipping in my face gives me a jolt of adrenaline. Yep, it's the wind doing that. Thoughts swirl and my head lightens so I roll up the window half-way. Maybe I hit the gym too hard. Maybe I'm dehydrated. But I know it's much more than that. Dammit, why did I have to be there that day? He obviously doesn't remember me, and I know that shouldn't bother me but it does. And now, I'm mixed up in this situation, and I don't know what to do. It's not in me to walk away, and I hate that this unmerciful pull took over and made me feel weak. Not to mention what his dark, tortured eyes do to me. And his powerful presence. But I'll be damned if I let that affect my judgement. I just have to focus on the now and forget about everything else.

I pull into the driveway and jog up to my front door, knowing Rocky is probably dying to get out. As I slip the key into the door, I wonder why I don't hear the usual heavy breath shooting from his nose through the crack in the door.

When I open it, I gasp but my startle is quickly replaced with a smile I can't contain.

Rocky is belly up on the couch, with his tongue lolling out, enjoying a vigorous rub.

"Lou, what are you doing here?"

"Hello, dear. I thought you had the day off."

I shut the door, drop my bag on the ground, and sit next to Rocky. "Remember we talked about my hide-a-key being for emergencies only?"

"This is an emergency," Lou says, taking Rocky's snout in her brown-spotted hands. She leans closer to him and acts as though she is talking to him. "My boy here was getting lonely. I could see his sad eyes staring out the window when I was sitting out front." Louise is my neighbor of the senior citizen variety.

I snap my fingers and point to the ground to get Rocky's attention. "Down." He jumps off the couch and sits at my feet. I turn to Louise where she sits, avoiding my gaze. "So why were you sitting out front? Tired of that beautiful garden we set up in your backyard?"

Lou folds her arms across her chest and purses her lips as she does when she's about to lay down one of her confessions that sound, coincidentally, like deflection.

"If you must know…I got locked out." Her eyes pierce me with a challenging look that says *go for it.* "I went to get the paper because that lazy little paper person can't seem to find my porch, and the door blew shut."

I don't have the mental energy to deal with this right now, but then again, I'm also not stoked about scaling her roof and climbing into her bathroom window like I did last time.

When I don't answer, she releases a stiff hold on herself and rests her palms on her legs. "I was going to go across the street and ask Mr. Simmons to help me but it's trash day."

I let out a breath and a giggle along with it. "And that's not good for anyone."

Mr. Simmons has a habit of forgetting his pants. He drags the trash to the curb in his boxers, waters his plants in the afternoon that way, and even stands at his mailbox filtering through his mail sporting that thin plaid material.

"I'm sorry to be a bother to you, Mollie. It's just that I—"

I put my hand over hers to stop her. "I know, Lou." I nod and get up from the couch. "Let's go see what we can do. And then we're going to get an extra key made that you can keep here at my place."

Lou's relief is displayed on her weathered face, and when she stands, I can tell she wants to give me a hug. But instead, she declares, "Well that's only fair now, isn't it? I have your key and now you'll have mine." That look enters her eyes and she takes in a prepared breath. "Course that takes our relationship to another level. Will you expect me to house sit? Walk your dog? Pick you up from the airport? Hang around like some side kick on a sitcom—"

I hold up both hands in surrender. *What have I gotten myself into?* I can't believe she had enough air for that, but it seems to be her trademark. I have always been one of those people in the neighborhood who keeps to themselves. I don't want to be the "have everyone over for dinner" or "let's housesit each other's places while were on vacay" kind of person. "One thing at a time, girl." I convince myself that Lou is the exception. How can you not feel bad for someone who just lost their husband? But if she thinks I'm going to start hanging out with her and Mr. Boxer Briefs at a barbecue she's got another thing coming.

We leave Rocky in the house and head next-door for our next adventure of breaking and entering. Before I start scaling fences, I decide to check the backyard first. The small garden I'd helped her cultivate over the last few weeks brightens her small space. A floral scent traipses under my nose with the cool breeze. I check the kitchen window first and it's locked, but I give it a good shaking just in case. Then I pass the sliding glass door and move toward the side of the house where I had climbed on the brick wall last time to gain access to a second-floor window. I glance up, shielding my eyes from the sun with my hand, and it looks like the window is closed. I turn back and see Lou watering some petunias and I plant my hands on my hips. "Really?"

"What's wrong?" She sets the can down on the ground. "I'm sorry, did you need my help?"

I shake my head and feel like a mother with a child, only Louise is old enough to be my grandmother and probably in her early seventies. "Let's just try the front and if we can't get in, we might have to call someone this time." I wait for her to walk back over and as she heads back toward the gate, I fall in line behind her. But then I stop and am needled by a thought. I turn on my heel and go back to the sliding glass door. I pull on the handle and the door slides open with ease. I release an exaggerated sigh. "Lou!"

She comes around the corner and sees the open door. "Oh, wonderful!"

"No, not wonderful," I say, trying to keep my voice from rising. "Why didn't you check this door, number one? And number two, you need to be more careful about keeping your doors locked."

"Well, make up your mind. Do you want it locked or not?"

And this is why I spend very little time around my mother, or pretty much people in general. "It's not safe for you living alone," I say as I follow her into the house and slide the door closed behind me.

"You're living alone." She enters the kitchen and glances around as if checking that everything is fine.

"Yes, but I can take care of myself and you're...well you're..."

"What? Weak? Old? A widow? Helpless? I mean, what were you thinking? I can take it."

"Lou, please." My voice is clipped, but I toss her a quick grin. "I'm sorry. You're not…old. I'm just used to taking care of myself. And I can defend myself too. And—"

"I know what you're going to say, and I'm still considering it."

I've been prodding Lou to come to my gym where they hold self-defense classes each month. "It's actually fun and a great work out."

"I have my mace that Bart gave me." She pats her heart and looks up quickly. "Rest his soul…the stubborn bastard." She opens the fridge and tells me, "Have a seat. The least I can do is make you some lunch."

I glance over my shoulder and hesitate a moment. "I should really…"

"Nonsense. I know you're off today…"

"Right." I take the seat and mentally pull up my to-do list. Being single, living alone, with no family in the area and almost no friends…yeah, I'm swamped with stuff. That doesn't mean I want to hang with Betty White over here.

She shoots me a knowing glance and points a finger at me. "You need more home-cooked meals."

"I cook." Sure, I only have four choices I rotate through every week, but I can do more than boil water.

"Trust me, I know it's not easy to cook for just one person." I watch her take in a slow breath and divert her eyes back inside the fridge as if there were a multitude of choices. "For a while, the Meals on Wheels folks brought me some nice dinners, but I didn't like feeling so dependent." She bends over and pulls open a drawer. "But cooking for two, I can do," she says on a high note.

It's not that Lou is a terrible cook; I'm not in the mood for her Good Housekeeping recipe of meatloaf or beef stroganoff.

"Actually, I should probably get back to—" I stop myself when she closes the drawer and turns to me with a dejected look on her face. I stand and smile. "Why don't we grab some pizza instead and then we can have the key made?"

She closes the door and places a fist on her hip, but I can see in her eyes I've already won. "Sure, pizza sounds dandy. But it's my treat and I get to pick the place."

"Where did you have in mind?"

"Best pizza place in Ventura. Bart and I used to go there every Saturday night, and when he got sick, we had it delivered."

As we head back to my place to grab my keys and purse and take Rocky for a potty break, all I can think is that I have a lunch date with someone who uses the word dandy and probably fantasizes about Clint Eastwood.

Twenty minutes later, we arrive at Pepitos. Some of the staff at the hospital have mentioned it before, but I've never given it a try. When we walk in, there's a bit of a line to order, so we take our place and as we stand there, my mind wanders back to Logan. In high school, he was so confident. He seemed so sure of every move he made and comfortable in his own skin. I know what he's been through since then, and I can tell it's changed him some. But when his eyes met mine, I sensed a certain confidence still there. And the looks he kept giving me confused the hell out of me because he should have been on the defensive the whole time with how I'd attacked him and his family. Instead, he softened instantly, and it was almost like he was glad to see me or something, and I have to admit it felt a little bit…dandy.

I feel a nudge on my elbow and realize Lou is trying to get me to fill the empty space in front of me from the line moving forward. "Sorry, I guess I spaced for a moment."

She gives me a slow nod. "Thinking about anyone special?"

I grab the end of my ponytail and twist it around my fingers. "Just trying to decide what to order." I gaze up at the menu casually. "What's your fav?"

"Was it that handsome doctor I saw you talking to in your driveway?"

My jaw drops and I swing my head back to her. "Lou! Were you spying on me?" Mortified doesn't begin to describe how I feel about there being a witness to the disaster that was that relationship. Okay, relationship it was not. I'd actually thought I'd stricken that from my memory banks.

"No, I heard a car and looked out the window. Just like my beloved Bart used to do." Her eyes go wide, and she places a hand on her heart, playing the innocent card with a dash of pity.

I roll my eyes and step up in the line. "I'm not seeing anyone right now."

"Why not? You're young, smart, beautiful, have a great—"

I put my hand on her arm to stop her from going on and on. I smile, not because I believe her words but because she says them with such sincerity I know she believes them. "It's just not a good time for me right now. I have a lot going on."

"That's what they all say."

"Who? Who says that?"

She shrugs and nudges me forward.

We're almost to the front so I turn to face forward.

Then she says, "I don't know…people. Single people, guarded people, lonely people, workaholics…"

Could I pretend I haven't heard her?

"…people hiding from the opposite sex."

"I'm not hiding," I throw over my shoulder. I'm not sure why I feel the need to defend myself in front of her, but I quickly begin spewing an argument before I can stop myself. "I have plenty of male friends," I say with a quick flip of my head before turning back to the front. Then I turn halfway with a thought to quiet her down. "In fact, I just connected with one from high school."

She brightens and touches me on the arm. "Oh? Do tell. What's his name?"

Gah! Backfire. I roll my eyes and turn forward again. "Lou…"

A throat clears before a deep voice says, "I think I know."

I freeze. It couldn't be. My cheeks warm, but I know I have to turn around, so I do so slowly, casually. Before I have a chance to put words to my awkwardness, he's got his hand out to Lou.

"Hi, I'm Logan, Logan Bridges."

"Logan?" She takes his hand with a look of surprise. "I know exactly who you are."

Logan points his shit-eating grin in my direction, and I want to blow his ego right out of the water. I'd never mentioned him to Lou so I don't know what the hell she's talking about.

"Really?" he says and then releases her hand. "I hope you've heard good things."

My head shrinks back like a turtle, and I pull my eyebrows together, hoping to convey my *wasn't me* face.

"I have," Lou tells him and then glances at me.

I decide it's the perfect time to get my wallet out, so I dig inside my purse and silently curse the guy in front of me for using a coupon, but at the same time wonder if I had said something to her. I peek up at Logan's profile as he faces her, noticing how his dark hair curls around his collar and I'm surprised to feel flushed.

"Your mother, Nina…she delivered meals to my husband, and then to me. Such a sweet woman," Lou tells him.

"Nina was my stepmother, actually. And she loved her volunteer work."

Lou puts a hand on his arm and leans in. "I heard about your family's loss, and I'm so sorry."

My pulse quickens, and I fiddle with the flap on my

wallet when I realize I hadn't said anything to him either of the times we'd seen each other. "Yes, um, me too, Logan." *Me too? What am I, twelve?*

He nods.

"Must be so difficult on your families. Losing two women. Your aunt as well? My goodness."

"Yes, ma'am...we're getting by, though." His dark chocolate eyes lock onto mine right before the man in front of me leaves the counter. I shrug and gesture, indicating I have to go. His lips press together, and a quiet ache builds in my chest as if I were about to step on a plane and not two feet away.

After placing our order, I move aside and nod at Logan, who somehow managed to press up right behind me while I had my back turned. His scent distracts me for a moment but a sigh from the woman standing behind him jostles me back to reality. "It was...nice to see you again." My lips bump up at the corners, and I don't fight them, though I feel a sense of guilt too. As I step out of the line, I wonder if I'm being swayed by dreamy dark eyes and lack of sex.

"You too," he says before Lou and I leave to grab a table.

As soon as my ass hits the seat, her simper is already pinning me to the red vinyl booth.

"No, Lou."

She shrugs playfully. "No, what?"

"No to whatever you were going to ask about...him."

She folds her arms and leans back. "Well I was just

going to ask if he knows you've got the hots for him—so that's a no?"

"Very funny."

I move my attention to my purse as if I'm looking for something. A moment later, I gaze up looking for Logan. Lou busies herself organizing the table condiments and wiping the crumbs onto the floor.

Logan sits in the chairs up front, probably waiting for a takeout order, looking down at his phone. As if he senses me watching, he glances up and catches me looking. I don't pull the fake I wasn't looking routine and quickly look away, because everyone knows that's the universal sign for *I was staring at you*. Instead I give him a small grin, which he returns like we've bartered some valuable commodity. I give my head a tiny shake when I feel my cheeks warming again, which is odd for me. Neither of us seems to want to be the one to turn away so we just keep staring like it's the most natural thing in the world. I examine his posture, his movements, the way he scrubs a hand over his short beard.

"I can only pretend to be busy for so long…"

"What?" I say, without breaking eye contact with Logan. But then her words register, and I blink before slowly turning my head her way. "Sorry, Lou."

"I don't mind, really. I'm just looking at your eyes sparkle and wondering what the story is."

"Story?" I take a peek back to the chairs and he's gone. I slump back in my seat and then mentally shake it off before continuing. "The story is…strange." I proceed to explain what happened at the hospital and how we'd gone to school together. Though it was the most Lou's ever not interrupted while I was talking, I couldn't bring myself to tell her everything.

"That's not so strange."

"How do you figure?"

"Every great love story starts with a…well, story."

I throw my head back and laugh. "That's quite a leap, Lou. 'Great love story'?"

"Well you know I'm a hopeless romantic."

I open my mouth, hoping an argument will stop her in her tracks, but nothing comes out.

"Don't try to deny it. I can see in your eyes there's something there."

"Something being the key word. I don't know, maybe I just feel sorry for him…and his family."

"Well then maybe it was fate that brought you two together. Another thing in every great love story."

I roll my eyes but can't help wonder if there's some truth to this theory. The fate part, at least. "I think you've been reading too many romance novels."

"Maybe so, dear, but I've been around long enough to know when I see two people who are drawn to each other. And you could use some romance in your life."

"My life is fine."

"Fine is existing…boring, lonely, pointless—"

"Okay." I hold up my hands in surrender.

"So, you're going to consider it?"

Our pizza arrives at the table, saving me from having to reply. But as I pull a piece onto a plate and hand it to Lou, she gives me a devilish smile. "What?"

She raises her brows. "I forgot the biggest selling point of all."

"What do you mean?"

"Something every great romance has."

"What?"

"Hot sex, of course."

5

LOGAN

I walk in the front door with two extra-large pizzas and enough wings for a football team. I realized at the last minute if I didn't have food here, I was less likely to get everyone in the same room at the same time. If there is one thing that seems to bring the Bridges together it is food—at least it used to.

When I pulled in, I saw Mason's car in the driveway—a miracle in and of itself. I assumed he'd walk in late with some kind of excuse about the business, which has become his wife, mistress, and best friend. It's not that I don't look up to my big brother and respect the hell out of him, but we are for sure two very different people considering we have the same mother and father. I actually feel closest to Ryder, even though we were apart for all those years. I never think twice about having different mothers.

I head to the kitchen where I drop off the food, turn on the oven to keep the pizza warm, and check the fridge for drinks—something I hadn't thought about while I was out. Seeing Mollie at Pepitos was like getting kicked in the head. Now all I can seem to think about is her, and all I want to do is find a way to see her again. That awkward smile she flashed when she turned around in line…hot damn, that was sexy as hell. I also caught a glimpse of that hint of a dimple on her cheek. I wanted to dip her back in one of those sailor kisses. And after that stare down across the room while she sat at the booth… I'm not above having an "accident" that sends me to the emergency room. Okay, now is not the time for sponge-bath fantasies.

I shake it off and realize I'm just staring into the fridge. There's enough sodas here, but as I suspected, Frank has not replenished the beer he has no problem drinking like it's his own personal stash. I scoot some things around—including some foil-wrapped mysteries I'm not about to deal with right now and a doll-sized plastic baby bottle—and notice one wheat beer hiding in the back corner. Hell, if anyone deserves the last one it's me. So, I grab it, pop the top off, and take a swig with the refrigerator still open.

I hear the click of heels on the kitchen tile behind me. Since Mollie was the only woman to come around this place for months, I know it must be the shiny dress shoes of my brother Mason. I turn to find him completely decked out in a dark gray designer suit with a black shirt and thin tie, of course making me look like farmer Fred in my ripped jeans, white T-shirt, and ball cap.

"What's up, bro? Got a hot date?" As far as I know he hasn't dated in over a year.

He ignores the comment. The responsible, professional one of us four has no time for my jokes, apparently. "I just had a meeting with The Meyers Group. They're looking to do some cabins in Solvang. We put a bid in. Russell Meyers worked with Dad before, so I think we have a good shot."

"That's great." I raise my beer in a mock toast and take another drink while I try to think of something more enthusiastic to say. I'd prefer to avoid the lecture from Mason about coming back to the family business. "Dad should be happy about that," is all I can think of.

He nods, but at the mention of my dad, we exchange our unspoken concern over how he's been coping with Nina's death. In his defense, how many men could survive being a widower twice without falling apart? I'm leaving this one for Mason to handle. He's the eldest, and I've got my hands full playing house.

Mason steps up into my space and reaches up to the cabinet above the fridge. He's got a couple of inches on me at just over six foot, but I've packed on enough muscle that the height is no longer a factor.

"Gramps's whiskey?" I say.

He pulls the bottle of copper-colored liquid down and places it on the counter. "Why not. I paid for it."

I exaggerate a sigh. "Put your ego back in your pants, man."

"You should come by the office some time. We'll talk options. We keep expanding, I could use you on the inside."

Mason has a degree in business and hasn't touched a tool in more than ten years, even though Dad had us all working summers and breaks, hoping to groom us so we'd all follow in his footsteps. I actually loved the building side of things. So, it pisses me off Mason's trying to sideline me into an office job. "You know that's not me, bro. I'm hands-on. But right now, the kids need me here."

He stares at me like he wants to say something but doesn't. He grabs two shot glasses from the cupboard next to the sink and then raises his brows at me.

"Naw, I'm good."

He shrugs and pours out one, but before he sets the bottle down, I say, "Yeah, hit me up."

We throw them back and Mason goes for a second.

I tap out a light punch on his arm. "Dude."

He gives me a sidelong glance. "You want me to sit through your family meeting, Mom?"

"You're being a dick." I walk away but as I leave, I throw over my shoulder, "It's about Belle…all the kids, really."

He might be running the show at the company, but I'm the one who moved back in to keep this family from falling apart. No way in hell he would have done that.

Twenty minutes later, I've got the kids set up with a

movie, and the rest of us all gathered in the living room —except Frank. His ass cheeks almost fused to the sofa cushions and the one time I need him here, he's gone.

No sooner do I set down those two boxes of pizza than a sea of dirty, harry knuckles crack against each other, reaching to grab up the pieces. I let them do their thing and wait for the storm to calm before I consider saying anything. The football game plays in the background, and it almost feels like old times. Another reason I dread dropping this bomb. But the longer I watch this scene, the more I know things will only get worse if we don't do something. I don't know if our family is cursed, but if I were a woman and walked into this place, you couldn't get me out of here fast enough.

And then I think of Mollie. I want to get close to her. At least be friends, but my body's reaction to her tells me I want more. When she was staring at me today... And she didn't even try to hide it, which really got my juices flowing. I like that she's a feisty little nurse, but at the same time, I catch her getting flustered. Still, she doesn't seem to like me that much, and when she gets to know me, know what happened to me...not sure I'd want to be saddled with that either. Those thoughts deflate me, piss me right off, but that's not what's important right now.

A loud cackle from my younger brothers pulls me from my reflection. They're standing inches from the TV fist-pumping the air because of the last play in the game. Ryder jumps onto the coffee table and yells,

"Hells, yeah," and then knocks the plate from Justice's hand, his pizza flopping onto the carpet.

"Rebel Ryder, get your ass off there," Gramps yells. He's wearing a bandana and leather jacket, which means he's been out riding his motorcycle. Nina had told him many months ago she didn't think it was safe for him any longer with his glaucoma. *So much for that.*

Justice turns with fire in his eyes. "You're dead."

Ryder leaps off the coffee table and bolts with Justice hot on his heels. They fly past Mason who's leaning against the wall texting as if nothing is happening around him.

"What the hell?" I mutter under my breath. "Dad." It comes out like the teenage version of myself. When he doesn't hear me, I step over to where he and Gramps are standing. "C'mon, Dad, really?"

"What do you want from me, Son?"

I don't say what I want to, or even what I should. "I'll be right back. Just do me a favor and get this under control before I return."

I snake a couple of slices before they are all gone, toss them onto a plate, and take them back to Colton and Belle who are watching *Frozen*. When I return, there are only two pieces left and I grab them before the chain gang notices.

Finally, I clear my throat and say, "Hey, guys, we need to talk." Of course, I'm ignored. "This is impor-tant!" Not even a glance my way, and I push back what should be a blow to my ego, considering I used to be able to snap my fingers and command a group ten times this size. Life. It sure as hell ain't no box of chocolates in this story.

As Ryder and Justice stumble back into the room mid-argument, an ear-piercing whistle blares over the group, and all eyes turn to Gramps. He pulls the fingers from his lips. "Now shut your damn traps and listen to the boy!"

I choose to focus on how bad-ass my gramps is instead of on the fact he had to bail me out. Tossing the plate with my untouched food onto the coffee table, I say, "I know none of you want to be here, but this is about Belle, about our family, and it's important so listen up. Starting right now, we are going to start acting like a family and not a damn circus." I quickly recount what happened in the hospital and when I finish, Justice chimes in. "That hot nurse that was here? She's cool, she wouldn't do anything."

"That's not really the point, you little pervert," Gramps says.

"He's right," I say. "She has an obligation and whether or not she makes that call doesn't matter now. We need some things to change around here, not just for Belle but for Colton. For our whole family."

"Like what?" Ryder says while sucking the meat off a chicken wing. "I mean what are we supposed to do? If Mom were here…" He throws the bone onto his plate, shoves himself onto the couch, and wipes at the corners of his eyes with his sleeve.

"Lots of things. But we all have to pitch in, and the most important thing is taking care of the little ones."

Justice smacks the back of Ryder's head. "That means you, runt."

"No, it doesn't!"

"Colton and Belle are your cousins and starting now, you're going to treat them like your brother and sister, and we're all going to take care of them…and each other. Tonight, I'm texting each of you a schedule with what you need to do and when."

"Hey, where's Uncle Frank?" Justice says, glancing around as if he just noticed. "Shouldn't he be the one doing this? I have school and football and I don't have time for babysitting." He stands and looks over at our dad. "Is this for real or what?"

Dad folds his arms and gives him the look I haven't seen since I left home. "Sit your ass down and do as you're told."

Justice turns back to me, salutes with the tiniest bit of middle finger jutting forward, and sits back down.

I clench my jaw and ignore him because this feels like progress.

I look over at Gramps and he nods his approval.

We talk about how to get started, in little ways and big ways. There's arguing, name calling, and excuses, all while food and drink are being shoveled into their mouths. But, it's something. It's being a family and trying to solve a problem. Well, almost, a family.

"I'm assuming you all got this covered," Mason says, sidling up to me.

"That's it? You're going to bail on us?"

"I'm working fifty hours a week and babysitting Dad.

I don't even live here. What more do you want from me?"

I glance to my younger brothers to see if they've heard the comment. They haven't totally grasped yet how bad my dad is handling things. How far removed he is from reality. He's just barely hanging on, but I'm praying with time that will get better. As much as I hate that Mason has a point, I can't argue with him right now.

"Can you just come around on the weekends more? Check on things. Come for some dinners during the week? You have to eat, right?"

He puts an arm across my shoulder. "You going to cook me up something real nice, princess?"

"Fuck, off!" I jerk away from his hold.

"Come on, Lo, I'm just giving you a hard time. I'll do what I can, okay?"

I give him a sidelong glance and pursed lips.

"I promise you, I'll try," he adds.

"Damn well better. All of you," I say, turning to make eye contact with the rest. "We need to prove to everyone that we're not going to fall apart just because of what happened. And if that's not motivation enough for you, then you think how you'd feel if somebody came in here and took Belle away from us. Faces fall flat and silence envelops the group of us.

Later, when the room clears and all our doing their own things, I clean the mess in the living room. I'm not even pissed that no one helped because it was good night. In a way, it made me homesick for my other family. My guys, our troop…those we lost. I rub the short hairs on my jaw and remind myself to stay in the present. Focus on my family in the here and now. Since I've been back, I rarely let myself drift back there. The fear of those lost memories coming back keeps me in check. Some things are better left alone.

With my arms loaded, I head to the kitchen, where I find my dad sitting at the table with his head in his hands. I pretend not to notice that look on his face when he glances up, because I just can't do it tonight. Not now. When you're the person everyone leans on, it's not always easy to stay standing at the end of the night. I start to clear the counter, but it doesn't take long for the guilt to set in. I turn around and lean against the sink, ready to be whatever Dad needs. But when he looks up, his smile is everything. "You did good tonight, Son."

My expression mirrors his. "Thanks."

"I'm going to do better too. I promise."

I nod because how the hell do I know how long it takes. He lost his wife and for the second time.

He gets up and lays his hand on my shoulder. "I never got a chance to tell you…"

My gaze meets his. "What?"

"I'm glad you're home."

6

MOLLIE

I glance at the time on one of the computers at the nurses' station and wonder why this day is dragging worse than Rocky's ass across the carpet when he's got a dingleberry. It's no different than any other day, but I keep feeling this sense of urgency, like I need time to speed up. I love my job. I live for my job. And not a day goes by that I'm not grateful for the opportunity, because God knows this was not something I thought I'd be doing or even thought was possible.

But today my mind is somewhere else, and that can be a dangerous thing in a place like this, especially for someone like me. I can't afford to make mistakes. *Get yourself together, Fisher*, I tell myself, disappointed.

Robert walks up beside me and leans in. "Hey, you."

His scent jolts me, sending my self-esteem straight to the toilet. I mentally shake it away.

"Everything okay?" Dr. Suave asks softly when I don't respond.

Hearing the concern in his voice should make me feel good. Once upon a time, when I'd forgotten I wasn't a brainless puppy, who drops her panties for perfect teeth and a pat on the head, it did just that. Now it puts me on high alert and makes me feel guilty and defensive. "Great," I say in a perky tone.

His smirk makes me glance away from him, a protective reflex from his lascivious lips and dangerous eyes. At least they used to be. Then I think better of my avoidance and stand tall, turning my face to him. When our gazes lock, he questions me with a perked eyebrow.

"What?" I say, trying to hold his stare. But his power in this hospital gives him the upper hand so I turn to the keyboard and tap into a file. *Make up your mind, girl.*

I can see from the corner of my eye his arms fold across his chest. My temperature flares up because I know exactly what he's thinking and he's way off base. He might leave a flat line of broken hearts in his wake, but I'm the blip on his screen. That ship sank before it left the dock. My indifference is the only way to send that message so I don't look at him with my next words.

"Just finishing up one more thing, and then I'm heading to lunch, actually."

"I am too. Want some company?"

I smile and close out my file like I'd just finished the formula for a life-saving antidote. "Thanks, but I have to take care of something while I eat." I reach under the counter for my bag and the sweater I can't be without in the freezer that is our cafeteria.

What I see when I pop my head up flushes my face with warmth. My cheeks pinch and then peak, fueled by giddy surprise when I spot Logan coming right toward me. I skitter to the other side of the counter, hoping to leave Robert in my wake, but the tapping of his shoes tells me he won't make this easy.

"Something or someone?" I hear Robert say under his breath.

Of course, I won't correct him. "You're here!" I decide to play into Robert's suspicions.

"Right on time too."

Logan's eyes widen so quickly I almost miss it. "You know me, hate to be late."

Somehow Robert arrives at my side, and Logan reaches out his hand to him. "I'm Logan." His tight blue T-shirt could have been an accordion before he put it on, and no one would know it. He has the kind of broad, smooth chest that any woman would trade her best pillow for.

Robert accepts the handshake but eyes me as he says, "Dr. Hall," in that deep, authoritative voice he uses when he explains things to patients and their loved ones. Then he puts his hands on his hips and gives Logan a once over. It should piss me off but when I see Logan's lips curve up, I can't help but do the same. It appears we both agree it's a jackass move.

As the three of us decide who will speak next, I see

Aubrey sashay past us. I let out a breath. I'm hoping she will be the distraction I need. Just a whiff of her "come hither" body spray, and Robert's usually sniffing right after her. But when his eyes stay glued to Logan, I step into my new best bud and take his arm. "We'd better get going. I don't have much time today."

"Later," Logan says with a short, mock solute.

"Yeah," Robert says half-heartedly.

A quick glance over my shoulder shows Robert, without the slightest of pauses, turns to run after Aubrey.

"Who was that tool?" Logan says a second later, obviously unconcerned Robert might hear.

"Dr. Hall."

"Yeah, I got that part. He's obviously got a rap sheet where you're concerned." He cocks his head and a beat later says, "Or did I forget I asked you to lunch?"

"No, but you truly saved me showing up here."

In a matter of minutes, we've gone from awkward acquaintances to fast friends, and I'm not even sure how it happened. I just know it feels good, right, so why are red flags waving at me behind my eyes?

When we arrive at the cafeteria, Logan tells me to have a seat. "I want to try something," he says without sitting himself. I watch as he heads to the counter, throwing a couple of smiles at me as he does.

I don't know what he's up to, but my stomach ignites like he's going to return with a winning lottery ticket instead of mediocre cafeteria food. Two nurses I know from another floor walk past him, staring at his ass like it's the dessert tray at a restaurant. Somehow, my gaze stays locked in when theirs leave. It is a damn sight to see in a pair of jeans that ride low, are not too tight but clearly reveal some solid thighs.

A few moments pass, and I see him reach for his wallet. And finally, the question hits me. What's he doing here, anyway? I'm guessing it has to do with Belle, but he wouldn't be so…relaxed if something was wrong. Whatever it is, I remind myself how this whole thing started and almost feel guilty for getting caught up in the moment. Eye candy is one thing, but getting involved when I clearly have a responsibility to remain objective is another. My excitement and smile fade just as he approaches the table.

"How long was I gone?" he says as he sits. "You look worse than when we were back with Dr. McCheesy."

I barely register the comment when I look down at what he brought me. "I'm fine," I say, confusion coming over me as I scan the tray full of food. "Oh, my God. Stalker."

"Pretty good, huh?"

A bowl of white rice, a plate with a small piece of salmon and some veggies, a cup of what looks like iced tea, and a napkin with a small sugar cookie all sit on the tray.

My mouth hangs open. "How…" I look at him, and he's just smiling with the most beautiful milk commercial, straight, white teeth.

"I've been thinking about you lately, Mollie."

"I knew it. Stalker."

He shakes his head and lets out a small chuckle. "No, seriously. I thought I didn't remember much about you at first, but some things have come back to me."

My stomach drops as I hang on his every word. I kept telling myself it was better for him to bring it up in case he really didn't remember.

"Like I distinctly remember you were the only girl at lunch time who didn't have a giant diet coke and burger with fries in front of her." He tilts his head as if the memory is coming at that moment. "And you were a bit of a loner."

I did eat alone quite a bit so it was hard to miss me. It wasn't what I was hoping for from him, but it's still sweet. "I can't believe you remember that." Maybe, in time, he'll remember the rest. And if he already has, there must be a reason he hasn't brought it up so I certainly won't.

I glance back to the tray, my appetite springing to life. "Hey, where's yours?"

"I'm not hungry. Besides, who do you think that cookie is for?"

"Um, me?"

He palms the back of his neck, grazing through some dark curls at his collar. "How about be split it?"

"I guess." I slump my shoulders for dramatic affect. Then I pick up the fork and bowl and pile some rice over the fish. "I usually don't like an audience when I eat so…" I raise my brows and gesture to the cookie.

He grins and reaches for it. "Okay, but I'm still going to watch you." He breaks the cookie in half and places one piece back on the napkin. "I get the big half…since I'm bigger."

For some reason, the silly comment makes me grin. I take a small bite of fish and rice and try to act casual as I chew.

"You know, you have gorgeous eyes…especially when you smile."

I'm sure my cheeks pinken, but when he shoves the entire half cookie in his mouth, I almost spit out my food along with my laughter. So much for eating together.

When the moment passes, I remind myself I still don't know why he's here. "How's Belle?"

"She's good." He nods and then wipes a few crumbs from his lips, drawing my eyes to his mouth. "In fact…" Suddenly, he pops forward and I blink away and back to his eyes. "We're all good," he continues and his face lights up. "We had a family meeting, the night I saw you at Pepitos…"

I nod my understanding and take another bite of my lunch.

"Yeah, whole family got together and talked—well, I'm using that term loosely. But the point is, we are going to get through this, and we're all pitching in to make a home, a good home for the kids."

"Good. I mean, that's…good." I immediately regret my lackluster response.

He narrows his eyes at me and opens his mouth, but his words are delayed. I'm sure my reaction wasn't what he'd hoped for. He puts his hands on the sides of his chair and pushes it back. "Well, I'll let you finish your lunch. Just thought I'd let you know."

"Logan, wait."

He stands and steps close to my chair. "Hey, it's cool. I just thought you'd care to—"

"I do care." I take hold of his wrist and stand as well, bringing us inches apart. He's probably an inch or so under six feet, a few inches taller than me at five seven, which leaves my face right at his neck. A woodsy scent wafts from him to right under my nose. For a moment, I almost lose my train of thought as I breathe him in, lower my lids, and watch his chest move.

He removes my hand on his wrist, startling me. "You know, none of this is easy for me. Since the day you said those words to me in this very hospital, my heart's been on the edge of tachycardia."

I widen my eyes but he continues before I can speak. "Yeah I'm not as dumb as I look."

I giggle and quickly move to cover my mouth. "Really? That was your follow up to tachycardia?"

"Shit," he says and turns to leave.

I grab his wrist again, this time pulling him so our gazes meet. "Sit."

He glances to the exit as if he's considering it. "This isn't your problem."

"It became my problem, the moment you came into my hospital"—I note my tone rising and force myself to keep it in check—"and I decided to talk to you instead of making that call."

He stares into my eyes with a challenge and something inside me softens.

"Please. I'd like the chance to…explain my reaction, my feelings."

He turns away and takes his seat again, lips a thin seam, arms folded.

I sit as well. Ignoring the food, I clasp my hands and rest them in front of me. "This whole…thing has really messed with my head. I need to make sure I remain objective, and I'm just afraid that I won't be able to."

His brows furrow. "What do you mean? Why wouldn't you be objective?" He pauses, searching my eyes for an answer. "Because we went to high school together? We barely knew each—"

"No." I shake my head, my pulse pumping faster with my growing frustration. I draw in a deep breath and sigh it out. "It's just that I, well, you and I— What?" I say when I see one side of his mouth curve up.

"I get it now." He's nodding with that whole smile now. "You like me."

"I didn't say that."

"Clearly." He cocks his head.

"Listen. I like all of you."

"Right. Which means to like me, too."

"No. I mean yes. I like you and I like your whole family, and I love Belle. But I could get in a lot of trouble if they find out that I had suspicions and didn't report them. I don't want anything to cloud my judgment."

"I guess you're just going to have to trust me…and resist me."

"Stop. This isn't funny."

He leans forward and mirrors my position with his hands in front of him. "I know that. Why do you think I'm working my ass off over here? I mean it's not my fault I'm irresistible. Belle shouldn't suffer because I'm so damn handsome and charming."

"You're an ass." I lean back into my chair to gain some space and avert my eyes toward the door. "On second thought, your charm is fading fast." A moment later, I slowly turn my gaze on him. "Besides, what about you?"

"What about me?" he says with a casual shrug.

"You like me."

"What makes you so sure? I mean how can you tell when you're looking at me through heart-shaped pupils?"

I huff and ignore the accusation. "Oh, so the other night at Pepitos…that was just your 'I'm sitting here waiting for pizza' look you were shooting at me?"

His jaw clenches and his lips purse as if he's fighting the grin. "Fine. I like you and you like me and we both love Belle and everything's great. What's the problem?"

"The problem is we can't be anything more than friends if we're going to do this right."

His lips move back into place, and he gives me a long, hard stare. I know the wheels are turning but have no idea what will come out when they stop. Finally, he says, "You're right." He pulls his phone from his pocket, taps the screen a few times. "So, what days are good for you," he says, eyes averted.

I scrunch up my face, trying to figure out what his game is. "Good for what?"

He looks up and cocks his head to the side. "You just said it."

"What? What did I say?"

"You said 'we,' that we couldn't be more than friends if 'we're' going to do this right."

My mouth falls open, and my breath snags in my throat. "Yeah, but—"

His challenging brow raise halts my words, and we're at a stare down for a few seconds before I try again. "Logan…I—"

"Let's just make this simple. Either everything you said was BS or it was sincere. One word. Are you in or out?"

I don't even pause because when given only two choices—the answer is obvious. "In."

7

MOLLIE

I feel like I'm walking up to a job interview as I approach Logan's house. *Why the hell should I be nervous?* He's the one who has something to prove. I stop and shake my head. With that attitude I'll be looking for things wrong. That's not why I'm here.

When I'd agreed to be "in" this thing with them, I wasn't sure what I was agreeing to and had a feeling Logan wasn't either. But then, he threw out this plan. I tried not to flinch when he suggested I come to the house two afternoons a week to hang with Belle—the only one not in school yet—and keep them on their toes.

Last night in bed, I thought a lot about Logan. On the surface, he's making a huge sacrifice. He's pushed his whole life aside to focus on helping his family. My heart aches for him, and at the same time it melts at the thought of the man he's become. No, become is the wrong word. He's always been that kind of person. I've always known that. I just hope he's not also hiding behind this new responsibility. I hope the reason he hasn't opened up to me is because he doesn't remember not because he wants to forget. To avoid it all. No matter what, I told myself Belle is the priority, and if he decides at some point to talk to me, then I will be there for him. If not, that's his choice.

I walk up the driveway and notice the garage door is only a third way up. I hear music and metal clanking. I bend down for a peek and see sweat-pants-covered legs. When my gaze travels up his body, it lands on skin instead of clothes. Shirtless, Logan is deadlifting a pretty hefty-looking bar. And holy hell, he did not have that chest in high school. Not that I ever saw his chest, but I'm certain he wasn't hiding that under his clothes.

He spots me and gives a little head nod before squatting to the floor with the weight. He stays low and we are now both kneeling down, staring. That smile, those teeth, that close-cropped beard—they're going to be the end of me. I promised myself to remain professional and then Lou has to come at me with all her romance crap.

"Are you going to open the door or what?"

"Sorry, it's actually broken. You'll have to scoot under."

Yeah, that's not happening. "I'll just go around to the front."

"It's locked."

I tilt my head. "So, go let me in."

"Don't be a baby. Just scoot under."

I blow out a frustrated breath and begin scooting closer and lower. "I did not sign up for this."

Just when I get into a position that looks like I'm taking a pee behind the frat house, Logan busts out laughing. He leans down and throws out his palms at me. "Wait! I'm sorry. I was just messing with you." Then he stands and moves out of my vision.

I straighten up and fold my arms. "You ass," I say to the door as it's rising up in front of me.

"Excuse me, but that potty mouth is not welcome here. We have children in this house."

"Yeah? No shit," I whisper and push hard at his chest.

He stumbles backward and looks like he might lose his balance. My brows shoot up, and I hold my breath, praying I didn't cause him to fall. Thankfully, he recovers and then chuckles. "You're pretty strong for—"

"Say it and you'll see how strong my foot is."

"I swear I wasn't going to. I just wanted to get a rise from you."

"Why are you so feisty today? Is it bunco night?"

"Hilarious." He grabs a towel and wipes across his forehead and then down his chest. My gaze is pulled along the towel's path like it's magnetically charged.

"Can I just be in a good mood? I'm working out, the house is quiet, and you're here."

"You training for the mommy decathlon?"

He drops his chin to his chest and fights a grin. "Payback's a bitch, right?"

"I owe you at least one more for that door thing."

And there's that golden smile again. *Are his eyes twinkling? Look away.* This time he doesn't hold back, like he is reliving my embarrassment.

"So," I say, gesturing to his setup. "You hit this stuff pretty heavy?"

He shrugs. "Pretty much."

"You're in great shape."

"So are you."

I avert my gaze from his and pad around the garage. "Shouldn't I be inside with Belle?"

"She's still asleep. Probably another twenty minutes or so."

"Well don't mind me then. Continue." After I check out his set up, which is pretty elaborate for a garage, I watch him pick up some metal hand bells and do some curls. When his eyes catch mine, I pretend not to be staring, if that's even possible.

Then another beautiful thing catches my eye. "Wow, nice Harley. Yours?"

He shakes his head. "No, it's my granddad's...and no one is allowed to ride it."

I laugh and try to picture that old guy running a hog down the street.

"I keep telling him he's too damn old to still be riding it."

"I guess it depends on how old he is physically and his skill level."

"Don't tell anyone, but Gramps used to be a Hell's Angel."

"No kidding?"

"It was a long time ago and he found the life wasn't for him, but he still loves his Harley."

"That's cool." I walk farther back and lean against a wooden shelf with toolboxes on it and notice a baby monitor looking out of place and giving me comfort all the same. "So how are Belle and Colton adjusting to living here?"

"Pretty good. But they were here a whole lot before anyway. Nina and my aunt Sheri were really close. People thought they were sisters instead of my dad and uncle being brothers."

"And what about you? Are you adjusting to moving back home?" I feel a little trepidation leading him into this territory when I'm so unsure if he wants to discuss it.

"I was in a, uh, transition period, anyway. So, it hasn't been too bad. As hard as it was to lose my stepmom, I'm actually glad to be close to my family again." He picks up the towel again and drapes it over his neck, holding the ends with each hand, causing his biceps to plump up. *Good lord.*

"You close to yours?" he says with a pointed stare.

Turning the tables on me, huh? I turn around and there's something else on the shelf that catches my eye. I pick up a notebook that is open to a page with writing and charts on it. "What's this?"

He chuckles sheepishly and sidles over to me. "That's my brother. Ryder. He wrote out a whole workout schedule for me. Wants to be my personal trainer for… just this crazy thing he wants me to do."

He's standing right behind me now, looking over my shoulder, and I can barely breathe with his closeness. This is something I have to get over if I'm going to be spending time here. I ignore the heat radiating off his sweaty body. "I think that's sweet." I look up and over my shoulder to catch his gaze. "He really looks up to you."

"I guess."

Our eyes lock in on each other, and I can see the doubt in his. He doesn't like what I said and I understand why. "So, what's the crazy thing?" I say, hoping to ease him. But now I see awkwardness, and he swerves his focus away and steps back.

"Hey, you said you had something you wanted to talk to me about?" he says, flipping on me again.

I wonder how long this dance will last, where we both avoid talking about anything personal.

"Yes. Well, it's just a thought. You said Belle is turning four soon?"

"Yeah, in a month. Why?"

"What about pre-school? Do you know if your aunt was going to enroll her?"

His brows furrow but not only in confusion. He seems offended and I think I know why. "Hey this has nothing to do with me not wanting to help out."

"That's not what I was thinking."

"What then?"

"Sure you're not trying to get Belle away from this house? Away from us?"

Mouth agape, I stare as my heartbeat quickens. "Oh,

God. No. That's not what I meant at all. It's just that she's at that age and without any female figures or girl-friends around…"

"She might turn out like one of us?"

I shake my head and touch his arm. "And that wouldn't be a bad thing. Hey, it was just a suggestion." I put my other hand on my hip. "I am here to help, after all."

"So, what are you thinking?"

"Lots of kids go part time. She could go two or three half days a week, and I'll still keep coming." I give him a small smile, hoping he sees I'm sincere.

"Smile bigger."

"What?"

"I need to see something."

"Well I can't smile now."

He stares at me for a second, like he's thinking. Then he bows his arms down by his sides like the hulk and flexes his muscles. "Urrgghhh!"

I bust out laughing, sporting a huge smile. "You're a dork."

He immediately straightens and turns serious. "There it is." He strokes my cheek. "God, you're gorgeous."

I barely shake my head, confused, but he seems to know what I'm asking.

"You have this tiny…wannabe dimple. It doesn't come out all the time. It's hard to see unless it's a big smile, but it's so…adorable. You should let it out more."

"I'm glad you're enjoying my facial deformity," I say

because I can't think of anything else while my body temperature continues to rise.

"I do believe I'm enjoying everything about you, Mollie."

Oh, God, the way he just said my name.

He takes my wrist and looks down at my bracelets. Suddenly, he seems mesmerized by them and runs two fingers across the top of one. I hold my breath and watch him carefully.

"These bracelets…" he whispers.

Then he looks up at me and those dark chocolate eyes spear me with an intensity that causes me to take in a sharp breath. He's still fingering my wrist and bracelets, and I can see his chest filling more with each breath. He pulls me toward him so our bodies are barely brushing each other with our breaths. "Mollie," he whispers.

All I can do is open my mouth because in that moment I don't know whether to push him away or reach up and place my mouth on his. I don't know whether to close my eyes and live in the moment or say the words I probably should have said that first day. I'm paralyzed with fear and confusion and before I finish my next thought, he's reaching his other hand to my face.

"You're incredible, Mollie," he says, running his hand over my hip. Then instead of leaning in, he pulls back. "And, I'm so sorry." He steps back farther. "I wasn't thinking. This is such a bad idea, but you're just so… well, I know why you're here and…"

I close the distance between us and run my hand down his arm. "It's okay. I get it."

His smile surfaces for a moment before he hides it away. "It's like I look in your eyes and forget myself. It's selfish. You agree. Bad idea, right?"

As much as it pains me to agree, I do. At least for now. This thing is much more complicated than even Logan realizes. I nod. "It's probably best."

"But we can be friends, right?"

I can see the hope in his eyes so I grin and nod harder. "Yes. Friends would be great."

"More than friends. A team."

"Yes, a team." I put my hand out for him to shake and he does. And just as I suspected, his touch is now more than a simple flirtation. It's a longing that won't be easy to fight.

We shake and when he releases my hand, he makes a fist which he moves in a small circle and holds out in front of me. I get it and put my fist out for him to tap on top. Then I do the same to him.

"And you're right," he tells me when we finish our apparently new friends' handshake. "I'll talk to Frank and see what he thinks about preschool."

"Great. Is Frank here?"

"Actually, I'm the only adult here right now which is odd." He points to the door. "Let's head into the kitchen.

I follow and we step inside. "Oh? Where is everyone?"

"Kids are at school, Dad's at work, and Gramps went

to get a haircut if you can believe that." He opens the fridge. "Water? Tea? Soda?"

"Water, please." He hands one to me and I sit on a barstool at the counter. "I like your gramps. He's cool."

"Thanks. I think he's pretty cool too," he says, leaning against the counter, still shirtless.

Trying not to stare at his pecs, I ask, "So what does your dad do?"

"My dad and older brother, Mason, work at our family's construction company. Mase has been pushing my dad to be more active in acquiring new jobs so they're out doing some recon…"

"So they're builders?"

"Dad is. Mason has a degree in business so…" He lifts a shoulder. "Dad had us all working summers and breaks, teaching us the trade. But Mason always felt he was better than manual labor."

His tone is a touch bitter, but I can't resist asking. "And your uncle? He works there too?"

He coughs out a laugh. "No, Frank is more of a desk rider. He did PR for years. You know, spinning company images and sneaky subliminal stuff like that. Got laid off over a year ago."

I lean back in the chair and glance around the room. It's clean, which is good but definitely lived in. Cluttery but not in a dirty way. "That must have been hard." When I don't hear his answer, I take my gaze back to him. He was watching me checking things out. "Sorry, I wasn't—"

"It's okay. I know. What were you saying?"

"Frank. That must have been hard for him."

"Oh…yeah." Then he seems to think better of it, sets the water down, and folds his arms. "No, screw that. Hard is everything that's happened since then. My aunt had to go back to work. She is…was a teacher. And she loved it, but she wanted to be with her kids, and not leave them with her has-been of a husband whose part-time job became wallowing in self-pity."

"So, you don't like your uncle too much, huh?"

"I know I sound harsh when his wife just died but look at the reality. You and I are here doing what we can to make things right." He looks at me with pleading eyes. "But, Mollie, he does love his kids." His voice softens. "Please don't get me wrong. I know Frank will come around. He's struggling with the loss, but I won't let him mess this up. Trust me."

"I do."

"And I promise I'll bring up the preschool thing." He gestures with his head for me to follow him down the hallway. "Let's go wake the Belly Bean."

Just the mention of her makes me giddy and I bop along behind him. We both pad quietly along the hall even though our intention is to wake her. We stop in the doorway and watch because we both know it's a beau-tiful sight to see—an innocent child sleeping. We exchange glances. Friendly glances that we are both trying to maintain.

After a few moments, he bumps my shoulder with his, indicating I go inside. I comply and take a seat on the edge of her little bed. She's on top of a yellow comforter and her arm is draped around what looks like a hippo. When her eyes finally flutter open, it's like watching the sun rise. Bright blue eyes slowly unveiled by lids pulling up long, thick lashes.

We spend the rest of my time there with Belle—reading, coloring, snacking, and talking. The boot limits physical play so we are making do. Every so often, Belle touches my face or my hair, and I don't mind because I know I'm the only women she has contact with. It almost feels too good, and I don't even want to face what's happening to me with this little one. She's winning my heart, and she's not the only one. Just before they have to leave to pick up Colton from school, Logan tells me he wants to show me something. He sets Belle up on the couch and stands behind her. "He's been practicing," she tells me. He begins brushing her hair and then separates the strands into pieces. Then he proceeds to do a braid similar to the one I gave Belle when she was at the hospital. When he's done, they both flash me triumphant smiles.

Yep, I'm so gone.

8

———————

LOGAN

It's almost half time in the game, and I look at my cell phone for probably the tenth time, hoping to see a message from Mollie. When she said she'd try to make it, I assumed that meant she would be here by now, but I'm about to give up hope—even as I mentally scold myself for hoping in the first place.

Justice invited Mollie when she was at the house this week. It surprised me—that he asked and that she accepted. A small part of me is nervous we are all getting too attached to Mollie already when she is only a temporary fixture in our lives.

"Hello, Justice's family," Turner's mom says as she chases after Turner's little sister. When Abby waddles by, I glance over my shoulder at Belle and hope she doesn't see her. We told her she could only come today if she didn't run around in that boot.

"Hello, Turner's Mom," I say back.

"Hey, Cath," Gramps says in a tone I don't recognize. I'm sure it has nothing to do with the fact that Cathy is divorced, and the school pride shirt she's wearing looks like it's Belle's size.

I chuckle to myself. Good for Gramps. He thinks my plan to have Mollie around is pretty convenient for me so I guess the apple doesn't fall far from the tree. I almost chuckle thinking about how true his words were, but of course I denied it to his face. He caught me spying on Mollie and Belle the other day. I hadn't meant to, but when I heard their sweet voices from the other room, I found myself being pulled down the hall, like when a song lights you up inside and makes you reach to turn it louder. I stood outside the door and listened to Mollie read my Belly Bean a story, and like always, Belle interrupted a million times. What's that? Why is she holding that? What happened to the boy? Just the sound of Mollie's replies affected me. I couldn't figure out what it was, but something about the sound of her voice felt so familiar, so comforting.

Justice hands off to the running back and he fumbles the ball. We're down by seven but with how bad they're playing right now it should be worse. I glance at my phone once more and figure Mollie is not going to make it. I'm disappointed but how can I be mad? I'm not. I just can't seem to stop myself from analyzing her actions. While I appreciate what she is doing for my family and why, I can't help wishing she is doing it for a different reason. Selfish as it is, I like having her around for me. Something about her presence makes me feel… present. In the moment. The past I miss, the past I crave, the past I dread thinking about—the past I can't remember… It all goes away when I'm near her. But I have to keep my expectations in check. I'm just surprised she would let Justice down today. And Belle for that matter.

I take another look over at the little runt who is sitting in a chair with her leg propped up, watching a video on my iPad. I held her piggyback style for the first quarter and my limbs finally gave out. Yeah, I could have powered through to prove something to myself, but that's the selfish mindset I don't have time for these days.

Gramps and Ryder flank her, standing with their arms folded like secret service in case an errant ball or player comes her way, Gramps pridefully watching his grandson on the field, Ryder looking for any foul up or excuse to give Justice crap after the game. Colton sits on the grass playing with a rocket.

A whistle blows on the field, taking my attention to a mound of players at the twenty-yard line. We are on defense now so I don't have to worry about Justice's skinny ass getting crushed at the bottom, though he is an expert at the fifty-yard dash right out of bounds.

In an instant Ryder is by my side shoving his phone in my face.

"Dude, stop. I'm watching the game."

"Look," he whines. "See the date." He points to the form with a huge grin on his face.

I sigh because I don't want to disappoint the kid, but he's living in a dream world. "Ry, I told you no. I can't even think about that now. It's just not possible."

"But why? I know you can do it. You said you'd try."

A squeal from Belle behind me and a tap on my shoulder alerts me my wait is finally over, and I smile. When I turn around, I'm surprised to find two women standing before me. Mollie is there looking enticing as ever, albeit a little frazzled, along with her neighbor I met a few weeks ago.

I give Ryder the death glare and whisper to him, "Put that away and get back over there."

As he jams his phone into his pocket, he says, "Would you rather a girl catch you digging up your nose or beating your sausage?"

Holy hell, this kid. "Go," I whisper with irritation but smile when Mollie's gaze grabs mine.

Ryder gives the two women hellos as he returns back to the Bridges clan.

"Hey," Mollie says tentatively, her eyes seeming to seek my forgiveness. "Sorry I'm late, but the piece O' crap that drives me around wouldn't start."

"Bummer, but I'm glad you made it." Our eyes lock for a moment and then I turn to her older companion. "Hello. Lou, right?"

"Yes, it's nice to see you again." She eyes me like I've got a blue ribbon pinned to my chest.

"You too." I gesture over her shoulder. "Let me introduce you to some of my family."

Mollie places her hand on my arm, and it's so natural I want to take it and entwine my fingers with hers. "I'll do it," she tells me and slides her hand away too quickly for my liking. "You watch your brother."

I turn to focus back on the game but really I'm on high alert to what's going on behind me. I wonder why Mollie brought her little golden girl. But when I glance over my shoulder and see the lights in Belle and Colton's eyes as they speak—yes, even Colton says a few words—with both women, I realize it doesn't matter. Then I chuckle at Gramps who seems to be playing it cool, pretending nothing is happening but the game in front of him. Mollie catches me watching and comes to my side.

She lines her body up right next to mine so our arms connect as if we are magnets. "Sorry about this," she says quietly. She tilts her head toward my neck and a burst of sweet sunshine hits my nose. "I asked to borrow her car and somehow here we both are."

"What's that smell?" I ask, completely overcome by it. "You smell like sunshine and rainbows—okay, I heard that out loud and now I can't take it back." I run a hand through my hair and give her a sidelong glance.

She giggles and shoves me with a little shoulder bump that makes me want to tackle her to the grass and pin her arms to the ground. Just a friendly tickle and roll session, which I'd conveniently use to my advantage.

But, thanks to the damn friendship pact, I have to take what I can get.

"My shampoo, I guess. Peach something… It was on sale. Did you even hear what I said?"

"Yeah." I shrug and put my hands in my pockets, turn back to the game before her soft gray gaze melts me into a helpless coma. "Lou's cool. I like her. Plus, listen to that angel's song behind us," I say, referring to Belle's chattering.

Mollie's hand lands on my shoulder.

God, you're killing me here.

"When you say things like that, it's so clear how much you really love those kids."

I don't say anything. I just nod and watch the game and hope she keeps that hand there.

After a few moments, her touch leaves me, and I swallow back the disappointment. "Where's everyone else?" she asks.

"Work…mostly."

"What about you?"

"What about me?"

"Do you think you'll want to join the family business?"

I tilt my head like the answer should be obvious.

"Okay, so did you ever want to?"

Tight-lipped, I shake my head.

"Oh, how come?"

I let the question hang a bit, hoping the switch to the offensive team gives me an out. I clap loudly and then cup my hands around my mouth. "Yo, Justice! Let's go, man!"

"You can tell me if I'm being too nosey. You said it's a family business. I figured you and your brothers might eventually all work there?"

I press my fist into my other hand and knead like I'm trying to crack my knuckles, only they never seem to crack. "Nah, I doubt that will happen now." I look at her, hoping to get my point across.

She puts her hand on my arm. "I'm sorry. I didn't mean to pry… I'm just interested in…"

"It's cool. It's just everything is different now. Mase says Dad has no drive, but honestly, I think my brother could run it on his own. Our family is in a different place now. Besides, the family in business was just pipe dream of my dad's."

I can tell she wants to know more, ask more, but I face forward again, regret bloating my gut. I don't want her to think we can't get to know each other. I certainly want to get to know her, but if that means talking more about me, I'm not up for that right now.

My uneasiness transfers from focusing on Mollie to my brother, who is about to throw a long pass on third down. I take in a huge breath and hold it. Justice fades back, looks for an open man, pumps the ball, and—oh shit—he ducks away from a linesman and bolts a few steps diagonally. "C'mon!" I say under my breath. I punch my fist and scrunch my face as another defensive player breaks free and heads right toward him. He's got time and space, but he can't hold on and performs his signature move. "Ah, hell." The crowd starts swinging their hands above their heads in a circular motion as if they're wielding an invisible lasso as Justice makes a run for the sidelines. The crowd screams, "Yeeee-haaww."

I drop my chin and can't help but laugh a little myself. The old me would have been pissed as hell. Probably give him a beating to toughen him up. Funny how circumstance and priorities change your life. Change you.

"I assume that won't go over well at school?" she asks.

"Home either," I say with a nod and turn back to the field as they set up for the next play. The crowd is chanting for that first down, and my pulse kicks up for my brother, who needs this more than those assholes giving him crap know. I clench my fists and send mental energy as Justice fades back and looks to his mark. I instinctively grab Mollie's hand and squeeze it.

"Come on, Justice," she says quietly. "You got this."

With his pass successful, we both pull close as the receiver maneuvers his way past first down and everyone cheers. I let go of her hand, though I won't apologize for my instinct toward her. Instead, I clap and enjoy the small victory for Justice, pretending I didn't just get as giddy as a freshman talking to the quarterback, just from the small connection with her.

"Speaking of home," she says suddenly. "You think I could catch a ride after the game?"

The fickle freshman leaps back under my skin, and I'm caught speechless. Women never rendered me that way before. There was always this natural confidence that led all my actions and responses to women. Maybe it's because I've turned into Carol freaking Brady these last few months or maybe it's because no matter what I do—how many hours of working out, how many weights I pile on the bar—I can't seem to get my mental fortitude back. "Oh...I...you need a ride?" *Nice recovery, jackass.*

"Well, Lou was going to run some errands, but I can go with her."

"No." My pulse quickens and I try to hide my buoyant smile. "The kids can go back with Gramps. I just have to get them settled into his car. I'd be happy to give you a lift."

9

———

LOGAN

Thankfully, our team pulled out the win, but Justice didn't let the timer run out without one more mad dash, this time out of bounds and without a defensive player within five yards of him. One of us had better get him used to uglying up that pretty mug of his before someone else does it for him.

The car ride to Mollie's felt like an exercise in telepathy. I had the radio on but at a reasonable volume for a conversation. Yet, our exchanges were limited to her giving me directions. There were glances. At her plump lips. Her shapely thighs as she crossed her legs. The V of her snug T-shirt. And of course, those light gray eyes that practically hold me prisoner whenever I look into them. Damn near ran a light getting caught up in them. Like that time in the pizza place, holding an unspoken conversation ending with her letting out a small laugh like I'd told a joke at a dinner party.

Getting out of the car, I wonder if she expects me to just drop her and go. I follow her to the door, and as she unlocks it, I hear these funny puffs of air coming from the crack of the door. She looks back at me and smiles. "That's Rocky. You're not allergic to dogs, are you?"

Just the mention of a dog sends warmth to my chest, and I'm not sure if it's simply my love of animals or the fact that she has one. She opens the door the second I shake my head. Two chocolate paws land on my thighs, but they don't stay there as he springboards off me, spins in a circle, and then sits at Mollie's feet slapping a long dark tail against the floor.

"Hey, suck-up, you know the drill."

Rocky eyes me one more time and then turns back to Mollie and gives her a head tilt.

She ticks her head up once. "Move it!"

A second later, a heap of brown muscled dog takes off to what seems to be the kitchen area and returns with—fuck me—a leash hanging from his mouth.

"That's amazing," I say. "I can barely get my brothers to pick up their stupid socks."

"Well it's his routine, except for when Lou pops in and confuses him. And he knows what's waiting after." She head-gestures to a Tupperware full of dog biscuits on a side table by the door. "Have a seat and I'm going to run him out to his favorite bush."

When she heads out the door, I take the opportunity to glance around and get a peek into the private world of my new friend. It's a small house, but feels homey. Not in a grandma sort of way but more of a gypsy, bright and colorful. One whole wall is purple, and there are light purple accents throughout the room. I see her through the window at her mailbox, the purple ends of her hair highlighted under the sun. I grin and find it difficult to pull my gaze from her, but I want to see more of her place.

Walking around the living room and peeking down the hall, I don't see any family pictures on shelves or the wall. Our house is littered with them, like Jabba the Hutt ate our family album and puked it up on all the walls. Though it is tinged in sadness, the thought brings me comfort. As dysfunctional as we are now, we are lucky to have had the upbringing we did. I feel a pang of sadness for Mollie, though. Without knowing any real details, she seems a bit lonely to me. We haven't defined this friendship yet, but I hope it means I can at least learn more about her. Get closer to her, even if that means close friends.

The door flings open from Rocky's nose as he pulls Mollie in. She unhooks him and retrieves his treat from the container. She hands it to him and immediately grabs his face and kisses his head. It's so sweet and unlike what I've seen from her, it makes my heart putter a bit faster. Not that she hasn't been sweet, especially to Belle, but she just has this sort of thin veil of toughness that protects her. Maybe that comes from being an introvert, though I wouldn't say she's still that girl from high school.

"Did you get a good look around?" Her tone is teasing, and her brows are arched, but I notice a sheen of sweat on her forehead. It seems unusual since the day isn't that warm.

"What? No, I was just enjoying your place. It's cool. Let me guess. Prince fan?"

"Of course." She laughs and walks past me, wiping her forehead. "How about something to drink before you go?" Her words are slow and breathy.

"A drink?" I could go for a beer after that game, but it's hard to tell what she means by "drink" especially when she seems a little off suddenly.

"C'mon." She motions me to the kitchen, and I follow in what is quickly becoming my favorite path in life: floating in the trail of scent she leaves behind her.

She goes right to the fridge and opens it, but now her face looks almost annoyed, and I'm wondering if I should bow out of here or what. "I can get going if…"

She's pulling out two water bottles, so I stop talking but continue to analyze her face. Maybe she's not comfortable having me in her home. She hands one to me, avoiding my eyes, and then she walks back toward the doorway, holding the other. "Be right back."

As I lean against the counter and chug the water, I can hear a faint mumbling. *Is she talking to me or the dog?* It must be a little lonely living by yourself. I've always been surrounded by people, so I can only guess what it's like for her. Still, until just a few minutes ago, she seemed like the type of person who didn't let much get to her. The kind of person who rolls with the punches and doesn't complain. I like that in a woman. In anyone, really. It's one of the reasons I felt so at home in the military. Everyone has two jobs: whatever you're responsible for and to back up whomever you're with when the shit hits the fan. And you don't bitch about it. As tough as it was, I miss it. Now I'm a damn head mistress for The Outsiders.

"Son of a bitch!" I hear her say.

Her words are faint but distressed enough to yank me out of my head. I double time it back to the living room, but she's not there. Instinctively, I head down the short hallway to my right and stop in front of one of the closed doors.

A moment later, I hear her. "It's okay, baby. You're okay."

Though her tone no longer sounds distressed, I don't fight my instincts and find myself pushing through the door. "Mollie..." I freeze and wrinkle my brow at the scene in front of me. Typically, I'm quick to surmise a situation but not this time. Mollie is sitting on the floor in a pair of tight black yoga shorts, a needle sticking out of her thigh. Rocky is lying across from her next to a newspaper that appears to have...is that vomit?

"Knock much?" She depresses the plunger of the needle and stands abruptly, Rocky mirroring her at her side. She pats his head and says, "Go to your bed, boy." Then she sits on the bed next to what appears to be some sort of pouch of medical stuff and busies herself with it.

I realize my mouth is open and decide I better say

something. "I'm… I apologize for barging in, but you sounded like you needed help. I take a step closer, and her eyes connect with mine, a warning just at the surface.

"I'm good."

"I don't mean to be nosey, but—"

"Then don't."

I sigh heavily and look over at the dog who's got his head resting on his paws in a big, puffy bed. "Let me clean this up for you," I say, walking over to the brown, clumpy mess. I lean down and fold the paper, wrapping it up tight.

"I'm not a druggie, if that's what you think," she says behind me.

I don't turn around. "It's not." I stand and head to the door. "Trash in the kitchen?"

"Yeah."

As I walk out of the room, my chest tightens. I find the bin and toss the paper in. I'm not sure if I should leave, but I don't want to. I can't, so I wait for her to join me in the kitchen.

"Sorry about that," she says, walking to the window and looking out. "Sometimes he gets nervous with new people in the house."

"Oh. I didn't mean to scare him. I love dogs." I come up behind her. "And if there's anything you need…"

"Hey." She turns, putting her close enough for me to lean in and touch foreheads but I resist. "Don't let what you saw change your opinion of me." Her voice is sharp, defensive.

I smirk. "I don't know what I saw, so I'm not sure how things change." I back up, needing to put a little distance between us. What I'm feeling—the need to comfort her, protect her after what I saw—is not what she's feeling based on her words and tone. "I guess I'm just a little confused. I thought we were getting to know each other these past few weeks. Trust each other."

She puts her hands on her hips and looks away. "So."

I half laugh, half cough. "So…I guess I'm just hur—surprised you kept this from me…whatever it is."

She's staring at me and jiggling her leg—something I noticed her doing before—like she's deciding.

"We're friends, remember?"

She licks her lips and sighs. "It's not a big deal. I'm diabetic, okay?"

It makes sense, but I don't know what I'm feeling right now. It's not pity but more like empathy and protectiveness. Yeah, she's tough as hell, but I hate to think of her struggling or in pain. I know her well enough that now's not the time to voice any of that. So, I play it safe. "Okay. Thanks for telling me." Then, as I take a couple of steps back, I mumble under my breath, "Explains the moodiness."

Her mouth falls open and she punches my arm. "Screw you."

As far as I know, this is not life threatening. Yet, I want to know more, to help her, to find ways to protect her, but I feel like that's the last thing I should want. "Hey, I'm just playing." I rub my arm and frown, playing it up to ease the awkwardness. But as we stand there, the playfulness in both our expressions fade. We only breathe and watch each other. Dangerous territory just like in my garage that first day.

Watching her, I want to pull her into my arms, but instead I take her hand. I want to press my lips against hers, but instead I lean in, touch her face. "I'm here for you if you need me," I whisper.

Her eyes widen and she lets out a choking giggle.

I furrow my brows and move back, releasing her hand.

"I'm sorry," she says. "That was rude." But she still seems to be covering a smirk like I'm some schoolboy with a crush on his teacher. "It was very sweet of you, but I'm a big girl. And I can take care of myself. Did you forget that I'm a nurse?"

"I know. And I know you're strong and you're independent, but you don't always have to be the one taking care of everyone else. Everybody needs somebody in life. Not just for this. For…whatever. "

She shrugs and cocks her head to the side, adorably. "Maybe I already have *somebody*."

"Do you?" She might think this is a fun game, but I'm totally serious.

Her gaze drops slightly before springing back to me, giving me the answer. That's when I realize I want to be her somebody, and it's very possible she wants that too.

When she turns away, I know the timing isn't right. She sits at the table, and I back up and lean against the sink, waiting for her eyes to meet mine again so I can make her understand I won't pressure her, but I will take what I can get, even if that only means another form of friendship. Preferably a closer one. "In all seriousness, I want us to be friends. And I appreciate you trusting me by telling me that."

She shakes her head and tucks her lips under her teeth while she plays with her hair. "You sure been throwing that trust word around, pot."

I scratch at the whiskers on my jaw and then immediately get the reference. "You calling me a hypocrite?"

She gets up from the table, saunters over to me until she's right in my face. If I wasn't a little bit nervous about what she's about to say, I'd be seriously turned on.

"When were you going to trust me and tell me about your leg?"

Shit. I'm floored. My mouth falls open, and for the first time in my life, a woman makes my face flush. What. The. Hell?

I lock gazes with her, and she raises her eyebrows at me. "What's the matter? Feel a little invaded?"

Yeah! "No. I was going to tell you, but it didn't seem important."

"Bullshit… You wanted your privacy just like I did."

I break eye contact and turn away, head toward the glass patio door. I stare out with my arms folded. "That's where you're wrong. I just didn't want to be…that guy. I didn't want you looking at me like—"

"What?" she says, coming up behind me and laying a hand on my arm. "A hero?"

"Hardly… No…" I can't finish it. I can't go there with

her. Not yet. Maybe not ever. So, I look over my shoulder at her. "How'd you know?"

"I know a lot of stuff, Logan." She turns and walks away, into the living room.

"What's that supposed to mean?" I say, trailing her.

She turns to face me and I wait.

"Do you want to tell me what happened to you?" She takes a seat on the couch, folds her legs under her and pats the spot next to her. "Might be good to talk about it."

"Oh, you get to be Miss Independent and I get thrown under the microscope?"

"So, we're both a little...tweaked. But mine is a simple story," she tells me as I sit and we face each other. "My genes gave me diabetes, and now I live with it and hope it doesn't interfere too much with my life."

"I'm sorry."

"Don't be. It's something I grew up with. You, on the other hand, have a much different story."

"Look, I appreciate it, but no. It's not something I want to talk about now. You know all the shit I got to deal with at home and leaving it alone, leaving it behind me, is the only way I can do that."

She looks down at her hands, and I feel like a complete dick, but I'm in survival mode here.

"Please don't let this ruin our...friendship. I just can't right now."

She shakes her head. "So, all that 'everybody needs somebody' speech was just bullshit?"

"No, of course not." I take the chance and place my

hand over hers. In this moment, I need to touch her and she needs it too. I can feel it. "Just give me some time on this one?" When she doesn't look up, I reach with one hand and lift her chin. "Besides, you've been my somebody since the day you got in my face at the hospital. You have been there for me. I'm the one who needs to return the favor."

"You got that right." The corners of her mouth push up into her cheeks, and it's like a halo sprouted from her head.

"Okay, then." I put my hand out to shake hers, and we both instinctively follow with a fist tap. "Now I'm going to get out of your hair and let you tend to Rocky." I stand and head to the door. With my hand on the knob, I ask, "What did you mean when you said you know lots of stuff?"

She pauses, gives me a nervous, tight smile. "I'm a nurse, Logan. I knew your military history, I've worked with patients with prosthetic limbs before, and...I could see it in your walk, the way you absently rub your thigh from time to time."

My heart stutters in my chest. "Great."

10

———————

LOGAN

I plow into the house and go right to the fridge, hoping no one is in the kitchen. I grab a beer, pop it open with more force than necessary, and then take a long pull. This shouldn't be a big deal. She was bound to find out. I just wanted it to be on my time. My terms. It wouldn't be the first time I had to face this with a woman, but this time feels different.

My phone pings and I pull it from my pocket.

Mollie: *You okay?*

Those two words knock me down a rung on my confidence scale. She's a caring person and that should make me feel good, but instead I feel like another one of her charity cases. Belle and me and our bum legs. We could be our own pathetic telethon. Only Belle will be rid of her boot soon, and I'm stuck with Titanium Ted for the rest of my life.

I scroll beyond Mollie's text to one from Jennings. *Why hasn't that dumbass given up on me yet?* We survived while our brothers died for their country. We don't need to cry over beers and make each other feel better for being lucky. And yes, I'm aware I'm an asshole for thinking it. But for all I know, we survived because our coward asses found a way out. I slam my phone down in frustration and take another long drink from my bottle.

I glance down to a sink full of dishes and pans, most of which are still covered in clumps of food. "Those motherfuckers," I say under my breath. I turn and look at the schedule I posted on the side of the fridge. Uncle Frank's turn for dishes. No surprise there. I pull open the dishwasher to see if that provides him an excuse. It's full. Justice was supposed to unload it. I pull the paper—which is now covered in drawings of middle fingers and penises—from under the Harley magnet that's holding it up. I crumple it and throw it on the counter. Why did I think anyone would care, let alone listen to me?

The anger and loss of control mingle with my moment of pity and low self-esteem, pushing my pulse into overdrive. I take another drink and try my breathing exercises to ward off the attack. I've gotten so good at detecting the signs, they rarely happen, so this one comes as a surprise to me. It's not supposed to happen like this. I'm basically a housewife. I have to be able to handle this.

I pull out a chair and swing a leg over so I'm straddling it. I fold my arms across the top and drop my head onto them. I picture my mother, what she looked like when I was seven, just before she died. She was one of those non-traditional mothers who'd randomly take you to get ice-cream on a school night or let you skip school to go to a museum. I'm not one of those people who forgot their parent after they died because they were young. I've held her face at the front of my mind like a super power I could access whenever I needed. My mom is gone, but I remain a proud, card-carrying momma's boy, and when I was lying in a pool of my own blood after being blown right off the road in Baghdad, it was her face that got me through those first moments I remember. Yes, I loved my stepmom too, but she never let me forget my mother. And as I got older, she relied on me a lot with my brothers, and that's why I feel like this is my place right now, as hard as it is. I only wish I didn't feel so alone in this.

After a few moments of breathing, I can feel my pulse slow. As it does, my mother's face fades, and I see Belle, and I know I need to stay strong for her and Colton and my brothers. Then Mollie pops into my meditative haze. All my senses come alive, and it's more than just her face. I can smell her, hear her, feel her. Calm settles over me. I keep my eyes closed, staying focused on the image of her. At the same time her image brings me peace, there is also something about her that is unsettling. I don't know if it is because of today or something else, but I don't like it.

A hand lands on my shoulder and I open my eyes.

"Those demons giving you a hard time?" Gramps says.

I run a hand over my jaw and then pick up the bottle from the table. "Just tired," I tell him. I stand and turn my back so he doesn't see my eyes. I never was good at lying to him. I open the dishwasher and start to unload.

Gramps comes beside me and places his hands on his hips. "Wasn't my turn."

I look at him and he smirks.

"Where is everyone?" I ask.

"The little ones are in bed, Rebel Ryder's watchin' Netflix on your computer, and Justice is in the shower."

"I don't care if he's tired from running scared shitless out of bounds. This was his job."

"Hey, where's the schedule?" he says. He looks around and sees the crumpled paper on the counter. He tilts his head and stares at me, dragging his thumb and index finger down his mustache. "Maybe you didn't give it enough time."

I grab the silverware tray and take it over to the drawer. "Yeah? Or maybe our family consists of a nothing but lazy, selfish, ingrates."

He grumbles and I add, "'Cept you, Gramps."

While I finish the silverware, he works on the glasses.

"Considering that's not news to you or me…and you've now got that little cutie to play house with, you seem pretty pissed off, kid."

Gramps only calls me kid when I'm about to get a lecture. And since I don't have the mental energy to deny him right now, I dig right in. I tell him about what happened at Mollie's house and how it felt to be called out about my leg.

"Damn, she is a feisty one."

"That's it?" With the dishwasher empty, I close the door and sit at the table. The sink can wait for now.

"What, you feeling sorry for yourself because you brought some metal home from the desert with you? Son, that's just a papercut. When I came home from Vietnam, some of my buddies were lucky to—"

"Yeah, I know. Can we not make this about swapping war stories, Gramps?"

Gramps holds up his hands. "All right." He pulls out a chair and sits across from me. "So, you're feeling like less of man?" He shakes his head. "You looked in the mirror lately, kid? It's been what? About three years since it happened? And you're here, looking mightier than I've ever seen you."

I scoff but in a way, he's right. My rehabilitation went way beyond what I needed. I became obsessed with fitness and building my body up. Hell, maybe I was overcompensating for my leg. "I guess being here... Doing all of this..."

"Emasculates you?"

"That's a big-ass word for an old man."

"I'm not so old in here," he says, pointing to his brain. "And here," he says, pointing to his heart.

"Don't get me wrong. I'm not saying this is women's work or anything like that. It's just not what I saw my life looking like. And Mollie… She complicates everything."

Gramps leans back in his chair and folds his arms. "This is your family, kid. Your flesh and blood. You fought and risked your life not just for your country but for your family. Now…you're still doing that." He smirks. "Just with a dishrag, hanging over your shoulder."

He's right. I know it. But I still feel like I'm fighting a losing battle. "I know, Gramps. But everyone's fighting me on this. Maybe they think because Mollie's here they don't have to try. She's not here to do their jobs, dammit!"

"Then, why is she here?" He lifts his brows.

"Because she cares about the kids. About Belle. It's nice for her to have a woman around."

"And?"

"It's not like that. Yeah, she's my friend but she's genuinely a nice, caring person. I mean she's a nurse for Christ's sake." I let out a breath. "That's not the point anyway. Do you know Dad forgot to pick up Justice from practice last week?"

"I thought he came home with that annoying Turner kid."

"They were out of town. Justice sat there for an hour before he finally called me. So, what the hell do you suggest I do?"

He gets up from the table and pushes the chair in. "Well, I suppose it's time I have a talk with my boys. Your dad and Uncle Frank needed time to mourn." He reaches out and tags my shoulder with a firm grip. "Now, they're gonna get my boot up their ass."

He walks away, leaving me with a grin I can feel in my gut. A grin that feels a lot like hope.

I toss my empty beer bottle in the recycle bin and eye the dishes in the sink. It'd be a whole lot easier to just do them. My decision becomes simple when Justice walks in wearing pajama bottoms, hair still wet from the shower.

He pulls open the cupboard and sticks his hand into an open bag of pretzels. "Had seven pieces of pizza after the game but I'm still hungry."

I nod. "Burn a lot of calories running away from the other team?"

"Don't start on me, Logan. I heard all the crap from everyone in the locker room."

"Yeah? Well you're damn lucky it's only words."

"What's that supposed to mean?"

"One of these days, someone on your team just might beat some sense into you."

"Just leave me alone, okay?" He grabs a handful of pretzels and turns to leave.

"Where the hell do you think you're going?"

"What do you mean? I have homework and I'm tired as shit."

I pull my lips into a tight line but don't say anything yet. I grab the crumpled paper, smooth it out on the counter, and then stick it back up under the magnet. I peer across the dimly lit kitchen as I tap the paper. "You need to load the dishwasher…and I'm not having this sit here all night long."

His face scrunches into a pained expression as if I've just executed some extreme form of torture on him. He leans over and looks at it. "Not my turn."

"You were supposed to unload and that's why all this crap is still sitting here. So now you get to clean it up."

"Duuuude, no."

"Dude, yes." I nod and walk past him toward the doorway. "I'm not even going to argue with you either. I wake up tomorrow morning and see these dishes still here, there'll be hell to pay. Take your chances…"

I contain my grin until I'm in the hall. Once I'm in my room, I sit on my bed and see that Ryder is still watching something on the computer. I rub my thigh out of habit but it doesn't really hurt that much. Then I pull out my phone to reply to Mollie.

Me: *I'm good. And I'm sorry I left the way I did. Can I ask you a question?*

Mollie: *Sure*

Me: *Will you be my somebody?*

Mollie: *Only if you'll be mine.*

11

MOLLIE

The light turns yellow and Logan slams on the breaks—reaching his arm across my body— just before the crosswalk.

"Sheesh! You had that. Why didn't you just go for it?"

He nods to my right so I turn and see a mother about to step off the crosswalk. She's pushing one of those jogging strollers.

"Crap. Sorry. Good call."

"Thanks." He lowers his arm but instead of returning it to his side, he lays it to rest across my thigh. I admit it feels pretty fantastic, and that worries me. Friends aren't supposed to make each other feel fantastic with only a touch.

"Guess you got pretty good at that sort of thing being in the Army." I might be pushing his comfort level, but he never seems to want to talk about what happened. I told myself it's not my place to push. As a nurse, I know it can be very difficult—sometimes even dangerous—for service people to return to normal lives, especially if they've had injuries or are experiencing PTSD. I've seen it in my patients, and I've witnessed it firsthand. I'll be patient, though, take baby steps, but I am desperate to get him to open up.

"Sure, but I've always been that way. Maybe it really came from having to help raise my half-brothers."

I fix him with a stare when I say, "So, you're a natural born mother, then." And I don't hide my mischievous grin. Until I feel his tight grip clamping down on my thigh just above my knee. I squirm and yelp. "Stop! Stop! I was kidding." I remove his hand and place it back in the safety zone on the console between us.

We are at another light so he takes the moment to stare at my gesture.

"Safety first," I tell him.

"Right," he says with narrowed eyes.

When he turns back to the road, I can't help but notice his bulging left bicep, flexing as he bends it to steer the car. I know he's got some things to deal with, mentally, but physically he's solid and cut and his leg doesn't change any of that.

I stare at the road and despite my promise to myself, I blurt out, "Why did you join the military?" In the space before he answers, I add, "Because if I recall, you got pretty good grades for a jock."

He throws a quick glance at me and moves his

hand to his own thigh. "First, I wasn't really a jock. But, yeah, I always had a feeling it was my path. Maybe it's because I'm older than two of my brothers but I've always had this protective instinct. And when nine eleven happened...it affected me. I felt like...responsible. You know? Like I needed to do something. Then Ryder was born and as tough as it was to leave him...to leave them both, I had to do it."

It felt like I'd held my breath through that whole thing, and I finally let it out. "Wow, that's really... awesome." I scoff and shrug. "Sorry. That sounds so...so, insufficient but I really respect what you did." I reach over and put my hand on his for no other reason than to show him I'm sincere.

"Hey, I respect what you do. You're the hero," he says with great sincerity in his tone.

I cringe and fluster, knowing I need to monitor my words. The awkward side of me creeps out as it often does when I'm uncomfortable. "I didn't say you were a hero." I pull my hand back and try to hide my grin.

He lifts his hand and moves it slowly toward my leg. "Looking for some of this again?"

"No, no, I'm sorry," I say as I block his arm. "You said it the other day." He retracts his hand and rests it back on the console. "But I never felt like a hero anyway," he whispers.

I take a deep breath and hold it before slowly letting it out. "If you ever want to talk about...anything, you know I'm here. Ready to listen."

His head shakes so slightly I barely notice. "I'm sorry. I— What I remember of it, I just want to forget."

And there's that crap feeling I should have avoided. "Don't ever apologize for being honest." I reach up and rub the back of his neck, and I watch as his chest fills. "I'll still be your somebody."

"Damn right," he says.

A phone alert goes off and we exchange glances. "That's my phone," he says. "It's by your foot. Must have slid off when I hit the brakes back there."

I reach down for it and can't help but read the text on display. I set it on the console between us. "It's Ryder. He wants to know if you're going to watch the show tonight. What show?"

He gives me the wide eyes like maybe I overstepped. "What?"

"Is reading each other's texts one of the duties of being someone's somebody?"

"It's not like I was trying to look…but now that you mention it, that could be included in the job description. Why? You got a woman texting you that you don't want me to see?"

He smiles without looking at me. "Would that be a problem?"

Uh, yeah it would. But I refuse to be suckered into this trap. I don't even know what the hell we're talking about, considering we never really defined what a "somebody" is. All I know is that we both seem to agree that more than friendship would complicate things too much. Still, I'm having too much fun with this to drop it. "Would it be a problem if I did?"

He lifts his chin. "I'd have absolutely no problem whatsoever if you had a woman you were texting."

I punch him in the shoulder. "Smart ass."

He flinches. "Hey, you're going to make us crash. Listen, if I had a woman, my somebody would most certainly know about it." He pulls into the parking lot of the preschool, slips into a space, and turns to me. "Okay?" And his gaze is so reassuring it's the only thing that matters in that moment.

"Okay."

"Can we go in now?"

I press my luck with a tight smile and a question. "So, what's the show?"

His eyes shoot upward and he seems almost embarrassed. "It's...well, come over tonight and see. You were bound to find out at some point...being my somebody and all."

"Mysterious...I like it." I look at the time on my phone. "One more question?"

He opens his mouth but hesitates.

"Not about you," I say quickly. "You never even told me how Frank responded about preschool. I mean obviously he agreed since we're here but I was interested to hear what happened."

"Let's start walking up and I'll tell you. There's only half hour left and I want to watch some before it's over."

We get out and he comes around to my side. "You

didn't say it was my idea, did you?" I ask, wishing I'd thought of that sooner.

"No and he was actually all for it. Not because it makes it easier on him either. He said Aunt Sheri had mentioned it before she died."

"That's good."

"Yeah, and as we speak, he's interviewing with a head hunter."

"That's great. Did something change?" I ask as we walk and his shoulder brushes against me.

He shows me a lop-sided grin and gives an exaggerated nod. "Gramps happened. Hate to admit he had to step in. He owns the house we are all staying in."

"Oh."

"Yep. And he sat down his sons like they were teenagers and told them to get their acts together, or he was going to make them move out."

"Wow, I knew I liked that man."

"Yeah, he made me feel like a chump but whatever, it's done."

I giggle and he stops me just before we reach the door by grabbing my shoulders. "Wait. Smile bigger."

I avert my eyes but my smile betrays me and goes wide.

"There it is," he says, referring to my dimple he seems to be obsessed with. The way his eyes panned from my cheek to my eyes to my lips, makes me feel like he's going to kiss me. My pulse quickens but I don't move. "I think it's my lucky charm," he says.

He fades back and I let out a breath before he pulls the door open for me.

Someone is at the front desk, so we wait by the door and suddenly I feel nervous, hoping I didn't push them all into something that isn't the right time. I must have missed something he said because he elbows me and leans in.

"Hey, you may have gotten this whole thing started, but it's the right thing." He watches me intently, and I marvel at how he always seems to read my mind.

"I know you all want to give the kids a good life, and I'm glad to be a small part of it. I just know you're on your way to moving forward in a way that will make Nina and Sheri proud."

"Thanks. And you're right." He nods and puts his hand on the small of my back when the front desk attendant becomes available.

I stay silent when he signs in and the woman checks his name in the computer. When she asks about me, he tells her I'm the nanny and still I stay silent, holding back a reaction on my face as well. She tells him it's fine this time since I'm with him but that Belle's dad will need to add me to the list if I ever come alone.

We are taken to a viewing room and once again his hand finds my back, something I could easily get used to. There are four monitors, two on the inside of the classroom and two on the playground. The woman from the front, whose nametag reads, Miss Tami, followed us in and is now standing next to one of the outdoor monitors. "The sound is distracting so it's only visual."

Most of the children are outside, with just a few doing activities inside. "There she is," I say, pointing to the monitor on our right.

"She's been doing very well," Miss Tami says. "A bit behind on the pre-K curriculum but that's totally fine."

"Curriculum?" Logan questions. Then he brings his attention right back to the monitor.

"Don't worry, Logan. It's just the word we use, but there's absolutely no pressure for her at this point. As I told your uncle, we believe in nurturing learning at the child's pace."

"Good." He nods but stays focused on Belle.

I watch him watching her because the look on his face is so pleasant, so prideful. I feel his hand grab mine and he entwines our fingers. Logically, it's out of place, but it feels too right to pull away.

A moment later...I feel his fingers caressing my bracelet, the soft one, which makes me think something is wrong. I see his brows pull together. I turn back to the screen and scrunch up my face at the visual of Belle getting right up in some boy's face. We can't hear what they're saying but she really seems to be giving it to him. The boy takes a step back and Belle moves forward with no indication of struggle after only getting her boot off yesterday.

"Don't do it, Belly Bean," he whispers. "Don't do it."

Logan squeezes my hand right before Belle fists the kid's collar and pulls him close as if she's in some black and white detective show, telling a thug to wise up.

We both stand and hold our breath as Belle releases

the boy's shirt and gives him a shove with the other hand. He stumbles backward and lands on his butt. An adult comes rushing over to him. Belle strides over to some snack tables, casually like nothing happened. She plants herself next to a little girl, draping her arm around her shoulders.

"Oh, my," Miss Tami says finally. "That's not a good sign on her first day."

Logan releases my hand and brings both of his in front of him as if in prayer. "I promise you, Miss Tami, this is not a normal thing for Belle. I'm sure if we talk to her, there's an explanation."

"I would hope not, but you should know we have a zero-tolerance policy against violence."

"Violence?" I say, my voice louder than it should have been. "They're preschoolers."

Logan gives me a quick side glare. "I understand. But it's her first day, and I'm sure she was just scared or something. I'll talk to her. Trust me. It won't happen again."

Miss Tami looks down her nose at him and then glances at the wall clock. "It's almost pick-up time. Why don't you give Miss Bridget and me a moment with Belle and then you can speak to her as well."

"Thank you. I will."

"And I assume you'll let her father know?"

"First thing." He smiles and nods, grabs my hand, and then pulls me out of the viewing room.

"Well, that sucked," he whispers to me in the waiting room.

"It's going to be okay," I tell him. When he looks at me with a noticeable crease in his forehead, I say, "Imagine how many times your dad was in this exact same position."

He laughs and nods, but when Miss Tami walks through the room and glances our way, he reins it in.

We both stay composed until the door shuts and then pull our collective snickers into a close huddle.

In the car on the way home, Belle is still grinning from her surprise seeing me. "Are you going to ice cream with us, Maui?"

I look back over my shoulder. "Have you been practicing my name, Belle?"

She frowns and shrugs.

"Answer, Belle," Logan tells her.

"I have but I like Maui better."

"Me too," Logan says under his breath.

I ignore him and say, "Can I hear it, please?"

She scrunches up her face and takes a deep breath. "Mau-lee."

"Better."

She raises both hands, palm up, toward her shoulders. "Are you going to get ice cream with us, Mau-lee?"

I look at Logan with raised eyebrows until he turns to me. Then I give him an added head tilt.

"Sorry, Belly Bean. No ice cream," he says.

"But Daddy said."

I could tell he was on the fence, not wanting to disappoint Belle but wanting to make this a lesson even more. Maybe it even scared him, this whole thing. I suddenly feel guilty for the pressure I added to his already intense situation. He is a good man and this is a good family. Just struggling to make it through devastating loss. There is nothing I can do to reverse this course now, though.

I touch Logan's arm and turn my body to face the backseat. "I know you thought you were sticking up for Alexis, but—"

"Logan says if we're tough enough to handle it, then we need to fight for people who aren't tough enough."

I can't help but smile. "That's true. But you're in school now and in school there are rules."

"Yeah, and it's hands off or there's no ice cream for you, little miss." He looks in his rearview mirror at her. "Next time just tell a grownup."

"But Justice said that's snitching. He said snitches get stitches, and I don't want to go to the hospital again."

"It's not snitching if someone might get hurt," I tell her.

"That rule doesn't count until you're older," Logan says in the mirror. "Okay?"

"Okay," she says, bouncing her feet against the car seat. "But if I get stitches, I'm gonna be mad at you."

12

MOLLIE

I'm sitting on the closed toilet seat across from a bubbly maiden wearing purple goggles. She submerges on one end of the tub and emerges on the other, looking like she's just performed an incredibly difficult trick.

"Wow, amazing," I tell her. "But how about working on getting clean now?"

"Gramps says just soaking in these bubbles gets me clean enough."

"He's probably right." I laugh.

Logan went to pick up Ryder from the bike jumps, whatever that is. I offered to stay, but I'm suddenly getting a bad vibe about being here. My visits are becoming more frequent and not everyone seems to think it's a great idea. In fact, I've gotten some looks that make me glad I'm not a mind reader. I understand why they feel some hostility toward me; I only wish Logan could have found a way to avoid telling them it was me who'd threatened to call CPS.

"So, what's this show we are watching tonight?" I ask Belle, feeling a little sneaky.

"Gramps woves *Pawn Stars*," she says and then blows some bubbles from her hands.

I remember Logan telling me that, but that doesn't seem like what he was talking about in the car.

"L-l-oves. Do your cousins like that show?"

She shrugs and dives down under the water. Guess I'll just have to be patient. I reach across her to the back edge of the tub and grab the shampoo bottle. When she pops up and sees me, she goes right back down. I tap her shoulder and she shakes her head, still underneath the soapy film.

"Belle, c'mon. I need to wash your hair."

"What are you still doing here?"

I turn and see Frank in the doorway, frowning down on me. I open my mouth but am too afraid to say the wrong thing.

Belle pops up and says, "Daddy! I'm taking a bubble bath."

"I can see that." His words are matter-of-fact. Then he turns to me. "I'll take it from here."

"I was just about to wash her hair if you want me to—"

"I'm perfectly capable of washing my daughter's hair…and I don't need a supervisor."

I stand, my chest tight with sadness and a little embarrassment. I look at the floor as I squeeze by him in the close space, and we change places.

"Mollie!"

I turn in the doorway and give her a quick wink. "You said my name."

"Are you leaving, Mollie?"

I look at Frank, and he turns his head without a word.

"I probably should, but I'll see you soon."

I move into the hall but stop when I'm out of view. Guilt peppers little daggers at me but this is something I need to do, at least for a minute. It's not like I think he's a horrible person. Maybe I want some hope, something to hold on to.

"Scoot over here, Belle." His tone sounds defeated. Maybe things didn't go well at the head hunters.

"I missed you today, Daddy."

No reply. I hear the shampoo bottle click open. My pulse kicks up at the thought I might be caught here, but I need to stay a moment longer.

"Daaa-deee! You got it in my eyes."

"You need to keep them closed."

"I did. Mommy never got it in my eyes."

"Here, wipe them with this."

"I want Mommy." Her tone just about breaks my heart. It's not whiney or mad but sad, defeated like her dad.

The front door opens and Justice walks in, catching

my gaze, which I can only imagine is filled with remorse.

"What are you doing?" he asks.

Nervously I turn my head back down the hall but realize I have no reason to go that way. I face him again and step forward, praying Frank doesn't come out to the hall. "How was practice?" I ask, hoping to get the focus off me.

"Sucked."

I stop in front of him and notice a red welt on his left cheek just below the outer corner of his eye. "Looks like a rough one."

"This didn't happen at practice." His voice is low and angry. He shoulders by me and goes to the kitchen.

I follow him but keep my distance. I stop in the doorway, watching him open the fridge and look around. From my view, it looks pretty empty.

"There's never any damn food in this place now!" He slams the door, whirls around to the cupboard and pulls it open before grabbing a box of cereal. I step in as he sits at the table and starts digging into the box and eating multi-colored rings by the handful.

"Are you going to make that your dinner?"

"Why? You gonna call the cops?"

What have I done? I try not to take the remark personally, though that's exactly what it is. But he's obviously hurting for more than one reason, and he and I have mostly gotten along up to now. "Of course not," I tell him, opening the freezer and taking out an icepack.

I wrap it in a paper towel and offer it up. "This'll keep the swelling down."

He stares me down, continuing to eat the cereal, so I set the wrapped icepack on the table in front of him.

"Do you want to talk about what happened?" I ask, gesturing to his face.

"Not much to say. Some of my teammates are getting sick of my ass. Say I ain't willing to take one for the team."

"I'm sorry. I know it doesn't seem like it, but things will get better."

As I'm easing myself into a chair, he says, "You can't come in here and start acting like our mom."

I pull my lips tight but don't speak. I can tell he's got a few more things to get off his chest as he sets the box down. His eyes become glassy. "Because if you were my mom…you'd make sure we had some good food to eat. And if you were my mom, you'd have some better advice than that shit."

I swallow hard and try not to let his words affect me. "I'm sorry, Justice. I know this has to be so, so hard for you." I've never been much of a crier but I feel the tug of tears behind my eyes and the constriction creeps up my throat. That won't help either of us, though, so I swallow again and breathe. "I'm not trying to be anyone's mom. I thought we were friends. I was only trying to help…"

He ignores my reply and continues his rant. "Everyone around here would be happy and nice instead of a bunch of assholes, who are actually probably worse since you started coming around."

"Hey!"

We both flip our gazes to the doorway, where Logan and Ryder stand. This is going to get much worse before it gets better.

"Ryder, go do your homework," Logan says firmly.

"I don't have any."

"Just go. Check on your cousins."

Ryder smiles when he walks by me, gives me a little wave. Then he turns back over his shoulder and points to his phone. "Half hour."

Logan shakes his head and walks up to the table. "We'll talk about your face later, but right now I want to know why you think it's okay to talk to Mollie that way."

Justice pushes back his chair and gets up. "I'm going to shower."

Logan grabs his arm and turns him around. "We're not done, not by a long shot."

Justice yanks his arm away. "You're not my dad…and she's not my mom. And since I don't see either of them here, I'll do what I want."

Logan gets right up in his face. "Is that right? Is that the kind of house you want to live in? Is that the world you want to live in? Where no one is accountable for anything?"

Justice turns his face to the side, avoiding Logan's piercing gaze.

"You wanna live in that world, then it goes both ways. I could make it so you have a matching set of those," Logan says, nodding to the welt on Justice's cheek. "If that's how you want to play it."

When Justice's eyes glaze over, I touch Logan's arm. "It's okay. He's had a bad night. He's going through a lot."

"I don't need you to defend me," Justice says, pushing away from his half-brother. He holds his hands up. "Okay, I get it. I'm sorry."

His tone is so clipped Logan looks like he's about to go off again. But instead, he softens. "You think your mom would be proud of this behavior? You disrespecting someone…a woman?" Justice swipes at his eye before Logan continues. "It literally pains me to see you treat Mollie that way." He pauses again, breathing deeply. His words and his demeanor affect me so profoundly I can barely breathe. With his hands on his hips, he lowers his head, staring slightly to his right. "You know…it may have been doctors who operated on me"—he gestures down to his leg—"gave me this damn thing, but it was nurses…people like Mollie who really saved me. She's here because she cares and when she's in this house, you'll show her some respect! And me for that matter."

I notice Justice's face transform when Logan mentions his leg. I have no idea what this family went through while Logan was away, fighting for our country, and then suffering without them, so far from his family.

Justice blinks away the tears he won't let fall. "I'm sorry. I just…I got my ass handed to me tonight, and I can't take much more. Can I go now?" He stares down at the floor until Logan gives him the okay.

I'm practically in tears myself, but I somehow hold it together enough to stand and walk over to him. "Listen, I appreciate that but I really should go."

His eyes are laced with concern. "Don't—"

"This whole thing… I never should have started this. I don't belong here."

I step away, but he grabs my wrist. "Please," he says. My heart lurches in my chest, and I let him pull me close to him. He reaches to my chin and nudges it up. "This…" He slowly lowers his lids and sighs. "This is Justice. He acts like nothing bothers him and then he blows up. You just happened to be in the line of fire."

I let my lids fall closed too, wishing we were both somewhere else, wishing that was all there was to this. I open my eyes and he's watching me now. "And what about Frank? He saw me giving Belle a bath, and it was like he'd walked in on the evil stepmother."

"C'mon. Frank's a dick to everyone." When he sees I'm not wavering, he clasps my fingers with his and brings them up between us. "I know this isn't easy for you. And I will totally understand if you just don't want to deal with it." Giving me a slim grin, he sighs. Then he bends his head down and whispers close to my mouth. "But I've gotten used to you, Mollie. You're my some-body…and no one ever said it would be easy."

His breath brushing my lips has the effect of a double shot of whiskey. And his words have wrapped around my heart and taken it hostage, so how the hell can I walk out now? I take our entwined hands and press them into his chest to nudge him back. "Okay." I smile. "But only because I need to see what this show is all about."

Humor brightens his eyes as they grow wider. He pulls me into the living room where his grandpa, or Bud as he told me to call him, and Ryder have already taken seats, Bud in the recliner and Ryder on the floor. Colton and Belle come running in and plop down on bean bags, Belle's hair still damp from her bath.

"Take it easy on that foot," Bud says to Belle.

Logan and I sit on the couch, and the suspense has me bouncing my leg.

"Hey, Gramps," Ryder says. "Would you rather put some old lady's dentures in your mouth or have to kiss her without them?"

"How about I tan your hide, Rebel Ryder? Or would you rather go and get your brother?" Bud says.

"Justice, c'mon!" Ryder yells.

"Dude, no yelling," Logan says.

Ryder jumps up and runs out of the room. I hear his steps thundering down the hall. Maybe he's still amped up from jumping his bike, or whatever they were doing.

"Is everyone coming to this?" I whisper to Logan.

He shrugs. "Sometimes they do."

Belle jumps up in her nightie and turns to us while Colton scoots over to sit against Bud's leg.

"Cousin Logan, watch me," Belle says and hunches over, curving her arms to her sides like she's the hulk. "Errghh!" she says, straining her muscles.

"Wow, so strong, Belly Bean."

Ryder comes bolting back into the room and practically slides back into his place. "He's coming."

Justice waltzes in and past Logan and me to take the seat on the other side of me. I sneak a quick glance at him and he mouths, "Sorry." I nod and touch his arm.

As I sit there amongst all the mini conversations, I enjoy feeling a part of this big family, something so different from mine growing up. But what is this show they are all excited about? Everyone is so casual it seems like any other night so what am I missing? I glance over at Colton and my heart constricts. It has to be tough being the youngest boy and with Belle getting so much attention. Just when I'm about to quietly say something to Logan, he seems to notice the same thing.

"Hey, Colt," he says. "Did Ryder tell you what we're doing this weekend?"

Colton gives him a minimal head shake.

When Logan glares at Ryder, he shrugs. "I forgot."

"Buddy, we're going to the car show. To see some really awesome race cars. Won't that be cool?"

"And someday, I'm going to race one," Ryder says.

Colton nods but seems unaffected. But Belle jumps up and stands right in front of us, placing her hands on Logan's knees. "Do I get to see the wace cars?"

"If you can't say it, you don't get to go, twerp," Justice says right by my ear.

I lean away, closer to Logan. The loud, chaotic atmosphere can be fun, but it's also hard to get used to when you didn't have any brothers or sisters, and had a father who rarely spent time at home. And now the only noise in my home is when Lou comes over to talk my ear off.

Belle tries a few times to say the word, coming pretty close. Logan pats her head while shaking his. "I'm sorry, Belle, but this is only for bo—"

I pinch his thigh, digging in my nails and hoping to save Belle from a lifelong complex. Logan flips his wide-eyed gaze at me but then catches on quickly enough. "You're just a little too young and there will be lots of walking. Your foot isn't well enough for all that."

She pouts and dives back into her beanbag.

I look at my phone, anxious to get this going. I text Lou and ask her to take out Rocky in case this thing keeps dragging out. I go back to my leg bouncing as Ryder and Justice argue about who will sit in the front seat when they go to the car show. My nerves finally get to me, and I blurt out, "Let's go!"

Everyone stops and looks at me before they all fall out laughing.

"Sorry, I'm just so curious. What are we going to watch?"

"You don't know?" Bud says. "We're watching—"

"Did I miss it?" Logan's dad, Ed, says walking into the room. He's holding what looks like a pizza box, only there's no way that's enough for everyone.

"Awesome! Cookie chain." Justice jumps up and runs to his dad. "I'm first!"

"No way. You're last," Ryder says, chasing after him.

Ed holds the box above his head as he skirts by both boys and then sets the box on the table.

"What's going on?" I ask Logan.

"Nina used to do this game sometimes before we watched TV," he tells me.

Ryder jumps in excitedly as he kneels down next to the table. "We pass around this giant cookie and each person takes a turn breaking off a piece for themselves."

"The key," Bud says, "is to break off a size that's fair for you to eat but not so big that by the time it gets to the last person the cookie's all gone."

"So, what happens if it makes it all the way around and everybody gets a piece?" I ask, looking around at everyone. "Is there some sort of prize?"

Logan turns to me with his face scrunched up. "Oh no. Nina said the fact that we were able to successfully be unselfish was reward enough. Well, plus eating the cookie." He lifts one shoulder.

"Then what happens if you get to the end and there's none left for the last person?"

Everyone is quiet for a moment as if enjoying the same memory before Ed explains. "Well, officially there were no consequences. But my wife was not a subtle woman, and she was always trying to teach the boys lessons in different ways. So, the next night at dinner would be proof enough that she was paying attention to the results."

"Yeah, remember that one time when Justice was like third in the chain?" Ryder says.

"Yeah, I crammed that whole sucker in my mouth in about three seconds flat," Justice puts in.

Gramps swipes his hand over Justice's head, messing up his hair. "And it was my turn after you!"

"What happened?" I ask.

"Next night dinner we were all having some sort of big chicken thing and Nina accidentally didn't buy enough so Justice's plate was filled with all of his favorites—Brussels sprouts, beets, and green beans."

"Nina sounds like an incredible woman," I say.

"Best mom in the whole world," Ryder says.

Everyone grows quiet again, faces a mix of solemn nostalgia. Then a small voice says, "Hey…what about my mommy?"

We all look at Colton, who has tears in his eyes. I expect one of the older men to console him because who knows where his dad went off to, or even Logan. But the voice that pipes up belongs to Justice. "Dude," he says and then scoots so close to me my thighs almost overlap. "Colton, come sit next to me."

Colton hesitates only a moment before rising to meet Justice's outstretched hand. Colton snuggles in next to him and rubs at his nose. "Your mom was the best too. And you know what, man?" Colton doesn't respond, only listens intently. "I always thought Aunt Sheri was the coolest ever so she's the best mom and the best aunt."

The back of my eyes burn, but I blink it away and focus on Belle, who is now sitting in Bud's lap, cuddling beneath the arm draped around her. For all the struggles and dysfunctions of this family, it certainly isn't lacking love and compassion and that goes a long way to making a strong and healthy family.

Eventually we get everyone back to a more festive mood and begin the cookie parade. Not surprisingly, it makes its way around the whole bunch of us and there is still a big chunk sitting in the box before us. I'm so not surprised.

13

LOGAN

I'm not a hero. But Ryder has always seen me as one, especially since I got back. And even though I returned missing part of my leg, he thinks I'm invincible. Thinks that's why I survived. Because I'm a freakin' invincible hero. But the truth is I was just another guy, doing his duty, fighting so others don't have to. Another guy coming home messed up. Physically and mentally. Thankfully, I've worked hard to get past the demons—well some of them, anyway—and to overcome my physical limitations, and I plan to come out even stronger. Ryder hasn't seen any of those struggles. He hasn't heard me cry out in my sleep, wake in a cold sweat, panting with my heart beating wildly. He hasn't witnessed me looking like I'm zoning out but in reality, I'm frozen with fear, watching fragments of that scene unfold behind my eyes because that's all that is left in my memory. He still just sees his big brother. His hero. I'll admit it does feel good sometimes, but mostly I feel like I'll let him down. Which is why I have no idea whether or not I can go through with this.

We finally get the show going, and I glance at Mollie to see her reaction. Her brows are knitted, and she looks like she's about to laugh.

"This is the show?" she asks.

"Yep," I say with a head tilt.

"I've seen this show before. That ninja warrior thing? Where guys compete in those ridiculously hard obstacle courses?"

"Yeah, it's badass," Justice says.

I can't tell if his tone is normal teenage attitude or still some lingering hostility toward Mollie but I don't say anything.

"This…is the big mystery?" she says.

I shake my head, seeing that Ryder is about to launch into his campaign.

"First, it's the coolest show on TV. We always watch it. And second…Logan is going to be on it, and win!"

"Really?" Mollie says with wide eyes.

"Whoa, I never said I was going to be on it," I say to everyone just in case. Ryder has been obsessed with this idea for months, texting me updates on tryouts, stats about previous winners, and the fact that a guy with a prosthesis made the qualifier last year. He makes sure

I'm hitting the weights, even giving me a list of things to do in my workouts. Part of me thought I was only humoring him or didn't want to burst his bubble, but there's a small spark that ignites in my chest at the prospect. The challenge of it. The chance to feel strong again—complete with official proof.

I turn to Mollie. "We've been watching it since Ryder was a little guy. He always used to say he was going to be on it."

"I just know you could do it," Ryder chimes in.

Gramps leans over and taps Ryder on the ankle. "You're the Rebel Ryder. So, you do it…when you're old enough."

"Yeah, and I will, but Logan first. He's stronger than all those guys, even if…"

"How about we all shut up and watch," Justice says, pointing to the TV.

Mollie taps my arm and leans in. "I think you'd be great," she whispers.

I roll my eyes and catch Justice watching us. My brother and I might butt heads way too much, but the look he's giving me now is not his usual attitude. I tick my head up at him as if to ask what's on his mind.

Me too, he mouths.

I blow it off like it's nothing, but the rare times he's like this get tucked away in my memory so I can bring them up later when he's being a little asshole. Now I need to make sure he gives Mollie the respect she deserves. Dad's here so he might just be playing it cool.

When the show ends, Justice is off the couch and

heading down the hall, staring at his phone. Belle fell asleep at some point during the final competitor, even though my brothers kept yelling at the guy. I start to get up to take her back, but Frank, who didn't join the whole time, appears right on cue, scoops her up and takes her back to her bedroom with Colton trailing behind him. If he really is coming around, then next on my list is getting him to accept Mollie and realize she is only trying to help.

"This old goat needs to hit the sheets," Gramps says, rising from his chair. Seeing that Ryder is the only kid left in the room, he says, "What about you, Rebel? Did all your homework?"

"Yep." He smiles and keeps his eyes on us as Gramps passes him to head out.

That just leaves my dad, who's been sitting on a barstool behind us. "Bedtime, Ryder," he says.

"I get to stay up later than the little kids," he whines.

"Now, Ry. Want to talk to your brother."

Mollie rises the same time Ryder does. "I should go too. Let you talk."

"No, stay, please," Dad tells her.

Ryder gives Mollie a hug and whispers something in her ear; I have a pretty good idea what about.

Dad comes around to the other side of the couch and perches himself on the edge of the coffee table. He has that look he gets right before he's going to say something serious. It's pain mixed with awkwardness. I hate to put Mollie through this, whatever it is, and I don't understand why he's asked her to stay. But then his grin takes form, confusing the hell out of me.

"What's up, Dad?"

"I just wanted to tell you two…thank you. And…I'm proud of you."

I look at Mollie and she's beaming brighter than the TV. She reaches out and touches his hand. "No need for thanks, Ed."

"Speak for yourself," I say, smirking.

He rests his hands on his knees. "I know things haven't been great around here and the lot of it has fallen on you, Logan. I just wanted you to know, I know. And it might be slow, but things will get better."

"They already are, Dad…"

"But?"

"But I'm wondering if this is all because Gramps gave you and Uncle Frank a tongue-lashing." I chuckle and put my arm over my face to block the pretend smack he threatens.

"He does have a way of getting through to people." Dad stands and turns to Mollie. "And I know Frank has been giving you a hard time, but I'm going to work on that. He was struggling before all this happened, so please don't take it personally."

Mollie nods and blinks. "I won't. And thank you."

"Now, I'm going to go make rounds and make sure everyone's settling in for the night. So why don't you two get out for a bit. Go have a drink or talk somewhere besides this three-ring circus."

I look at Mollie questioningly, and she shrugs so I

take it as a yes. We quickly grab our stuff and sneak out before any munchkins or annoying teens stop us.

I left home before I had a chance to hit the bar scene. Probably good that I didn't. So, I take Mollie to the only one I'm familiar with—The Brass Bell. Mason has mentioned it a few times, so I know it's classy. But given that it's a weeknight, I'm surprised to see my workaholic brother the second we stride in—and he's not alone. Which makes me realize it's been a long damn time since I've seen him with a woman.

When it's just the two of us, Mason and I are almost as awkward as Dad and I. Those two are more alike than he cares to admit. And it doesn't escape me that I'm the odd ball in the family. But no matter our differences, he will always be the big brother whom I clung to when our own mother died. Hell, I climbed into his bed like Ryder climbs into mine.

Tonight, he stands, smiling, and waves us over like we're old friends. *Who is this guy?*

I put my hand to the small of Mollie's back and guide her over. She hasn't met Mason yet, so we make introductions all around. He tells her how good it is to finally meet her, then shoots me that look of approval. I suppose I'll have to set him straight at some point, if that look means what I think it does. His companion's name is Megan, and she looks almost as uptight as my brother typically is. Guess he's playing the laid back one tonight. I'm just glad he's doing something besides work. But they're both wearing professional attire like they came from a late-night meeting.

"You must be the nurse," Megan says to Mollie who looks as surprised as I do.

"I am."

I catch Mason eyeing me, and he immediately turns to Mollie to avoid my gaze. "I was just telling Megan that it's great Logan has help."

Mollie opens her mouth to speak but I can't help jumping in. "Well, she's not helping me. She's helping the family. Helping out with Belle."

"Yeah, that's what I meant," he says with a side glance.

"Right. Well maybe you'd know if you came to the house more." I regret the comment that just came out of nowhere. Old habits.

"So, we're going to do this again?" he says and then looks apologetically at Megan.

Going down that road will only make us both look like asses, and I don't want to ruin this for my brother, so I'll be the lone ass. "No... I'm sorry, ladies." Then to Megan, I say, "So how do you and Mason know each other?"

She glances at Mason. "Oh, he didn't tell you?" Mason sips his beer and stays focused on his blonde date. "My company is commissioning Bridges Construction for a project in Solvang."

"I love that area," Mollie says.

Megan and Mason exchange honeymooner smiles, and I'm beginning to understand. It's not just a date. It's about money.

"It's a rare gem," she says.

I remember Mason mentioning a meeting. "Renovating cabins, right?"

"Yes, and adding a few."

"I thought you said the developer was The Meyers Group," I say to Mason.

He puts his hand on Megan's shoulder in a too familiar way. "And this is Megan Meyers."

"Russell is my dad," she adds.

"Wow, that's great." My response is genuine, but I hope Mason doesn't screw this up by sleeping with his client. With the awkward timer about to hit zero, I say, "Well, Mollie and I are going to head to the bar."

"It was nice meeting you both," Mollie tells them.

"You too," they both reply together.

At the bar, I ask Mollie what she wants to drink. "Whatever beer you're having… You are having a beer, right?"

"Hell yeah." I lean in next to her ear. "My kind of girl."

"Well, I'm not as cool as you think. I have to be careful of mixed drinks and the sugar."

I'd almost forgotten about that. I guess being a nurse gives her one up on the disease, if that's what you call it. "Hey, you're still cool in my book." I gesture to the bar. "Is it cool we just sit at the bar or you want a table?"

"No, the bar is great. More to look at."

I can't disagree with that. Mollie has her hair down in soft waves. I've wanted to touch it all night but resisted and now in this "non-family" setting I can't take my eyes off her.

"Oh yeah?" I ask, wondering what she was referring to. I look at the tall bartender with the fancy hair and back at her, lifting my brow.

"I don't mean that. It's just cool watching them make drinks."

We grab two open stools and sit when the bartender comes over and takes our order. The bar is busy enough that it's entertaining but not so loud we can't have a conversation. Still, I reach over with both hands, grasp the bottom of her wooden stool, and slide her over so she's closer. "Tough to hear each other talk," I tell her.

She nods and shows me her pearly whites. The bartender sets down our ales, and she immediately reaches for hers and takes a big sip. *Yep, my kind of woman.* She sets her beer down and shoots me a curious grin.

"What?" I say, wondering if I've got something in my teeth.

"Sometimes I smile in awkward situations, or when I get nervous."

"What have you got to be nervous about?"

"For one, you're staring at me," she says, bouncing her gaze from my eyes to over my shoulder.

"I'm guessing you're used to men staring at you."

I see the faintest of pink creep up her cheeks. "And…" She gathers the ends of her hair, strokes at the purple and then flings it back over her shoulder. I could watch that all night. My own little Mollie channel. "Don't you see this is the first time we've been together where the sole purpose is spending time together?"

I narrow my eyes at her a moment. Then I turn away and stare into the bar mirror as if lost in thought. Without looking back at her I say, "Shit, you're right." I take a long pull from my beer. "Now you've got me nervous." I snap my fingers and then turn to look at her. "Only way to fix this is to do something purposeful."

"What does that mean? Like we have to do something productive? Want to make a list of—"

"Or, I could kiss you." I fix her with an intense stare.

Her mouth falls open, her eyes wide.

"Well, that's a start," I tell her, "but I was hoping for something a little more…sensual?"

She chokes on a laugh and then smacks my arm. "Nice try."

Her wrist is resting on the bar and I catch sight of her bracelets. I reach over, put my hand on her arm and brush my thumb across the soft woven grooves of the middle one. "I wasn't kidding."

"Tell me why you do that?" she says as she places her free hand over mine.

"Do what?"

"That…with my bracelet. You've done it before."

Now that she mentions it, I recall that I have. "Maybe I just like to have a reason to touch you."

"Is that all?"

Her question hits me square in the chest because now I know I've done it to Belle's bracelet too, but if I tell her that she'll probably think I've got OCD or maybe I've got some secret obsession with jewelry. "I thought you were a nurse, not a psychologist. What's the big deal?"

Her eyes peer into mine, like I've just asked her to marry me or something. "Tell me something about yourself, Logan. Anything."

14

LOGAN

"You think we don't know each other?"

"Do we?"

I take another drink of my beer and she follows my lead. Hell, yeah, I want to get to know her, but there are things in my life I'd rather not think about, so how can I share? I'm a freaking manny, and before that, my life was the military and my recovery. "Too bad I didn't marry you in that class when I had the chance." I pull my phone from my pocket. "I just remembered I need to call Justice and tell him to drag the cans out to the curb. He'll just ignore me if I text."

She cocks her head like I'm avoiding her questions, but she doesn't say anything.

"When I get back, we'll talk all about jewelry. We can do makeovers too if you want."

I step off my stool and over to the hallway by the restrooms. When I call Justice, he doesn't pick up. I leave a lame voicemail that I'm sure he'll ignore. Then I quickly check my messages and when I look up, a guy is standing next to Mollie, talking to her.

I see her smile at him and it doesn't look any different than the one she shows me, which kind of pisses me off. I'd expected one of those plastered polite deals that uninterested women give men until they leave.

As I sidle up right behind the two, she laughs, and my heart is strangled when her wannabe dimple appears. *That's my fucking dimple.* I don't say anything, waiting for them to acknowledge me.

"You need something, buddy?" the guy says, looking me straight in the eye. His face says annoyed, as if he'd invested the night instead of arriving literally seconds ago.

"Not a thing…except maybe for you to go find a seat somewhere. You're blocking my chair."

He ignores my words and dips his head in Mollie's direction. "He your boyfriend?"

"No," she tells him.

That blows me out of the water. Of course, I'm not her boyfriend, but telling him straight up "no" wounds me.

"Maybe I could get your number," he tells her.

Am I not standing right freaking here?

I laugh. Out loud, because no matter what, it's

ridiculous that she'd give a guy her number when she came with me. Isn't it?

"Hey, man. We're trying to have a conversation here."

I can hear him, but I'm no longer looking at him. My eyes are burning a hole into the side of Mollie's head, waiting for her to set him straight. Then I see the slow twist of her body, her eyes flicking my way, and the easy grin take over her mouth. Either she's really enjoying my pain, or she's getting off stringing this guy along. Either way, I'm relieved that smile is not for this jackass.

"She just said you weren't her boyfriend," the guy reiterates.

I already feel like a first-class idiot, but my next words will boost me into champion status. "Yeah, well, I'm her…somebody. So, you can leave now."

He scoffs. "What the hell is a somebody?"

"It's the person who makes sure you don't do stupid shit like giving your number to a douche at a bar."

He looks at Mollie as if she's going to correct me. She shrugs with a head tilt but her face clearly gives him confirmation. When he turns his attention back to me, she covers her mouth to hold back a laugh.

"Screw both of you." He takes a step back and lifts his drink. "She's not hot enough for me to kick your ass."

When I see he's not going to come back, I take my seat next to her.

"Oh, my God!" she says with a laugh. "I didn't take you for the alpha male type."

"I'm not an alpha male." But if she could see the vision my anger conjured up, she wouldn't believe my words. Seeing another guy press up on her… It brought out the beast and I wanted to claim her as mine, take her home, and show her just what we could be together.

"You're definitely not the stereotype." She thinks for a moment. "You're sort of like a pit bull disguised as a labradoodle."

"Whatever that means." I take a much-needed gulp of my beer. "And thanks for nothing, by the way." I meant the words as a joke but as the reality of them sets in, I grow angry and I can't look at her.

After a moment of cold silence between us, she touches my arm. "Hey, you're really pissed?"

I shake my head, partly more annoyed with myself that I let the negative thoughts take over. I turn to her. "I know we said we would just be friends, and I want to be your friend…but it just keeps feeling like we're inching toward something more." I sigh and gesture past her. "And I guess that little scene gave me a dose of reality I don't want to think about."

"For the record, I couldn't have cared less about that guy."

"I figured, but he represents possibilities, and I guess I'm jealous of that."

She snickers and I can see it's obviously at my expense. "So, you're jealous of my possibilities?"

"I guess I am, yeah," I say matter-of-factly. I touch her face with the palm of my hand, and I feel her press into it. "I know you've been feeling the same thing I have, so why do we need to stop it?"

She blinks slowly. "We both agreed it would be better…safer to be friends. I still think that's important."

"I do want to be your friend, but maybe we could be something more." I grin and raise my brows. "Like friends with…"

"Benefits? Is that what you were going to say?"

I shrug. "Only if it sounds like a great idea to you." I hold my breath, waiting, though I'm totally winging it.

"Really?" she says, looking nervous—wait, I think that's annoyance.

I let out the breath I was holding. "Well, no, not really. I would never expect that from you," I tell her and realize I genuinely mean it. "I was thinking more like friends with…perks."

She giggles but tilts her head as if to challenge my proposal. "Perks?"

"You know, like doing things like this where we go out, away from the family. Maybe touch each other a little more, or maybe I could even kiss you instead of fighting it." I lean in so our faces are close enough to feel each other's breath and I whisper, "I mean who doesn't like a little kissing, right?"

Her eyes avert mine and she backs away, picks up her beer. "You've been fighting an urge to kiss me?"

"Hell, yeah. And I know you have too. It's not like I would expect sex."

Her head snaps back in my direction. "Good, because that's definitely out of the question."

"Well, yeah…I guess. I mean…why?" I immediately regret the question because I don't want to hear some excuse that has nothing to do with my leg when we both know it's a factor.

"Dammit, Logan. I see the wheels turning behind those eyes. Don't start acting like this is about your leg."

"What? I wasn't. So, it's about the kids? You still don't trust me...my family?"

She puts her hand on my thigh, assuring me she has no idea what it's like to be a man. I try not to focus on the heat transfer and wait for her answer. I put my arm around the back of her chair as she assures me it's not my family and it's not my leg, though I'm drifting in and out of fantasyland, so I don't catch all of her words, until I hear the word baggage. I catch her gaze and freeze. "Mollie, who the hell doesn't have baggage?"

"I know, but before I get in a relationship with anyone, I want to feel like we can open up to each other, get to know everything there is to know. And you and I...we haven't exactly been open books with each other."

I get it, but I'm not ready to give up. "Won't those things come naturally if we just...get a little closer? Seems to me friends with perks is just the way to get past that stuff."

She turns in her seat, facing me straight on, her knees pressed against me. "So, you're saying you'd be willing to open up to me about what happened to you?"

I guess this isn't as clear as I thought. "I don't know why this is so important to you."

She pauses, seeming to consider her words, but all she says is, "It just is."

"Look, I did all this in therapy. But the truth is…you can't talk about what you don't remember."

She looks conflicted. Sad. "You really don't remember? Not anything?"

I run my hand threw my hair, growing more frustrated by the minute. Maybe she's right. If I can't talk about this stuff, maybe I'm not ready for this. For her. "Look, all I know is one minute, we were in the Humvee shooting the shit and making fun of Finch's missing tooth, and the next thing I knew I was waking up in Landstuhl Regional in Germany."

Mollie's eyes turn glassy before I get to the end of my sentence. "I'm sorry."

That right there. That is why this is so fucked up. What's the point of trying to drudge stuff up? "Yeah, me too. I'm not trying to be closed off. But like I said, I don't remember the worst parts and I'm grateful for that. I only recall fragments that come and go. To be honest, I'm scared as hell that one day it will all come back. Shrink said it was possible." And let's face it. Does Mollie really want to know I'm the kind of guy who would shut out the only other survivor just because I don't want to face what happened? Jennings didn't deserve the freeze out I gave him. I take a deep breath, reach out, and grab her hand. "So, you see, maybe if I don't think about it or talk about it, I can keep it at bay."

"I shouldn't have pushed you on this, Logan. I'm sorry." A tear spills down her cheek, and I brush it away with my thumb.

We stare at each other in understanding for a few

moments before my attempt to lighten the mood. "Well this has turned really fucking depressing."

She shakes her head and sighs. "This is all my fault. I—"

"Hey, I get it," I say, thumbing another tear. "My past makes you nervous so you need to know, now let's turn off the water works." I smile, hoping to get one in return.

"But I can see now how much this pains you…and I won't pressure you to talk about it anymore."

I take in a cleansing breath, relief filling me. Just sharing that small piece took me too close to the darkness I've been trying so hard to avoid. "Thank you."

She finally smiles but her eyes don't match, so I try harder, hoping to salvage the night. "Um, is that a yes or no on the whole perks thing?"

She leans into me, puts her hand behind my neck, peering into my eyes before pressing her angel soft lips to mine. It's not a lustfully hot prelude kiss, but it's more than enough. Because it feels like a promise. It feels like possibilities. "Let's play it by ear," she says.

15

LOGAN

In the darkness, I shudder from the cold, sweat painting my skin. I've finally slowed my breathing after waking with a scream caught in my throat. I'm grateful I don't call out any more. That was before I moved in here, and I'd hate to scare the kids. Though some things have gotten better with time, I still feel the lost, lurking memories fighting to break from the shadows. I dread that day. All I want is to keep the good memories intact and keep the flashes of horror buried in my subconscious. My friends…my brothers…are gone, and I just want to remember them during our best days. Not our worst.

I drift off again and sometime later, I feel a gentle shaking on my shoulder and blink awake to the blurry dimness of my room. Figuring it is still too early to get up, I flip over to face the wall.

"Logan," a whispered voice says behind me.

At first, I ignore it, hoping it will just go away.

This time the whisper comes with another shoulder shake. "Logan, come on."

"Okay," I grumble. I scoot to the edge, assuming some kid in this house had a nightmare and this is always their destination.

I feel the covers being pulled from my body, and I flip back over to give someone an earful. My brothers, Justice and Ryder, are standing there, staring down at me. "Dangerous territory," I grumble. They know better than to wake me at, whatever the hell time this is. Startling me from a sleep is a risky endeavor. I've never hurt any of them, but Justice once witnessed a mild panic attack I'm sure he could have done without. And at this moment, panic hits me for a different reason. I quickly sit upright. "What's wrong?"

"Nothin'." Justice grabs my sweatpants from the floor and chucks them at my chest. "Get dressed."

Before I can give them the third degree, Ryder starts jumping up and down like he's using an invisible jump rope. "It's training time, Lo. Come on. You promised."

"I promised this? You waking me up at"—I pick up my phone to check the time—"you've got to be kidding me. And you do realize it's a Saturday, right?"

"I told you, man," Justice says to Ryder, smacking him in the arm.

Ryder sits next to me on the bed. "We have to step up

your workouts if you're going to qualify in regionals." Even in the dim lighting, I can see the pleading in his eyes. It is at this moment, I realize how much this means to him. I guess I thought it was sort of a fantasy thing, and the idea would just fade away. Yeah, the workouts are great and aren't much more than I was doing in the two years of hard-core physical punishment I gave myself after the standard PT. But now the shit is getting real. Especially if Justice is on board.

I hold my fist out for him to bump. "What's the plan, Ry?"

Ryder's lips curve up and he looks at Justice, whom I assume was only along for kicks or maybe to do his own workout for football. "This was my plan, but we need to hurry up," Justice says.

We're not in the car long before we arrive at our destination. "What's he doing here?" I ask as we get out and I spot Justice's annoying friend, Turner, walking out of the gym.

Justice runs over to him and gives him some dopey jock handshake.

"Turner's dad owns this place," Ryder tells me with a grin like he's at Disneyland. "He's going to let us use the gym any time before or after hours."

Suddenly I feel the pressure of the situation. It's becoming more real by the minute. "What's the catch?" I say to Ryder as we walk over to them. If Turner's dad is anything like his son, it is the question to ask.

Turner heard my question and reaches out to pat me on the back like I'm about to head into the ring to fight

Rocky. "My dad's so psyched about this. It's his favorite show. He wants to meet you and then you guys can do whatever you want for the next two hours."

"And…" I struggle for a polite way to word my next question.

Turner's head bobs. "All he wants is the gym name on your shirt if you make it."

Are these people for real? Everyone seems to be buying into this possibility, so I better be damn sure I'm on board. My gut twists at the thought of letting everyone down. If I fail, the disappointment will be crushing for everyone. But, if I don't even try, what will that do to my brothers? What will Ryder think of me? When we walk in the door to the empty gym, I take in the huge place with endless training possibilities and my nervousness turns to excitement. *Yeah, I can do this.*

As we are getting settled, Turner comes back with a man I assume is his dad.

"Roger," he says, holding his hand out. "Great to meet you, Logan."

I feel awkward meeting him this way when this whole thing was set up by kids, but still I shake his hand and give him a nod. "Yeah, you too. Sure about all this?"

"Like I told the boys, I'll always support my fellow military."

"Thank you. I appreciate that."

"Well I've got some stuff to do in the office, so I'll let you get to it. Let Turner know if you need anything."

He begins to walk away, but I stop him when I say, "It's a long shot, man."

He turns with furrowed brows.

"Just thought you should know. I don't know if Justice told you but I—"

"Hey, it's cool. Just the thrill of the competition is enough for me. I did a brief stint myself. Kosovo. Before I got sent back." He points to his right eye. "Looks like it works, but can't see a thing." He shakes his head. "Tumor."

Before I can say I'm sorry, he turns a corner.

The boys and I start with a warm-up jog, and I'm surprised to see even Turner joins us. No matter what happens with this crazy pipedream of my brother's, I will take this moment and enjoy the memory for years to come. Though it's so completely different from my training in the Army, we are our own little unit—running, talking, laughing. But as I suspected, I outlast them all and they fall off one by one.

When I'm ready to hit the weights, I jog over to them sitting against a wall, staring at their phones. It was bound to happen at some point.

Turner is the first to pop up. "Ready to see the best part?"

I assume he means the weight room so I trail behind him. My brothers jump up and run past me to join Turner. We climb the stairs to the upper level and before we get to the top, I can already see some of the equipment. "Is this for real?" Ryder says and runs up the rest of the stairs.

I have to admit, the obstacle course is pretty impressive. It's not nearly as elaborate as the show but at first glance, I can see this building more strength, balance, and agility.

When I reach the top step, Justice slaps me on the chest with an animation in his face he rarely shows. Not that he's a somber kid, but kids his age just seem so subdued. "How freakin' awesome is this, bro?"

I can only smile and nod because I really am speechless. Not just because of the equipment and the opportunity but more because of these boys. My heart warms from their excitement. After so much heartache, there is hope and possibility for us all. But once again the thought of disappointing them creeps in. I must have let it show on my face because Justice turns to me, closes the distance between us. Quietly he says, "Don't worry about it, Logan. Just go for it. No matter what, Ryder's going to keep worshipping you." His smirk takes the pressure off this serious moment he created.

"Yeah, what about you, little punk?"

"Hell no!" He flips the bill of my ball cap so it flies off my head and then takes off to some hanging ropes. He leaps to one and swings with his mouth open and tongue hanging out.

I don't react and bend over to pick up my cap when I hear a voice behind me.

"Nice ass."

I spin and see Mollie standing there in workout clothes with her arms folded.

"Nice ass? Really?"

"Just thought I'd try it out and see how it feels. You know since I've got my perks card."

I lift my brows, a little confused and surprised. Before I can even respond, Ryder comes running over.

"You made it!"

"Yeah, sorry I'm late, Rebel." She loops an arm around his neck and tilts her head to touch his.

"Did I miss something?" I ask both of them.

"Mollie and I have been snapchatting."

"What the hell is snapchatting?" I snap my fingers a few times. "Is that some new-age rapping?"

They look at each other and laugh before walking past me to the equipment. "So lame," Mollie says to Ryder. It's like I've entered a parallel universe where everyone is happy and loves each other.

I decide to play my part and go along with this temporary scene of amicability, knowing once we get home, my brothers will go back to annoying each other and me.

We take some time to acquaint ourselves with the equipment and try out each area. When the boys grow bored, they head across the street to see if the McDonalds is open yet. Mollie and I take to the ropes.

"Race you to the top?" she says with a feisty gleam in her eyes.

I try to contain my smile, knowing she'll see it as a chauvinistic gesture on my part. "You sure you're up for it?"

"Whatever." She practically snarls it at me.

"Hey, it's not that you're a woman… I've had training. I work out all the time."

"I work out."

"Okay," I say, but even I hear the condescending tone in my voice.

She clicks her head to the side, like something just occurred to her. "But first..." Mollie keeps one hand on her rope but takes one step toward me. She leans over with soft lusty eyes, and I start to wonder if maybe my tone was fine. She reaches up and strokes my cheek, sending my heart into my throat and Logan junior ready to do some climbing of his own. I place my hand over hers and run my fingers down to her wrist and then lean toward her, ready to enjoy one of our newly established perks and get a feel of those plump lips. I'm just about to grab her waist and pull her in when she flips her hand under my arm and tickles my armpit.

I'm really not that ticklish but it does catch me off guard, and I let go of my rope. She immediately hops on hers and uses my body like a ladder to give her a boost. She literally steps on my shoulders on the way up, one of her flailing feet knocking my hat off once again. Who knew she was so cut-throat competitive?

Not only was I thrown off by her kick-ass move, but I am so surprised she had the guts to do it, I throw my head back and expel a burst of laughter before noticing she's quickly making her way up to the bell. I steel my amusement and leap onto my rope. I work to catch her, but she's a good body's length ahead of me.

The rope is not a problem for me but I can't take my eyes off her while I try to catch up. If she wasn't so adorable, I would have surpassed her. But instead I make it to the top a half second behind her. We both ring our bells and slide down, panting and grinning at each other.

I run my fingers through my hair and look around for the cap I can't seem to keep on my head.

"Now that was fun," she tells me, snatching my hat out of my hands the second I retrieve it.

"I think my hair must repel that hat. Maybe you should keep it."

"It's my prize for winning."

Standing taller, she puts it on and holy shit does she look all kinds of adorable. I move in closer to her, reach down, and straighten the bill. She parts her lips when she sees me staring at them so I slip one arm around her waist. "What do I get?" I say softly, bending my head down close to hers.

One corner of her mouth quirks up, and I feel her rise up on her toes. "There's no trophy for participation," she whispers. Yet I feel her pushing her body closer to mine.

"Then I'm contesting your win." I cup her chin and tilt it up. She may have gotten the jump on me, but I'm in charge now. I brush my lips across hers, and I can hear and feel the shot of air she pulls in just before I cover her mouth again, this time with considerably more pressure. Our tongues sweep gently across each other's as one of her arms comes and hooks around my neck. The touch of her hand on my bare skin causes a heat flash up my neck. I pull back and look at her. I want to see in her eyes if she's affected by this as much as I am. Soft and light, her gray eyes reflect exactly what I'm feeling in this moment. I slide my hand inside her hair to the back of her neck and pull her back to me so I can feel those sweet lips again when I hear a loud slam and the echoing voices of three obnoxious and untimely teens.

Mollie shrugs and takes a step back. "I'm still keeping the hat."

I nod, hoping next time it will be one of my T-shirts instead. And nothing underneath. I may not have won that race, but I should get the Nobel prize for my ingenious perks plan. But even as I feel triumphant, watching the guys come over, I hope I don't screw things up with Mollie. I don't know what we did to deserve her but if I piss her off, I'm sure there will be hell to pay at my house.

"We got some extra juices and stuff if you guys want some," Ryder says, setting down a couple of bags.

"I want to hit the weights before we go," Justice says.

Turner leaves to help his dad clean mats while the rest of us head downstairs to use some of the machines.

While Ryder follows Mollie around, I take the opportunity to give Justice some tips on weights and see if I can get him to talk about his exit routine on the field. No doubt the shiner he got was because of it. "Quarterback's gotta stay lean," I say, moving the pin up for him. "But you could afford a little bulk."

"Whatever, hulk."

"Are we going to do this? I'm just trying to help."

"Maybe I don't need your help."

"Guess not. As long as you can keep outrunning them…oh, and I don't mean the other team's defense."

"You suck."

"Guess me and Mase didn't knock you around enough when you were little, huh?"

He gets up in a huff and stalks to a different machine. "Look ninja warrior, just let me do my thing."

I follow him and stand right in between him and the mirror. "There's no avoiding getting hit. You can't run from pain all your life. Hell, you should know that just being in this family."

He pushes up, working his traps but his eyes are averted to the side. "No shit."

I kneel down, knowing I'm doing a crap job convincing him and totally aware of my hypocrisy. "I won't harp on this, but if you don't get it together, coach is gonna cut you." I stick my face in his field of vision. "Do whatever you have to do, but get over this. And if you want me to help, I'm here."

His eyes finally shift to look directly into mine. He releases the bar and his shoulders sag. When he opens his mouth, Ryder yells from the far corner. "Lo! Hurry. Mollie looks sick!"

Without a thought, I jump from my machine and race over. Ry has his hand on Mollie's back as she sits on a workout bench, hands on her knees, leaning over. As soon as I kneel down next to her, she starts shaking her head. "Just…give me a sec," she says breathlessly.

I glance up at Ryder who looks terrified and I can't blame him. Having a scare like this after losing his mother must be frightening. Though my heart now feels like it's beating double-time, I keep my voice calm. "What can I do?"

I feel Justice come up and stand behind me but he doesn't say anything.

Mollie's breathing worries me but the fact that I can't see her face almost makes me panic. Overdoing it at the gym is fairly common but with her health issues, this could be something more. I gently place my hand on the side of her head, but I won't do anything without her approval. "Can you look at me, Mollie? I need to see your face."

She lifts it only slightly so I try to smooth back some of her hair. Her hands move to her stomach before she lifts her head all the way. She looks at me, frustration in her eyes, skin turning pale like she might pass out or vomit. "I'm sorry, guys…"

"It's okay. Just tell us what you need." Almost as if she told me with words, I see it in her eyes.

Over my shoulder I say, "Justice, run and get Mollie's bag from over there." He's gone before I finish so I turn back to her. I smooth my hands down the sides of her head and tuck the hair behind her ears. "It's going to be okay…right?" I ask with a tilt of my head.

Mollie nods and puts on her brave face just as Justice arrives with her bag. I pull it open and rummage through it. First, I grab what I assume is a travel medical bag and hold it up but she shakes her head. Then I see a small bottle of apple juice and I know that's what she needs. I open it and hold it to her lips. She sips, keeping her gaze hooked with mine.

We stay that way, the four of us, for a few minutes, until finally Mollie stops me. "I'm good now." She looks at each one of us with a tight smile and then says, "Three heroes are more than one girl deserves."

"Not you, Mollie," Ryder says. His face is awash with relief and he reveals a small grin. "Besides, you're like family now. Right, Logan?"

I nod, looking at Mollie, hoping I've masked my fears. "That's right, bud." It's so clear to me now how attached we've all become and the implications are terrifying given our family history.

"Mollie…" Justice shoves one hand into his pocket and plays with his phone in the other. "I never really told you how sorry I am for what I said." He looks her in the eyes only long enough to catch a forgiving smile and then looks at me as if he needs to be let off the hook.

"It's okay, Justice. Really." She touches his wrist but pulls away quickly as if she's totally aware how uncomfortable he is.

"Why don't you two go tell Turner we're leaving," I say, putting an end to all the awkwardness.

They go without complaint, and I scoot in next to Mollie on the bench.

"It doesn't happen that much," she says as if reading my mind. "I slacked. I'm sorry."

I turn my body toward her and grab her hands. "Hey, just because you're a nurse doesn't mean you're not human."

I can see she's fighting something. My chest aches for her because I know what she's feeling.

"I know better." She presses her palm into her head. "It was stupid of me not to notice sooner."

"Shit happens. And you have to stop thinking like a person who can only count on themselves. You've got three heroes now, right?"

She leans in and kisses me on the cheek. "Three heroes led by a pretty hot somebody. I can't lose."

16

MOLLIE

There are small moments in time so meaningful it almost breaks your heart to know they will soon be over. For many people those moments are milestones like getting married, seeing your child born. I feel so far away from anything like that. But in my little world, one of those moments is happening right now, watching Belle as she spins around in her full-length, blue princess dress, wearing green chucks on her tiny feet, and holding a plastic rifle. She's me—living somewhere between the feminine person society is trying to arrange her to be and the tough female real life created. On second thought, maybe Belle isn't torn at all. She knows who she wants to be and she wants it all. When I first saw her, I thought being around all these males was going to be tough for her, maybe even detrimental. I believed they couldn't give her what she needs. But I can admit when I'm wrong and I was dead wrong.

Belle jumps on her bed and starts kicking her legs out with the rifle strapped to her back. "I'm kidboxing like you Maui."

I sit on the edge and fold my arms as I stare at her. "You can say my name correctly now."

She plops down on her knees and takes my face in her hands. "I know. I just like that name. It's beautiful, like you."

"Thank you. And it's called kickboxing. Not kidboxing."

She slides off the bed and takes her stuffed baby tiger, tucking it under the covers. "Is it time for dessert yet? My baby needs to nap."

"We'll check in a minute. They said they would tell us."

Lou and Logan's grandpa are in the kitchen, supposedly doing the dishes. When I told Lou I was going to hang out with Belle tonight because all the boys were going to be late coming back from the car show, she finagled an invite by dangling her homemade lasagna as bait. She insisted the boys needed a homemade meal and they could eat the leftovers.

"I like your grandma," Belle says, coming to sit next to me. "Can she be my grandma too?"

I laugh. "Lou's not my grandma. She's my...friend." The pause when I almost called her a neighbor makes my heart heavy. As annoying as she can be at times,

Lou's been a good friend too. Makes me feel like I have someone in my life. I thought I liked my solitary existence. Being an only child, it's been that way most of my life. No sharing or hand-me-downs. Even in college I lived alone most of the time when I could afford it. My friends were surprised when I became a traveling nurse for a few years and even lived overseas alone. I still enjoy my alone time, but Lou has grown on me, and I know she needs me even if she pretends she doesn't. And just because I've found myself thrown into a big bunch of Bridges doesn't mean I don't want Lou in my life. A fleeting thought crosses my mind and my hearts clenches. I wrap my arms around Belle and squeeze her, as if I'm trying to get my fill, store it up just in case.

"You're leaving?" she says in my ear. I can hear the sadness in her words.

I pull back and look at her. "No, not at all."

"I thought that was a goodbye hug."

I pray that it's not. That it never will be, because my heart is nestling itself inside this family and if something happens and I get pushed from the circle, I don't know what I'll do. The more time I spend here, the more attached I become and the more they accept me. I've even had a few positive encounters with Frank. I can't help but wonder, if Logan and I take things too far and it doesn't work…

I stand and lead Belle from the room. "Let's see if we can help them get dessert ready."

When we walk into the kitchen, Lou and Bud are all puffy cheeks and squinty eyes, and she has her hand on his arm. I give her a sidelong glance like a parent catching teens making out. She throws her hands in the air. "Oh heavens, dessert." She jumps up and sticks her head in the fridge. "I know, I can be a little ditzy…a tad scatterbrained, a forgetful Fran, a—"

"Lou!" I interrupt, reaching for the glass pan she's pulling out. "It's okay."

"Ooh, chocolate." Belle's eyes twinkle.

"Not too much," Bud says and Belle's beam dims a bit. "It's late."

We each have a small piece of Lou's delicious chocolate pudding creation with Oreo sprinkles on top. As much as I truly enjoy the time with them, I'm getting tired of answering Belle's endless questions while watching Lou and Bud flirt like I wasn't there.

"Maybe we ought to head back," I say as I pick up the pan to put it back in the fridge.

Just then the door pops open with Logan carrying a sleeping Colton over his shoulder. The image makes my uterus vibrate like the needle on the Richter scale. I try to act casual, though I am in his kitchen holding a glass baking pan like a wife waiting on her man. Our gazes catch each other, and his says he's just as happy to see me as I am him.

"Where's everyone else?" I ask.

"Dad decided to stay the night in LA with the boys." He walks through the kitchen toward the hallway. "I need to get this little lump to bed."

"He have a good time?" Bud asks.

"Most happy I've seen him in a long while," Logan whispers before stepping into the hall.

I give hugs and goodnights to Belle and Bud, and then he takes her off to bed, leaving Lou and I to gather our things. Typically, I'm not here so late but I find myself stalling, not wanting to leave without getting to see Logan one more time.

"Do you want to ask that man candy for a ride home so you can stay?" Lou takes the dish from me and puts it back in the fridge.

"Of course, not. I just…well, I thought you wanted to tell Logan about the lasagna."

"Mm-hmm." She nods and gives me a look like she's calling me out. "Bud knows how to re-heat it. Are you going or staying?"

"Good. You're still here," Logan says, returning to the kitchen.

Flutters begin in my stomach and float to my heart. Ever since he told that guy he was my somebody—no matter how undefined that term was—I look at him with stars in my eyes. Something I didn't want to happen. Then with this whole "perks" thing, I can't seem to keep my cool around him. And the heat I've been feeling is the kind that makes you stupid. I feel like I've been bouncing all over the place. One minute pushing up on him and flirty, the next holding back.

Another case in point of my stupidity—my blunder at the gym. It's rare I let myself get that far without noticing the signs. I'm an independent woman, dealing with a disease that affects my daily life, trying to be responsible and help a family survive after loss, and all I can think about is his lips against my neck while sliding his hand up my thigh.

"Is that so?" Logan shoots me a sultry look.

Clearly, I've missed some of the conversation during my internal monologue. "Sorry, what was that again?" I'm looking at Lou because somehow, I don't trust Logan not to mess with me.

"I was just telling Logan that you've been waiting for him."

"What? No...I was asking you if we should wait because—"

A cocky smirk lifts one corner of Logan's mouth, stopping me mid-sentence.

"Shut-up," I tell him even though he didn't say a word.

"You two obviously need to clear up this confusion so I'm going to go." Lou picks up her purse and pulls out her keys. "Logan, you can take Mollie home, right?"

"Happy to. And thank you so much for going to all the trouble tonight." He opens the door for her and gives her a hug.

I'm glaring at her but more out of embarrassment because I'm truly glad to have some time with Logan.

"Are you hungry? I ask when he shuts the door. I try not to look at him but when I head to the fridge, he grabs my wrist.

"Starving." He pulls me back to him, against the wall that is his chest. His other hand snakes under my arm, coming up to the back of my neck before he leans down to kiss me. It's hard and greedy and literally takes my breath away. I try to pull my wrist from his grip, but he holds me tighter so I use my other hand to run my fingers through his hair, pulling his mouth harder against mine. Then his lips soften, and he leaves me with a few light kisses before pulling back. "Want to go to my room?"

The question alone causes heat to spark and spread through me. But as much as the offer tempts me, I don't want to take this too far too fast. Not to mention he lives in a full house with little ones wandering around. "Logan…"

He's still holding my wrist with one hand and now his other hand has joined it and is playing with my bracelet. "I want to be with you, Mollie. But not here, like this. I just want to spend some time alone with you since you're here." Smiling, he dips his head, and I instinctively bring my lips to meet his. I nip their full-ness as he strokes my wrist, and I imagine him contin-uing his exploration as I lie under him.

"Okay," I whisper but wonder how the hell I'm supposed to stop this when it feels so good to keep going.

I let him lead me to his room, and I feel like I'm in high school, sneaking into my boyfriend's bedroom. "Wow, nice room, Greg. When do Peter and Bobby get home?"

He gives me fake angry eyes as he plops down onto the bed. "What, not enough purple for you?"

"Yeah, actually." The décor, if you can call it that,

consists of tans and browns. There's not much in terms of personal items like it used to be a guest room.

"This was my old room but everything got packed away when I left. Since I didn't know how long I was going to be here, I haven't done anything with it." He scoots up and over, leaning his back against the pillows. "You gonna sit? I've got Netflix. Wanna chill?"

"Funny." I crawl up next to him and lean my body into his solid frame as he clicks on a small TV, which rests on the shelf of his bookcase. It's the most comforting thing I've ever felt. I might be able to handle not being naked with him if he'd wrap his arms around me and hold me like this all night. "So why didn't your dad and brothers come home?"

He gently brushes my hair out of my face. "There was some dirt bike thing tomorrow. Ryder's way into X games stuff."

"I thought he was into this whole gladiator thing you're doing."

"He is. Pretty much anything adventurous or dangerous, he's into it." He pauses and looks thoughtful, maybe even a little sad. "Actually, he used to do a lot more before his mom died."

"Is that why you agreed to try out for that show?"

"That's part of it. It means so much to him."

"And what does it mean to you?"

"It means, I'm doing something besides being a manny."

I tap his chest with the palm of my hand. "You have to know how important you are to this family."

"I guess. So anyway, Dad let them beg for a while to stay in a motel and go tomorrow, but I think he said yes to try and make up for the last few months."

"I think that's great. It'll be nice they have some special time together."

Logan puts his arm around me, pulls me in closer. "Special time sounds good to me." He rubs up and down on my arm, his thumb just grazing the side of my breast. He's barely touched me and fire ignites deep in my center.

Before I can decide it's a bad idea, I set my hand down on his thick thigh and rub up and down. When I look up into his eyes, I see the heat. The wanting. He kisses me softly and whispers into my mouth. "I want you so bad it hurts." He presses his parted lips to mine and slips his tongue inside my mouth. Sensual and hot, his mouth devours mine until I'm panting and have to pull away. He snuggles into my neck as I slow my breathing and peppers me with soft kisses. "Damn, you smell good." His hot breath against my ear sends me spiraling, and I arch my body into him. He slips and arm around my waist and rolls half-way on top of me. "Tell me to stop," he says, "before I ravage your body."

17

MOLLIE

top? Yes, we should stop.

The only light in the room is coming from the flickering television, which has been muted this whole time.

"Logan," I respond breathlessly. "*Stop*…making me so…hot."

He cups one of my breasts through my shirt.

I clutch his broad shoulders. "Stop…making me want you so badly."

He runs his hand down the length of my body to my ass and squeezes.

I wrap a leg around his waist, and then…he brushes his lips right into the side of my cheek as if he knows my face so well, he knows the exact spot of my dimple without me smiling. *Damn.* "Sto— Don't. Stop." I'm practically panting and about ready to wrap my other leg around him when I hear a door open in the hall and tiny footsteps.

We freeze. Lock eyes. Wait. Logan gives me the softest kiss on the lips and then mouths, little feet.

"Is the door locked?" I whisper.

"No," he whisper-laughs.

I give him a mini punch in the arm. A toilet flushes before we hear more footsteps and then silence.

"Should we go to your place?"

The short reprieve has given me a moment of clarity. My body obviously went on autopilot and was ready to fly off into the sunset with Logan. But as much heat as there was between us, I felt something much stronger. I'm not sure either of us is ready to stomp that out with sneaky sex in his family's home.

"Your delay is disturbing," he says, rolling off me and staring at the ceiling.

I turn on my side and face him. "Logan…" He turns his head in my direction. "I think it was pretty obvious what I wanted no matter what I'm about to say."

"No perks?" he says with a purse of his lips.

"Um, if those weren't perks, we were doing something wrong."

He turns on his side and leans up on his elbow. "The perks were incredible. I want more. I want it all and I think you do too."

"All?" I cock my head.

"Not just sex, Mollie. All of you. You're not a perks kind of woman. You're too good for that. I want to be all in with you." He takes my hand, kisses my fingertips, melting my heart in the process. "You in?"

And once again he asks me a simple question with a complicated answer—just like that day in the hospital cafeteria. I sigh because it's exactly what I want, but there's still so much between us. So much we should talk about. "I'm scared," I say honestly.

"About what?"

"Too much. Honestly, I feel safer sticking with the perks."

He furrows his brow. "What's that supposed to mean?"

I hesitate because if I bring up his family, he might take it wrong.

"Just tell me," he prompts. "You've done nothing but be there for me, help my family… How can I be upset at you for sharing your feelings?"

I take a deep breath and decide to lay it out on the table. "I've always been sort of a loner…"

"'K. Any other confessions to reveal?"

"Stop. I'm serious. This huge family of yours, being a part of it, is all new to me." I look down at our joined hands. He's playing with my bracelet again, but I can't get sidetracked with that right now. One issue at a time. "And you…and your family are all I seem to think about."

He lifts my chin so I meet his gaze. "That's a good thing, Mollie."

"It is good. And bad."

"It's only bad if you think I'm going to screw up this

good thing you've got." He releases my hand and sits up. "I get the picture now."

"I don't think you do. It's not that I don't have faith in you." I sit up beside him. "Maybe I'll be the one to screw it up. Maybe we'll find we just aren't meant for more than friendship. Maybe once we find out more about each other—" I stop myself before my emotional rambling goes off in the wrong direction. "It's just… really tough for couples to find their way back to friendship when it doesn't work out. I know this sounds really selfish of me, but honestly, it's just one layer to the onion. It's cliché, but it's complicated and you know it."

He turns and looks at me, pleading. "So, the odds aren't great. Haven't you ever taken a chance? You said yourself this is all new to you. Keep going. See what more life has. Let me—us—be a big part of that." His words don't match the defeated look in his eyes. Like he's given in but letting me know it hurts him.

"Hey, I'm not saying no, Logan." I run my hand down the side of his face. "I'm just saying that we should take it slow. Spend more time together that is not about the kids. Get to know each other better. Neither of us has willingly shared that much of ourselves."

He nods but doesn't say anything.

"Are you up for that?" I ask.

He nods again, takes in a deep breath, and sighs it out. "Yeah, I'm up for whatever gets me you." He leans in and places a soft kiss on my lips and lingers there. "I want to know everything about you," he says against my lips. After lingering a moment longer, he pulls away and gets off the bed.

"What are you doing?" I ask.

"Taking off my pants."

"Um…" As much as that excites me, I'm confused. My wide eyes narrow on him. I move to the edge of the bed and face him while he unbuttons his pants. I'm speechless as I watch his fingers pull down his zipper.

"You want to know me?" I hear him say as he drags his jeans over his hips and down his thick thighs.

"I want to know everything about you," I answer and force myself to pull my focus from the snug blue boxers that hug his rippled thighs back up to meet his dark brown gaze. Understanding comes over me at the look in his eyes. I scoot and he sits on the edge of the bed next to me.

He slips his shoes off and pulls his jeans all the way off and then removes his shirt, before standing once again.

"You need your shirt off for this?"

"You wanna see the whole package, don't you? Besides I'm not standing her in a shirt and my under-wear. It's all or nothing."

I hide a smile but it quickly fades when I see his broad, cut chest rippled with muscles and illuminated by the light of the TV. Muscles I'm pretty sure were there before he was injured but are likely bigger now. He sidesteps until he's right in front of me, my gaze almost eye level with his chest, and I start to doubt my resolve to take things slowly. I run my hands over the ripples and then down his hips, across his taut thighs, and down to his knees. He's the sexiest man I've ever laid eyes on, and I wouldn't change a thing about him. He lifts his right leg, placing his prosthetic leg and foot on the bed.

"Touch it," he says. "Might as well get used to it."

"So, you…keep it on—during?" I ask hesitantly. I run my hand over his knee and down the length of the prosthesis.

"Whatever floats your boat, baby."

I know he's making light of it to mask the awkwardness. But it also shows me how much I mean to him if he's willing to share this part of himself.

Without a word, he reaches down and presses a metal piece that looks like a button and I hear a slight click. He pulls off the apparatus and sets it on the ground. Still standing, balancing, he removes the first layer of material.

"That's the silicone liner with the pin in the end that goes into a socket in the prosthesis," I say.

He looks at me and I dip my head in a nod.

"Exactly. I should have realized you don't need the 'how to' part."

After he sets that piece aside, he removes another material liner. His leg goes down just past his knee by an inch or so. I've seen amputated limbs plenty of times in my work so nothing about this fazes me. I place my hand at the end of his leg and gently rub a few times before trailing my hand back up toward his thigh. I lift my gaze back up to his. "Yeah, so?"

Logan leans over and places his hands on my thighs without so much as a hop to steady himself. He presses down with some of his weight but keeps his eyes trained on mine. "I've got great balance…with or without it."

I skate my hands along the corded muscles of his arms, over his shoulders, and to his face. Just touching his close-cropped beard turns me on. "I bet you do." We share a smile of understanding. "Any other benefits I should know about?"

"I can deadlift more than you weigh so…"

His suggestion brings an image of him holding me with my legs wrapped around his waist. "Nice." I clasp my hands around his neck and pull him closer, covering his mouth with mine. Our tongues brush against each other, my pulse quickens, and all I want is to feel the weight of his body pressing me into this mattress. I lean back, pulling him with me until we are lying back on the bed.

His lips move to my neck and down to my collarbone. I weave my fingers though his hair, wanting to lead his kisses to every spot that's calling to him. My whole body is humming for him, and just when I consider throwing in the chastity towel, he turns his head to the side and rests it on my chest. Our bodies move with our breathing, rising and falling deeply together. I caress his head, and he does the same to my hip. I may have tried to make this moment playful, but my eyes blur with tears. I've never felt this close to another human being in all my life. I'm speechless but also afraid to ruin it with some lame words. And I'm surely not going to state the obvious and tell him how his leg makes no difference to me. I will show him that in due time.

I'm not sure what's going to happen next but I decide it doesn't matter. We lie with each other so long my eyes drift close.

I don't know how much time has passed but wetness in my hands awakens me. The room is dark so he must have turned the TV off at some point. I'd fallen asleep caressing his hair and now his head feels soaked. From what I know and what he's told me, my first guess is he's probably had a nightmare. I wipe his forehead and smooth the dampened hair away. "Logan," I whisper.

His head shakes and his whole body clenches around me. One of his hands grips my arm a little too tightly, and I'm so scared if I wake him too suddenly I could make it worse. But I can't do nothing, so I try again. "Logan," I whisper a bit louder this time. "It's okay, Logan. I'm here."

He gasps and lifts his head. I can barely see his face before he rolls off me and onto his back.

"You okay?"

"Yeah, I'm…good."

I give him some time to get his bearings. I turn on my side and face him, place my hand on his chest. After a couple minutes, I scoot closer and lay my head next to my hand. "How often does that happen?"

I listen to him breath and wait.

"Depends. Used to happen all the time. Then it got better and was only once in a while."

He clearly leaves his thought unfinished so I wait again. When I grow impatient, I ask, "And now?"

"For some reason, it's been happening more lately."

Though I had a feeling he'd say that, my gut still twists in knots. My throat thickens, and I don't say what I'm thinking. "Do you remember the nightmares?"

He pauses and this time I don't wait. "Was it about what happened to you?"

"Assuming so. When I wake up, I never remember— Well sometimes I remember bits of it...like what we were doing right before."

"I know you said you don't want to remember. Are you afraid the dreams will bring it back?"

I can feel his chest moving more rapidly but I still press on. "Maybe you should—"

"Let it go!"

His harsh tone startles me. I've never heard his voice so agitated, and knowing I brought it on brings tears of frustration to my eyes. But I won't make it worse by crying. I pull in a deep breath. "Logan, I—"

"Mollie, no." His tone is pleading now, softer. "I'm sorry." He lifts his arm and wraps it around me, pulling me closer. "Mollie, please, I don't want you to be afraid of me."

"I'm not. I'm just worried about you. You mentioned therapy. Do you still go?"

"No." His voice still has a hint of irritation to it, so I stay quiet, and we both merely breathe for a few moments before he speaks again.

"It's pretty standard. When you go through all I did.

The accident, the operations, getting used to the leg… they expect you to do lots of talking."

"Do you think it helped?"

"I know you want reassurance. PTSD is a big thing and it did hit me hard at one time. But the therapy? It's not me. I grew tired of it pretty quickly. I'm not putting down the process for those who can benefit from it. Like I said, I just want to move forward."

"I know." It's all I can think of as my mind whirls. As hard as I tried to hold it back, I feel a tear slide down my face and land on the hand my cheek is resting on. I'm scared and nervous and sad, and I don't know how I can get passed this if he just brushes it off calling it an "accident" and acting like it never happened. And at this point, I know I can't be fully honest with him and that's not the way to start any relationship.

I don't know how long we lie in silence as I try to come to terms with this, knowing I can't push him to talk. As if reading my mind, he speaks. "Please don't worry about me. For my sake or yours. I'm not going to come unglued or anything. If the memories come back, I'll deal with it."

"I'm sorry, Logan."

"Don't be. It was the worst and hardest thing I will probably ever go through in my life. I lost some good friends, part of my leg, and a piece of me that will never be the same again. But I came back. I adapted. I fought through the pain of rehab, and I didn't stop there. I came back harder and stronger."

I turn my face up to him and press a small kiss on his lips. "And next you'll be a gladiator."

He laughs against my lips. "It's a warrior…and you never know. I'm doing it to prove I can do it. Win or lose."

"You're an amazing man, Logan, and you don't need a contest to tell you that. I know you're doing it more for Ryder than you and I think it's sweet."

"It has seemed to be the only thing taking his mind off losing his mom."

"I like your brothers. You're so good with them. I always wished I'd had an older brother like that. Someone to watch out for me and notice when I was sad or even someone to give me a kick in the ass when I'm screwing up."

"I'm sorry you didn't have that. And now I feel like a dick I didn't know that. I really don't know much at all about you, Mollie."

"Not much to know."

"I doubt it. But whatever there is, I want to know it all. A somebody would have asked you more questions. No wonder I'm stuck in the somebody zone."

I laugh. "Don't worry. I have a feeling the meter's running and you won't be there long."

LOGAN

It's been at least forty minutes, and I still don't know where Mollie is. I stood beside the nurses' station for fifteen minutes before the annoyed looks from two other nurses drove me away. I texted Mollie when I arrived, but she must not have her phone. Some guy in hospital garb said he'd tell Mollie I was here if he saw her. Now I'm just wandering the halls, but the longer I'm here the worse I feel. I don't know how she does it—being around death and illness and tragedy. Maybe if my mother and step-mother hadn't died and I myself hadn't spent months in one of these places, I'd feel differently.

I smile and nod at an elderly woman coming out of one of the rooms telling whoever is inside to have a good sleep. She's smiling too but I can see the pain in her eyes, the weariness.

I tell myself I'll wait another ten minutes and then leave. Mollie wasn't expecting me anyway; I just found myself driving here, needing to see her after the night we shared last weekend. She hadn't come by the house for a couple of days, covering for someone out sick. Sometimes I worry it's all too much, and she's going to stop coming over to help.

I move inside a small area with phones, restrooms, and vending machines. I lean up against the wall and peruse the contents of the machines. It's an open doorway so I can still see the nurses' station that Mollie will hopefully come back to.

I pull my phone out to check my messages when I hear two women talking. One of them says, "Two thirty-five B keeps complaining about his TV. Says there's not enough channels."

"Tell him this ain't no damn hotel," the other one replies in a southern accident.

The women continue their bitch session so I take a couple steps to the side to see if I can get a look at them. They're both wearing a different color than Mollie wears so I assume they're assistants or something. Then I see past them, Mollie coming out of one of the rooms with that doctor I met when I was here months ago. He's standing in the doorway as she passes him, and his expression and focus on her feels too familiar. My blood boils at their closeness and what looks like more than two co-workers talking. When she passes, his hand lands on the small of her back, and I stiffen and push off the wall. I note the change in my breathing, quick and shallow, but I stay in the enclave, halted by one of the women's words.

"Looks like those two are at it again."

I just went from mad to crushed. I think about how I can leave without her seeing me. I don't know what this means. Of course, there could be nothing going on between them but if there was at some point, it's an image that will be tough to burn from my brain. I'll picture that assface touching her every time she's here. No matter what is between us, I can't let another man touch her.

Mollie and Dr. Dickhead stop at the nurses' station, and she notices the two women watching them. She shoots them a nasty look, and they appear to get the hint and s t e p farther away. Then Mollie's gaze pans to the left of them and sees me standing here looking like a total jackass.

As if nothing has happened, her face lights up. "Logan," she says brightly as she comes around the desk and over to me. The gossip girls watch her as they leave, and I move forward out to the walkway.

"Hey," is all I can get out. Despite what I saw, I'm still happy to see her. I can't help wanting to be near her, touch her, hear her voice. When I told her that night I wanted to know everything about her I meant it. So, maybe it's my own stupid fault I didn't know she and Dr. Dreamboat had a thing. I just hope it's not still a thing.

"What a nice surprise."

She touches my arm but I'm eyeing the doc. With one hand around her waist, I pull her close and kiss her right on the lips so what's his face knows what's up. "I missed you."

"Missed you too." She grabs my hand and pulls me down the corridor. "Come take a walk with me. I'm actually just about off."

We share a glance as if we are both remembering what happened the other night. I feel great about it myself but we haven't talked since so I'm not sure if she feels differently now. Maybe that's why I haven't heard from her. I've never shared myself in that way with a woman before. Truthfully, I've only been with a few women since I lost my leg. It was always casual, and usually I just gave them a heads up. None of them became anyone to me after, even if they wanted it. Sometimes I wonder if I didn't want to face them after they saw the broken parts of me.

Mollie leads me out to a patio area, and we sit on a little wooden bench. The night is chilly so I take off my jacket and drape it around her shoulders.

"Such a gentleman." Mollie laughs and pulls it off, placing it across her lap.

"You're not cold?"

She shakes her head. "What are you doing here?"

"I told you."

She squints and then grins, obviously remembering the one thing I said to her—that I missed her. Then, like the dumb, egotistical ass that I am I ruin the moment. "I've always hated Geometry."

She wrinkles her brows and twists her lips up to one side. "'Kaaay."

Feeling antsy, I get up from the bench and stand across from her. "If this is some kind of triangle thing, I'm not into it."

"What the hell are you talking about?"

"You…and Dr. McDouchey."

"Whoa, dude, step off the page for a second. This isn't a romance novel. Robert and I are colleagues, friends…sort of."

"So, you guys never hooked up?"

She averts my gaze.

"That's what I thought. You two were looking pretty damn familiar coming out of that room."

She gets up from the bench and swings my jacket over her shoulders. Somehow it makes me feel better. "He's my doctor, Logan."

"And?"

"And I wanted to have him check me out after what happened at the gym that day."

I close the distance between us in an instant, laser focused on what she just said. "Are you okay? Is there something to be concerned about?"

Her pause worries me and I cup her face, bring her attention back to me. "Tell me. I need you to explain so I won't worry. I know nothing about this stuff. Please."

She grins. "I'm sorry, Logan. There's nothing to worry about."

I pull her to my chest, probably overreacting. With all the bad things that have happened to the women around me, I'm paranoid. I stroke the back of her head. "Are you sure?"

She slips her arms around my waist. "I was just being careful, getting a regular checkup. I can't take any chances with my job. Robert is the only one who knows and when he asked me how I'd been feeling, I told him, and he insisted on checking me out."

I bet he did. I hold her for a while longer, listening to the crickets chirp, and feel a slight breeze skate around us. "Those chicks you glared at think you and the doc are getting it on."

"Good."

I pull back and fix her with a look of confusion. "Good?"

"Yeah, I don't want those little trolls knowing my business. Let them gossip. I don't care."

"I'm sure your doctor doesn't care either. What happened between you two?"

"We went out once. That's all it took."

She obviously doesn't want to elaborate but I think I can tell from her expression what happened. Of course, I know she's been with other guys, but I wish she wasn't spending her days with one of them. "Isn't there another doctor who you can see?" I take one of her hands and my fingers run along the length of her bracelet, a habit I can't seem to stop and don't know why. I only know something about the act soothes me and right about now I'm in need of some relief.

She stares down at our hands for a few seconds before looking me in the eyes again. "No. I don't want to see anyone else because I don't want anyone else to know. I'm sorry, Logan, but you're just going to have to trust me."

What choice do I have?

I nod my answer, and she brings our hands up between us. "You're doing it again," she says, dipping her head. "Touching my bracelets like that."

"I know." Just like Mollie's presence calms me, touching her bracelets does too. "They're such a part of you, I guess I like knowing you're here...with me." But even as I say it, I realize that doesn't explain why I've done that to Belle when she's wearing the bracelet Mollie gave her.

My phone rings in my pocket and I reach for it. I see it's Mason calling, and I immediately worry something's happened with Dad. Though he's doing much better around the family, I haven't heard from my brother how our dad is doing at work.

"Mason, what's up?"

"You need to get over to my place as quick as you can."

"Is it Dad?"

"No, it's Justice."

"Justice?" I look at Mollie, unable to hide my concern. She looks just as confused as I feel. I shrug. "What happened? Is he okay?"

"Yeah...I think so. He should be. Look, he's high off his ass. Or drunk or something. Just come over."

"On my way."

I relay to Mollie what he said, and she tells me to pull the car around while she gets some things.

The whole drive to my brother's house, I wonder how Justice ended up with Mason. I know why he didn't call Dad, but if he was in trouble, why didn't he call me?

I feel Mollie's hand on my thigh. "It's going to be okay."

"I know. Unless I decide to beat his ass."

"Don't be too hard on him. I'm sure you—"

I clasp her hand in mine. "You're right. I know."

Mason pulls the door open, still wearing his suit from the day, his tie loose and his top shirt button open. Sometimes I wonder if he dresses to make himself feel more important.

"Where is he?" I say, coming in the door after Mollie.

"In my room."

I start to walk down the hallway and Mason grips my arm. "Hold up a sec."

"I want to see my brother and make sure he's okay."

"He's had a rough night if what he says is true. He doesn't need you getting on his shit right now."

I'm blown away by his response. Mason has always been the strait-laced one of us and he's telling me to chill? I pull my arm away and start to move around him but he side steps and stares me down.

"Why don't I go in first," Mollie tells us. "You two can talk and I'll check him out, make sure he's all right." She walks off down the hall before either of us can respond.

"Last door on the left," Mason says.

"I don't like this," I say more to myself. "Even if he's fine, I want to see for myself. Find out what happened."

"How about a beer?" he says, heading to the fridge.

When Mollie closes the door behind her, I turn away and sigh. "Why not." I head toward the kitchen and slide onto a bar stool. I finally take a moment to look around, realizing there are some distinctive changes to the place. Not that I'm some master decorator, but Mason couldn't barely be bothered to put out a photo after a year living there. His house used to feel like nothing more than a second office. Now the subtle touches—art on the wall, a few strategically placed woven baskets, and new dark wood coffee table—have me wondering if this is Megan's doing.

Mason pops the cap off a bottle and hands it to me before doing the same for himself. He stays on the other side of the counter and stares at me like he wants to say something.

"What?"

"I know you were going through hell over there in Germany, bro...but that look on your face just now..." He shakes his head. "That's just how we all felt not being able to get over there to see you."

Sadness and regret swirl in my gut. "I'm sorry. I know it must have been hard." I take a drink and eye him. "So why are you telling me this now?"

"I just wonder..."

"What?"

"If Nina and Sheri hadn't died if you'd have ever come home."

The emotional cocktail that was swimming around turns to stone and falls to the pit of my stomach. I don't even know what to say. Because he's got a point. "Honestly, I'm not even sure. After Germany, I was hardcore into my rehab." I hold the bottle and stare into it. "It's the only way to be if you want to come back from something like that."

I look up and he's nodding. "It was all I was capable of, and maybe it was selfish but making it back stronger was not only good for me. It meant no one had to take care of me." I take a long pull on my beer. "What does this have to do with anything? The point is, I'm here now. That should count for something."

"I guess." He takes a drink of his beer and sets it on the counter. "I know you think you're making this big sacrifice right now. I get that because I sure as hell wouldn't want to do it now. But I would have if I wasn't already working."

If the fact that he had a job and I was injured and unemployed is supposed to make me feel better, he's not as smart as he pretends to be. "I know, Mase."

"And since you've come back, you think I'm not doing shit."

I admit I felt that way in the beginning. Only because I was shocked at the transformation my life had made. Those bombs didn't just blow off my leg; they blew up my whole life. "I may have misread the situation some. But...just because you're working with Dad doesn't exempt you from any other responsibility."

"That's just my point, man. Who do you think was

here for the family when you weren't? You were gone a long time. And the way you came blazing in here tonight like you're Justice's dad. Like you're the only one he needs or wants. But Justice came to me. Turner said the only person he'd let him call for help, was me."

"Turner? That little shit was a part of this? That figures."

"No, he wasn't. He was helping him from what Justice says."

I look down the hall, feeling anxious to get back there but grateful Mollie is with him.

"You're lucky to have her," Mason says, drawing my attention back to him.

Though I don't feel like I have her, I say, "I know. So, what happened tonight?"

"He swears he didn't intentionally do this to himself."

I narrow my gaze at him. Justice isn't a liar, but he's gotten in his share of trouble, including snaking alcohol from the house for him and his friends. "You believe him?"

"Didn't sound like a party to me. More like a setup."

"What the hell? Who?"

Mollie comes out of the room and joins us in the kitchen. She politely declines Mason's offer for a beer and proceeds to tell us that Justice is going to be fine and is resting after emptying the contents of his stomach in the toilet.

"Did he tell you anything?" I ask after Mason and I both thank her.

"He's embarrassed and hurt, which tells me someone did this to him."

My blood is boiling at the thought of someone messing with my brother. I know I can't step in and solve all his problems but this is bull. "Did he say who or how?"

Mollie takes the stool next to me and places her hand on my arm as if she knows her touch will calm me. "He only said that he was hanging out with friends and there was food and drink there but nothing illegal."

"Something must have been spiked," I say. "Unless someone slipped him something."

"I don't think he wants to tell," Mollie says. "Doesn't seem like he's afraid, but…"

"He doesn't want to get labeled a snitch," Mason says.

"I don't get it. He's a great-looking kid, totally sweet, and he's the quarter back. I thought guys like him were immune to the whole bullying scene."

"Maybe, but this is more like hazing." Mason points his beer in my direction. "Those punks on his team are pissed at him."

Mollie gives a tight smile and tilts her head. "Football is already that important?"

"Yep. And they hate that coach keeps giving Justice play time. He's got that golden arm. It pays off most of the time and I'm sure coach is working with him and hoping it's only a matter of time before he gets over his fear of being hit."

My phone buzzes in my pocket, and when I pull it out, I don't know whether to laugh or swear.

"What is it?" Mollie says after she sees my expression.

I stand. "Now he texts me. It's Justice. He wants me to go in and see him."

She laughs. "He's ringing the bell for you, nurse Logan." She gestures her head in the direction of the room. "Your brother left a Gatorade by the bed. Make sure he drank some of it."

"You'll be all right, here?"

"Heck yeah. I'm going to pump your brother for information about you."

I knew he'd be fine. But seeing his wiry frame sprawled out on my brother's king-sized bed makes my heart heavy with worry and sadness. My brothers—especially Justice—put up the tough front but they truly are boys without a mother.

"Stop staring at me. I'm awake."

I step into the room and pad over to the bed. "Pretty boy looks like crap," I tell him as I take a seat on the bed.

"Thanks."

"That's the shortest comeback in history. You are messed up."

"C'mon, dude. My head is spinning and I don't have the energy to pop off to you."

I lift the bottle of red liquid from the side table and hold it up to him. He shakes his head and then brushes the fallen hair from his forehead. "No. No more of that crap."

I set it down and give him a taut smile. "This has to

stop. This is no joke. You could have gotten seriously hurt."

His eyes narrow even more than they already were. "What do you want me to do? Go to the coach and add snitch to their bitch list?"

I know that will only make it worse but he may not like what I have to say. "I'd never tell you to give in to bullying…" I pause and take a breath. "Almost never. What you need to do is be a leader on the team. That's what quarterbacks do. And the first order of business is getting over your fears."

There is a long pause and I wait it out. Usually he mouths off about his golden arm and how coach thought he had this great potential. Finally, he whispers. "I don't know if I know how."

"I'm gonna show you."

"What? Army style?"

"Whatever. Look, you're coming to the gym with me. You can work the obstacle course, improve your agility. And then…you're going to have to take some hits. Even if I have to do it myself."

His eyes go wide and he turns on his side toward me. "You're like twice as big as me and most of the guys on the field. You'll crush me."

I smile and give his shoulder a little shove. "So, we'll start with Turner's skinny little ass. That ought to break you in."

We sit for a while longer and it looks like he dozes off. Maybe he just shut is eyes so he doesn't have to talk. I don't ask why he called Mason and not me. It seems petty and Mason was right. They had years to bond while I was away. It doesn't matter that I was fighting for our country or even that I was injured. My brothers grew up and grew together without me. I need to understand that and be patient while I gain their trust. I don't just welcome the chance. I am grateful for it.

LOGAN

With a towel wrapped around my waist, I hop over to the toilet seat and sit down in the steam-filled bathroom. My heart and mind are both racing, anticipating the night ahead of me. I'm taking Mollie on an official date tonight, and I feel like it's the first date I've ever been on. When was the last time I took a woman out? Treated her special? This isn't just any woman, though. It's a woman who makes me smile just from the thought of her—her humor, her generosity. So many things I can't put words to. A woman who calms the lurking fears that try to invade my consciousness. Strangely, there's also something about her that scares me. Something that warns me not to get too close to her. Yet that's all I want. I wish

I could decipher what that is because it doesn't feel like your standard relationship issues.

"Dude! Stop staring at your ugly mug and get out." Justice bangs on the door with this foot.

"Go use another one," I tell him through the door. For once I'm not giving it up.

Surprisingly, he doesn't reply. He's been a little less mouthy lately, after he almost became the star of an after-school special.

As I lotion up my chest and arms, I stare down at my amputated leg. Mollie didn't even flinch when she saw it. She's a nurse. Professional. I shouldn't expect anything less. But her eyes weren't evaluating me like a patient; I felt relieved at the acceptance I saw there. Still, acceptance and caring are a whole different story from desire. It sucks to know that for the rest of my life I have to wonder about that. I know it's on me. Something I need to work on and accept, but I hate the expectations even if I've only put them on myself.

One thing I do know is that it took all my mental and physical strength to stop what was happening in my bed that night. The feel of her velvety skin as I ran my hands down her torso. Her sinuous body writhing underneath me. Since that night it's been all I can do to not think about it—every minute I'm with or without her.

I use the sink to help me up and look at my face in the mirror. Thankfully I don't look as tired as I feel. I couldn't sleep last night, experiencing phantom limb pain, which I haven't had in a long time. It's pretty common but still a shitty thing to experience—pain when you don't even have the damn limb you feel the pain for. I tossed and turned and finally fell into an exhaustive sleep sometime after 2:00 a.m. And by the way I woke up, I know I dreamt about that day. I can always tell even if I don't remember. People get hypnotized to remember stuff. I want to get hypnotized to keep the memories at bay. If that makes me a coward, I can live with that.

What I can't believe is that I'm actually unsure what to wear. *Since when did I ever care about my wardrobe?* I miss the days where everything was uniform. I did, however, pick the place with no problem. I'm taking Mollie to a beach house restaurant on the pier she mentioned she's been dying to try. I know she'll love sitting on the wooden deck, and they've got great Mexican.

When I'm just about finished up, another knock sounds on the door.

"I have to go pee," my tiny cousin's voice—another one that makes me smile—says. And for a moment, I feel happy and sad all at once…for almost missing out on this opportunity and for understanding how parents feel when their kids are growing so fast you actually miss the kid they used to be. As if missing an actual person.

"Hold on, Belly Bean." I gather my things and open the door. My room is right across the hall so I typically hop back and get myself "wardrobed up" in my room.

"We should take a bubble bath together," she says as she passes me.

I pause in my doorway, holding back a grin. "Um, I don't think so."

"But why?"

"Because you're not allowed to bubble bath with boys until you're married or thirty. Got it?"

"Okay."

She shuts the door and then I shut mine, grateful I didn't have to respond to another "but why."

I planned to spend the rest of the afternoon ensuring I don't feel guilty leaving for the entire night to be with Mollie, even if I'm putting that on myself. But there really isn't much for me to do. The house is fairly clean. Justice and Dad are about to head out to his game. Ryder is at a friend's house, and Uncle Frank is taking his kids to Denny's for dinner. I'm floored. How is it that no one needs me right now?

When I think about it, things have been running pretty damn smoothly lately. It's been a team effort, but I can't help but believe it wouldn't have happened without Mollie's presence. Even the times she's just here hanging out, everyone seems more relaxed, more patient with each other. Must be some magical Florence Nightingale thing.

As I head toward the door, I spot the one person I hadn't accounted for. Gramps is dozing in his recliner, a half-empty bottle of beer on the side table. I don't want to wake him but gramps doesn't have a cell phone. I stop in the middle of the room, deciding whether or not to leave a note.

"I'm not asleep," the old man says.

"I'm heading out, Gramps. Need anything?"

"What are you, my waiter?"

"No one's going to be home so what are you going to do if there's an emergency?" We let the landline go a few months back. "You really should get a cell phone."

Gramps reaches into his front shirt pocket and pulls out a black device. "You mean one of these gadgets?"

My eyes widen. "Where'd that come from?"

"It's mine. Lou talked me into it."

Lou?

"Back in my day, you know how we talked to our friends?"

"I know. You leaned sideways and yelled over the roar of the bike."

He shakes his head. "Now I need teenagers to show me how to dial a number."

"Then why'd you get it?" I smile because I know the answer and just want him to say it.

"You better head out, Romeo. Don't make that pretty girl wait."

Before I go, I program my number into his new phone and see he's only got one contact: Lou. Gramps hasn't been with a woman for as long as I can remember. His wife walking out all those years ago must have hit him too hard.

As I head to Mollie's to pick her up, I can't help but wonder about prior generations of the Bridges men.

Maybe hundreds of years ago, some witch laid a curse on one of my ancestors for cheating with the scullery maid. Of course, I don't believe that, but it's quite possible the Bridges men are just unlucky bastards who either lose the women they love or run them off for whatever reason. I might have my own issues, but I'll do whatever it takes to be worthy of Mollie. This I know. Still, the thought is bittersweet since Mollie is going out of town soon to visit her parents for the holidays. We've spent so much time together lately, my heart constricts thinking of how empty it will feel without her.

I ring the doorbell and Rocky's paws appear in the window. A moment later, the door opens, and Mollie comes out, shutting the door behind her.

"Hi," she says, placing a palm to my chest.

Before I can dwell too much on why she didn't let me in, I notice her hair. The purple is gone. I liked it, but she looks even more striking with her sleek black hair framing her gorgeous face. She's wearing a deep purple sweater, a short black skirt, and black boots. Holy crap that space of skin between skirt and boot draws me in like a magnet, but that's dangerous territory right now. I force my gaze back up to hers and once again am blown away by her beauty. I step closer and grab a section of her long hair and run the pads of my thumb and forefinger down the length of it. "I like it."

"Thanks. I was planning on making a change anyway but since I'm seeing my parents I did it early."

"They don't like your…color?"

She lifts her chin with her lips pulled tight. "Um, no. They're VCR, pager, mom jeans type of people."

"Mom jeans?" I chuckle and wonder how she manages that relationship, but I also hope they don't make her feel bad for her choices, especially when all I want to do is make her feel good. I skim my hand over her waist to her back. Then I lean in and place my lips against her ear. "I love everything about you," I whisper. Her head dips against my shoulder, and I can't help but enjoy the deep rise and fall of her chest with my words. I place a single soft kiss just below her ear and feel her inhale against my neck.

"You smell amazing," she says.

I don't want to take this night straight through to the finish line so I back away to look into her eyes. "It's called…soap." I smirk and grab her hand in mine, lacing our fingers, and nothing has ever felt so right. "Let's go eat these famous tacos you been dying to try."

"I heard the margaritas are just as good if not better."

At the restaurant we belly up to a small high-top round table in the bar area and immediately order two of their famous Cadillac margaritas. The place is pretty authentic-looking in its Mexican décor, and if the smell wafting around is any indication, I'm sure the food will be amazing.

We each pour our side shots of Cuervo into our glasses, give them a whirl, and take a sip. "Whoa, these are strong."

She raises her brows and sets her glass down. "Oh, yes. Faster buzz and less sugar for me."

"How hard is that on you? Keeping track of everything all the time?"

"Sometimes it really does suck. Actually, it was worse when I was a kid. Now, I figure most women are watching every damn thing they eat anyway so I'm not that different."

I love her positive spin on something she clearly has a right to bitch about. "Whatever you're doing is definitely working." And just like that, all I can think about is seeing her naked. "You're in great shape."

"Says the ninja warrior."

I shake my head, trying to think of something that doesn't sound douchey but she jumps in before I come up with anything.

"Have you heard anything yet?"

"No, but I sent my tape in pretty early."

"Ryder must be going nuts with the waiting."

"He is. City auditions are still weeks away so I'd rather focus on other things." I lean over and put my hand right next to hers and rub my thumb on the back of her hand.

Mollie sips her margarita but keeps her steady gaze on mine. The heat transferring between us right now could melt the salt right off the rim of our glasses.

"You two ready to order?"

Mollie pulls her eyes away first and addresses our tall, lanky server. He barely gets a glance from me when he places chips and salsa on the table. I'm more interested in drinking in Mollie's beauty and getting pleasure from her awkward grin as she gives her order.

She clearly knows I haven't wavered in my stare. The left side of her mouth quirks up slightly, and I can tell she's holding back a grin as she asks the waiter to add extra guacamole. I slide my arm across the back of her chair and finally relent when she elbows me in the ribs.

"For you, sir?" the waiter asks.

"Whatever this beautiful girl just ordered, you can double it."

"Flexible eater, I like that," she says when the waiter walks off.

"Sure, I guess…that doesn't mean I don't enjoy the finer delicacies." I dip my head but keep my eyes on her, no hint of a grin because I'm dead serious.

Her cheeks flush a rosy shade, and I hope it's not from being shy or embarrassed because I plan on bringing that heat to her skin for the rest of the night.

"Well, I'm not sure it's a delicacy, but I love Mexican food."

Since she chose to ignore my innuendo, I decide to go along at her pace. I stick to small talk for a bit and then dive in to some personal questions. "So…tell me about your friends."

Her mouth purses and twitches to the side as she grabs a chip and eats it, the chewing conveniently giving her time.

"You do have friends, don't you? Maybe a BFF?"

She lifts her glass and tilts back a large swallow. "I guess I have to admit that the closest thing I have to a BFF…besides you"—she grins—"is Lou." She slips two of her fingers through her hair and pulls a thick piece forward. "Sad, huh?"

"Not at all. Lou's awesome. I'm pretty close with my gramps."

"Age is just a number, right?"

"We'll keep telling ourselves that."

We clink glasses as if we are toasting our mutual pathetic social lives.

"I was never the BFF type anyway," she says. "Then I did some traveling and work kept me so busy."

"Hey you don't have to explain to me. So, what kind of travel did you do?"

She pauses and plays with the stem of her drink, and I just want to tangle my fingers through hers. "I took a couple years off to work as a traveling nurse."

"That's amazing." I shouldn't be surprised she's even more interesting than I knew. "And, what kinds of places did you—"

"Would you two like another margarita?"

We both nod and laugh like it's an obvious answer.

"My pleasure. And your food should be out shortly."

I finish off my drink, ready for the next one, but aware I better watch how much this girl drinks. I want her free to make decisions later tonight. The mariachis start up, and Mollie glances across the restaurant in their direction, exposing a delicate section of her neck. My gaze goes right to it and travels down her collarbone to the slight bit of cleavage showing in her V-neck sweater. I can almost feel my lips grazing across her heated skin. I reach over and cup the back of her elbow, bringing her attention back to me. Her light gray eyes sparkle at me, and when she blinks, I'm certain she's reading my mind.

I'm just about to pick up our conversation when she jumps in.

"So, do you have any close friends?"

I should have seen the question coming. Maybe I could have braced for the knife piercing through my gut. I decide to ease into it. "Having three brothers was sort of like built-in friends. But I left home after high school so there wasn't much chance to make friends." I pause when I feel a sting behind my eyes. A burning that not only represents a hole in my heart but makes me feel like a coward.

"Are you okay?"

I feel her hand on my arm and I instantly place mine over hers. I refocus and find her eyes, unaware I'd drifted away for a moment. "Yeah, sorry. I did have… They're gone, though. Most of them anyway." The predictable guilt washes over me thinking of Jennings.

The waiter brings our new drinks, and we both just watch him in silence. When he leaves, Mollie pushes hers aside and leans over. "Did you want to tell me about them?"

I take a deep breath, knowing this could be a defining moment for us. She wants to go slow, to get to know each other. She clearly knows I have baggage. I want more than anything to get over these hurdles so we can be together, which is why I showed her my leg.

That was me, being vulnerable and opening up. But this…feels so much harder.

"I don't want to pressure you, Logan—"

"You're not. Truth is I let my friends down. I haven't been true to them."

"What do you mean?"

"I've told you I can't remember…that I don't want to remember what happened to me. But in doing so I also don't let myself think about my last moments with my friends who didn't make it."

Her eyes glass over. She blinks and widens them. "I'm sure your friends cared about you as much as you them. They wouldn't want you to suffer."

I breathe in deeply, trying to cleanse out the bad air. "Someday I might not have a choice. It might all come back to me."

Mollie seems even more shaken, and I suddenly feel bad for taking a dark turn on our evening. She picks her drink up and holds it to her lips. "How about you tell me one pleasant memory of you with your friends?"

Grateful for the mood change, I nod and she sips. And in no time a memory pops to the surface and I chuckle. "I met Morgan first. Everyone called him Mo. And when we started hanging with Vin, the three of us were inseparable. Like the three musketeers. But one day Sarge started calling us the stooges."

"'Cause of Mo?"

"Yeah. But those dudes were the opposite of stooges. Class act men."

"Like you." She grabs my hand and squeezes. "King of

the stooges." As she's laughing, I pull her closer, slide my other hand behind her neck, and cover her mouth with mine so quickly hers is still open from her gasp. The kiss is hard but I keep it short and pull back only slightly so my lips are still floating in front of hers when I say, "Nya, ah, ah."

"I'm going to miss you," she says, turning our silliness serious.

I pull back, my chest tight. "Yeah, me too." I don't want to make her feel worse so I don't say what else I'm thinking. I can't imagine spending Christmas without her.

"I know the holidays are going to be hard for you." Her lips pull to a thin seam. "It's been a while since I've seen my folks…"

I mirror her expression. "It's okay." But it's not. And in this moment, I realize how much I've come to rely on her. Not only with the kids, but emotionally. But I refuse to let this night become a downer. "I'll just have to suffer through it." I rub my jaw like I'm thinking when really I can't let myself. "I'll get by without my somebody, somehow." I wink and move my thumb over the top of her hand, but I regret my words. I regret not saying what's in my heart because she's not just my somebody. She's quickly transforming into my everything. And—crap—I now realize my revelation caused me to miss part of what she was saying.

"…and it's only a couple weeks and I'll be home right after Christmas."

The food comes and we eat and talk and flirt and

touch and stare. Hot damn do we stare. Food messy, lettuce falling out of tacos, sauce dripping, and all the while our eyes are getting it on something fierce. I'll call this act one and pray act two involves all the other body parts in Mollie's bed.

2 0

MOLLIE

"Stop staring at my ass." I glance over my shoulder and narrow my eyes at Logan.

His head shoots up as he trails me to my front door. "You don't know."

"Then why do you keep walking behind me?"

"I'm being a gentleman."

I reach my front door and turn to catch a devilish grin on his face. I actually love that he was staring at my ass, and that face—I could get used to staring at it. "Of course, you were."

He stops two steps from me. "Either way, it's a compliment, right?"

I try to keep a straight face so he won't think he's right, but I fail. So, I look down and filter through my purse like I'm looking for my keys. *Lame move.*

He closes the distances between us so his clothes brush my arm and his scent lingers under my nose. "Smile bigger," he says softly.

"What? Stop." I pull my keys out and feign ignorance.

"C'mon, I wanna see it."

Of course, my grin betrays me and grows wider because I know exactly what he wants.

He rubs his thumb in the tiny groove on my cheek, and I lift my gaze to meet his. *Smoldering.* When he replaces his thumb with his lips, embers blaze across my skin and then swirl around my belly. Butterflies take flight from the pit of my stomach as he drags his lips over to my ear. "You know one of my biggest fears?"

I shake my head but don't even attempt to move away.

"Another man touching my dimple. Let alone even looking at it."

I don't know what to say. I've never had a man claim my dimple before. But hearing the words and the passion behind them have turned my legs to jelly. I turn my head so my lips are even with his, wrap my arms around his neck and pull his mouth to mine.

Our kiss starts slow, sensual, and then grows needy. The mere brush of his tongue against mine causes my pulse to quicken, and my body arches into him. He's holding me firmly around my lower back, and we shuffle backward until we're leaning against the door. He pulls away from the kiss for only a moment, dragging in a breath, and I do the same. Then he brings his lips right back to mine. My keys are still in my grasp, and I'm surprised I have the fortitude to keep them from stabbing him in the neck. Our kiss continues like a teasing dance, him leading at a more frantic pace now. I never want to stop, and yet I know the keys in my hand could mean having so much more.

Then, my phone rings in my purse, and we both ignore it like it doesn't exist. His lips move to my cheek and brush over the spot he's claimed, and just knowing how he feels about it makes my head spin. When he reaches my neck, I moan at the same time my phone pings with a text. I want to feel his hair so badly so I run over his soft, thick waves with my one free hand. My phone pings yet again, and Logan pulls back.

"You better check that."

Our breathing is so heavy someone walking by would think we ran here. I pull my phone out—which continues to ping—and shake my head, trying to decide if I should laugh or scream. I have a missed call from Lou and several texts. I flash my screen at Logan.

Lou: *I'm at your place and I hear noises.*

Lou: *Someone's on the porch but I'm afraid to look.*

Lou: *Rocky is no help. He's just lying here.*

He shrugs. "Guess we better get in there."

With my libido now in check, I shout at the door before I put my key in. "Lou, it's us."

Lou is sitting on the couch with Rocky's paws draped across her lap and her phone in hand. "Thank God."

"Sorry we scared you," Logan says.

"Lou, what are you doing here?"

"I brought the suitcase you wanted to borrow." She gestures to the bag that is off to the side. "And I made you two some brownies for dessert…low sugar." She smiles and gestures to the coffee table. "It was no trouble at all. Then Bud and I started chatting and I got distracted."

The thought of her and Logan's gramps getting close warms my insides. Selfishly, I hope it takes the pressure off me to be such a big part of her life.

Logan and I exchange glances, and I'm sure he's wondering if he should go or she should. Then he takes a seat on the couch next to her. "I'm really glad you and Gramps have hit it off. I've been trying to get him a cell phone for months."

While they make small talk, I excuse myself to the kitchen where I pull one of my mini kits from the drawer and test my levels using the app on my phone. I was pretty good at dinner but I'm just making sure in case I decide to have a taste of brownies or some wine. It's so much a part of my routine that my mind wanders and sadness comes over me. As much I was anticipating tonight and what might happen, I tried to keep the fact that I'm leaving away from my mind. But suddenly, I'm already missing Logan and I haven't even left yet. More than anything, I want to make tonight special, give him something to think about while I'm gone.

I finish my business and collect some glasses, a bottle of wine I already had opened, and some napkins. When I return to the living room, the two are laughing like besties, sitting right next to each other and staring at Lou's phone.

"Louise Ann Garner, are you looking at the naughty videos again?"

Her eyes widen and she sits up straighter. "I told you that was an accident. I was just showing Logan the pictures of Rocky wearing the shirt I made him."

"Okay. I wouldn't want you to corrupt Logan's innocent eyes." I set the bottle and glasses on the coffee table and sit on the couch next to him.

Logan doesn't pull his attention from Lou, which is nice but at the same time, I want it on me. I lean back against the cushions while Lou continues to scroll through pictures and Logan appears completely enthralled. *How has this senior citizen hijacked my date?* Just when I'm about to lean forward and douse my neglected feelings with chocolate or booze, I feel his hand slide onto my thigh. Without looking from Lou, he finds my hand and laces his fingers with mine, and it's all I need to bring me back to my happy place. Of course, he's being polite to Lou, and now he's showing me why.

"Well," she finally says and pops up from the couch. "You two don't need me hanging around. I better take off. Skedaddle. Scram. Split. Get the hell out of do—"

"Bye, Lou," I say and stand along with Logan.

When she shuts the door behind her, something in the air shifts and I feel unsure. Nervous. I pick up the brownie pan like some housewife on crack and practically shove it at Logan. "Dessert?"

He chuckles. "I'm good, thanks."

I freeze for a moment and then blink a few times in case he didn't notice my awkwardness already. "I'll just take this to the fridge. Have a seat."

I rush off, stick the pan in the fridge, and take a moment to get a glass of water. Everything was so natural and right on the porch, and now it's like I'm starting over with time to think and doubt. I can't play games with Logan, but I'm also not sure if he's strong enough to take this all the way. He doesn't really understand what being together could mean, and I'm still hesitant the whole thing could be a disaster, and I'll lose not just him, but all of them. I shake my head at myself. My own selfishness. If I truly care about him, then being in limbo like this isn't best for him either.

I set the water down and take a deep breath, planning to go in there and lay it all out. Be honest about everything I'm thinking and feeling. He's strong. And he deserves honesty.

Before I can turn around, I feel him at my back and a chill creeps up my neck. His hands grip my arms and his hard chest pressing against my shoulders feels like the safest place on Earth. He leans his head down and puts his lips at my ear. "I wish you didn't have to leave."

My heart skips a beat and then thrums wildly. There's no way out of visiting my parents at this point. "Me too. But we still have a little time together. Thanksgiv—" I scoff when I realize my assumption.

"Of course, I want to spend Thanksgiving with you."

I grin, though he can't see it. "I have to admit…it will be tough being away."

He runs his hands down my arms before slipping one around my middle. "How long?"

"I'll probably be there a couple weeks, home a little after Christmas maybe."

I try not to flinch when his hand slides beneath the hem of my sweater and skates across my bare skin. "I can wait, Mollie. If that's what you want."

I don't want to wait, but I can't get any words out.

"You said we should go slow. Get to know each other. Be open." He brushes my hair to the side, exposing my neck. "I may not know everything about you, Mollie. But I know you. I know your heart and your will and your determination…and your vulnerability." He places soft kisses at the top of my shoulder, searing my skin. In between kisses, his voice is velvet. "I'm not sure how it happened, but I feel like I've known you my whole life."

I wrap my arm around his neck and let out a soft sigh. "I want you to know it all." Turning my head to the side, I part my lips, calling his to mine. "To have it all."

He wastes no time joining our mouths and stealing my breath with his warmth. A warmth that quickly turns to fire as we taste each other with soft slow nudges and nips.

Dizzy with need, I pull back to look in his eyes, breathing heavily. His hand cups my chin, keeping my face, my lips, close to his. "I might have some broken pieces that aren't fully repaired…and I might have some

blank spaces I can't remember…but the rest is all yours."
He kisses me once, gently. "If you'll have me."

"You're the best man I know, Logan." I spin in his arms to face him. To feel more of his body. To get as close as possible. His hungry lips devour mine in a kiss that is…everything. Not just a prelude, but a promise. I can feel it all the way to my toes and back up. A kiss so powerful, the force of it is physically moving us, our feet shuffling us out of the kitchen as we keep our lips connected.

He spins us and my back lands against the wall leading to the hallway. Logan groans into my mouth as he lifts one of my thighs and pulls it up against his hip. When I feel myself being lifted off the ground I pull back. "Your leg…"

"How much do you weigh?" He hikes my skirt up and reaches under both butt cheeks to lift me against him.

"One twenty." With my arms around his shoulders, I wrap my legs around his waist as he pulls me up, my back coming off the wall.

He stumbles. "One twenty! You sure?"

My heart skips a beat. "Okay, one twenty-five."

He quickly recovers his footing and laughs before kissing me again and pressing my shoulders back into the wall.

"You jerk," I say against his mouth. Logan holds me there and kisses me like I'm light as a feather, and he has all the time in the world. He grinds against me as our mouths move together like we'd been rehearsing for this very dance our whole lives. And in this moment, I know it's right. We are right.

As much as I'm swept up into his kisses, I'm still aware that my arms are clinging to his shoulders when what I really want is to set them free. Feeling all his hard ridges and muscles pressing against me beneath his clothes is so sensual, so teasing; I'm not sure how much longer before I start tearing every stitch from his body. "Take me to my room?" I whisper into his mouth.

He pulls back and pins me with dark eyes filled with lust and uncertainty. "You sure?"

"Never more."

I see the fire in his eyes as he hikes me a little higher on his sturdy frame and strides down the hall.

My skirt pushes up higher on my waist, the bottom of my black panties sticking out. When he gently places me on the bed, his eyes linger there a moment. I watch as his chest heaves, taking me in. He runs his hands down one of my thighs to my boot, heating my skin along the way with his strong rough hands, before removing it. He repeats the actions with my other leg and then helps me shimmy out of my skirt, before reaching for my panties and sliding them off. His dark, hooded gaze on my body sets a flame on a course throughout my whole body. "Oh, Logan."

As if a switch was flipped, our movements increase to a frantic pace, and I race to unbutton his jeans. We each take care of our own tops, whipping them over our heads, more than ready to bare our skin and our souls so we can join together. I release the clasp of my bra.

When it falls away, his chest fills, and a groan rumbles out of him. "You're...*everything*..." He leans over and covers my breast with his mouth in a soft, slow caress. His tongue lingers there, and then he pulls slightly away leaving his warm breath to spread on my damp skin. "So beautiful, Mollie."

With my heart raging inside my chest, I arch my back and pull his head back down to me for round two. But the torture is so sweet, my breaths are coming even heavier now, and I can't wait any longer. Logan reads my body as well as he reads my mind. In an instant, he shoves his jeans and boxers down to his knees, pulls me by my thighs until our bodies meet, finally giving us what we've both been longing for. The connection with him I've been craving for so long.

It is everything and yet it still isn't enough. His body is too far from mine in his standing position, so I reach out to him. He obliges and lowers himself until his hard chest presses into mine. He turns his head, brushing his lips behind my ear. "You feel so amazing." He pants against my ear, and his hot breaths are like bolts of electricity shooting straight to my core and winding me into a tight coil of sparking nerves, firing off in every part of me. He uses his strong arms to push back until our stares meet. "Logan," I gasp.

He nips at my lips, his tongue lightly sweeping the surface. "Say it again," he says breathlessly.

"Logan..."

He laces one hand with mine and continues to move while his eyes stay locked with mine. It takes only moments of peering into his burning gaze and succumbing to his relentless rhythm before my body gives in to release and I'm soaring. I wrap my legs and my free arm around his body, an involuntary reflex to keep this man tethered to me for as long as possible.

When our bodies slow and he finally lowers and stills on top of me, I close my eyes. "I never wanted that to end, but…"

"I know. Me too." He rolls to my side and cups my chin. "That was the most amazing experience of my life and I wanted to live in it for an eternity."

"Guess we'll just have to do it again."

He sighs and kisses me softly on the lips. "And again." He kisses my cheek. "And again." He runs his hand down to my hip and his face grows serious. "But next time I need to be closer, and for me that means…" He pauses and his eyes turn down to where his hand is. "Would you be okay if—"

"Logan…" It dawns on me what he's trying to say, and I don't want him to have any question in his mind. "I turn on my side and touch his rough cheek. "I want to know every part of you. What you do to me—how you just made me feel—it was amazing. And being as close as we possibly can will be more amazing."

He grins and leans into my palm. "You sure?"

"I want what you want." I kiss his cheek and then his neck and whisper. "Now finish getting naked and get in bed with me."

He nods and then sits up before pulling off each shoe. After he gets his jeans off, which were still pushed down past his knees, he begins removing his prosthesis. I sit up and run my hands up and down his back before placing soft kisses where my hands were, one after another.

When I see he's ready, I scoot up the bed and lie back on the pillow. I watch as he stalks over to me and right on top of me, once again gifting me the sinful weight of his body. I clasp his shoulders as he takes my mouth with his. This time the kiss is just as sensual, just as exciting, but somehow more powerful, more needy, as if his life depended on this consumption of me. And I take it all willingly, feeling so overcome by it all a tear streaks down one side of my face.

When he joins us together, I moan his name and then cry out in ecstasy, in joy of this moment. The feeling of being so close with one person—it's indiscernible where you begin and they end. He buries his head into my neck as we both reach our peaks and free fall together. His lips press into my skin as his heavy breathing slows and our bodies relax into each other. Neither of us moves to break the connection or even speak, and after a few moments, I feel myself slipping, unable to fight the euphoria guiding me into half consciousness.

LOGAN

Sometimes it amazes me how two-faced life is. I have to laugh because when one is given the choice between laughing and crying, why the hell not—choose laughter. Life can be such a struggle, so heartbreaking and confusing. Or, it can be simple as shit. It's all how you look at it. No, that's not entirely true. It's not how you look at life; it's how you look at the pieces of your life.

Right now, I'm sandwiched between Mollie's body and the back of the couch, watching the original version —like there's even another option—of *Willy Wonka and the Chocolate Factory*. Colton and Belle are sprawled out in sleeping bags on the floor in front of us and everyone else is either asleep, at work, or out with friends. The four of us just finished having leftover turkey sandwiches from a pretty damn good feast last night for dinner.

Our first Thanksgiving without Nina and Aunt Sheri was both difficult and a blessing. We missed the presence of the two incredible women who, by the grace of God, gave this family the strength it needed to survive without them. But we welcomed two very special women who've helped guide us from survival to living. Mollie and Lou were bright lights at our table and we all treated them like celebrities. I think we were all grateful we had someone else to focus on. And of course, someone to make a ton of kick-ass fixings. Gramps did his turkey as usual, but Mollie and Lou worked tirelessly to provide enough food for all twelve of us. The only other person not family at the table was Mason's girlfriend, Megan. Dad said the blessing and a surprisingly tender tribute to both women we lost. Even with that reminder, the day was exactly what we all needed.

Lying here and reflecting on that day, it's the most relaxed and content I've felt in I don't even know how the hell long. Now if Mollie could just keep still and not wiggle her ass against my crotch, then it would be spa-on-the-edge-of-a-lake relaxing. Don't get me wrong, her ass digging into me would be heaven on earth if the kids weren't here.

Violet Beauregarde blows up into a blue ball and the four of us laugh—Colt freaking laughs. He had a friend over last week, too, and Uncle Frank took Belle and them to the park. Sure, we're not the perfect family yet, not even close, but we are all making progress. And for that, I'm grateful.

Mollie reaches up and slides her hand right across my cheek, as if she's been sitting in my brain reading my positive thoughts. *Man, she's so gorgeous, inside and out.* And just like that, an ache rises up in my chest. Because of course, life can't be perfect, which is why I'm choosing to focus on the pieces of life that are. I don't know why my nightmares seem to be coming back, not to mention stronger, but I can't think about that. I can't dwell on that when everything else is going so well in our family. I can't think about why I wake up in a cold sweat while lying next to Mollie after making sweet, sweet love to her. I also can't dwell on the fact that she'll be gone soon to visit her parents for Christmas. The thought of not touching her for so long has literally made my hands shake.

I grab her wrist and kiss her palm, reminding myself to be grateful for any moments we have together. That's what losing people you care about does to you—it makes you see the clock is ticking.

Just before the credits roll, Justice and Ryder come into the living room, and I'm surprised to see them together.

"Where were you guys?"

"We were watching movies at Turner's house," Justice says.

Ryder has that look on his face, and I know he's got his own agenda. "Mollie, did Logan tell you?"

"Tell me what?" She scoots herself up and I sigh. Party had to end sometime.

Ryder drops down right next to her, leaving me to struggle to a sitting position. "They loved Logan's audition tape. He gets to compete in a qualifier now."

Mollie leans forward to narrow her eyes at me across Ryder's body. I shrug and run a hand through my disheveled hair.

"He'll be only the second competitor on the show to have a prosthesis," Justice says just before heading down the hall. "I'm out. See ya, Mollie."

"Goodnight," she says.

"Who cares about that? Maybe they don't even know about your leg," Ryder says, turning to me. "You're going to kick ass either way."

"We'll see, Ry. Don't get your hopes up. We talked about this, remember?"

"Yeah, whatever. Hey, Lo. Would you rather get your nuts caught in a car door or zipped up in your zipper?"

"Dude, not now."

Ryder jumps up from the couch. "Does Dad know about this? Is he awake?" He glances down the hallway with wide eyes.

Before I can say anything, he's sprinting down the hall. I glance over and see that Belle is asleep and Colton is awake, watching us. "Hey, buddy, why don't you go brush your teeth and I'll take Belle to her bed.

He gives me a nod and gets up, but instead of heading down the hall, he comes over and gives me a hug. Then he turns and hugs Mollie. Her face brightens as she looks over his shoulder at me. I just shrug.

"He's never done that before."

Her smile is so sweet I can't help but lean over and press my lips to her mouth. "Who can resist a hug from you?" I say, then put my hand behind her head and drag my lips down her neck. "I could use one of those hugs… preferably while naked."

"Hey." She pushes back so we are eye to eye. "Why didn't you tell me about the show?"

I should have known nuzzling her neck wouldn't distract her. But telling Mollie would have made it real. I wasn't ready for that. "I don't know. Maybe I'm not going to do it." I stand and walk over to Belle, checking if she is really asleep. She's actually pretended a few times just to stay up longer.

"Liar. There's no way you're not doing it."

"I'm not sure I'm up for it." I start to tell her why but I stop, unable to say the words. Instead, I put my finger to my lips, telling her to be quiet as I lift Belle up into my arms. I hold my precious cargo for a moment and look down at her angelic face. I don't know what the future will bring, but one thing is certain. No matter how long I stay here or how big these kids gets, I will always watch over them, and I'll care for Colt and Belle like they are my own siblings.

Mollie steps up beside me and strokes Belle's hair. "She's so beautiful," she whispers.

"I know." Her breathing is so peaceful I get lost for a moment. I wonder if I'll ever feel that kind of peace again. Even if I don't, my heart is content if those I love have it. It's hard to believe I can love them all so much when I'd been away for so long.

I feel Mollie's hand on my back and look over at her. She's grinning but it looks almost like laughter. "What?"

"Nothing. I was just going to say she…they are all lucky to have you."

"I was going to say the same about you," I tell her. Then I pad down the hall and into Belle and Colt's room. I lay her down gently, and she doesn't even stir. Like a rock, this girl.

"D'you brush your teeth, buddy?" I ask Colton who's already in his bed too.

He nods but I'm not sure I believe him. "Then why isn't your shirt wet like always?"

"I'm getting better." He stares me down and then we exchange smiles because we both know I'm letting it slide either way.

When I return to the living room, Mollie is giving me the stink eye.

I stop right in front of her and cross my arms over my chest. "What?"

She puts both hands on my forearms. Her skin is so soft, her touch so gentle, that instead of going where my mind always goes when she touches me, I take it in the complete opposite direction. "Your patients are lucky to have you too. I bet they feel like an angel laid her hands on them when you take care of them."

She shakes her head in slow motion. "I'll thank you

for that later. But right now, I know you're just trying to distract me."

"No."

"Yes."

I lean over and brush my lips against hers, warmth glowing in my chest. But I still have my arms crossed.

"Not gonna work either." She runs her hands up my shoulders and around my neck. "You better get your mind and your body on the same page, Logan," she says in a sultry voice.

I can't resist and I wrap my arms around her waist. "Oh, there's no conflict there. I think you're mistaken."

She looks to the side and laughs. "Why are you working out so hard, going to the gym, running those courses…if you're not sure you're up for it?"

I knew it was coming, but I still don't know what to say. Mentally avoiding it seems to have run its course. "Can't we just make out on the couch?"

Two wide gray eyes peer into mine, waiting.

"What can I say, I like training."

She runs one hand down my cheek and across my chin. "You're not going to disappoint Ryder."

I sigh and pull her closer. "I know, dammit. How the hell did I let him get me into this?"

"I think you thought it wouldn't happen. And now you're nervous. So what? You've never been nervous before?"

"Sure. More than nervous. Scared as hell. But not to look like an idiot in front of the whole country."

She kisses my chin where her hand was and then

pulls my face down closer to hers. "You couldn't look like an idiot if you tried, and you know it. I think…that you think…that you're doing this for Ryder, and maybe you are. But I can tell part of you wants this."

How does this woman know me so well? I shrug and let her go on.

"You're a strong, sexy, determined man, and I just know that you'll be inspiring. No matter what happens."

I hide my small smile in the crook of her neck and whisper, "Can you be naked and say that again?"

My breath tickles her and she squirms in my arms. I run my hands up her back to her shoulder blades and hold her in place while I gently suck on her neck.

She laughs but then feigns anger. "I will kill you if you leave a mark on me."

Frank walks in right as I'm taking her down to the couch, and we both pull to a sitting position like two teenagers.

Thankfully, he only nods as he walks by, looking exhausted. He's been working part-time at the Indian casino, trying to save money so they can get their own place.

With Frank in for the night, Mollie and I sneak off to her place and spend the rest of the night tangled in her sheets, soaking up as much of each other as we can before she has to leave. And that outlook I'm trying so hard to stay true to? Focusing on the good pieces. That's going to be a hell of a lot harder without Mollie by my side.

2 2

LOGAN

Days of finding private moments together have been incredible, even with her departure looming overhead. Mollie stirs in my arms, but she's still asleep. At some point in the night, we both dozed off, a tangle of slick, naked limbs. She called me when I was half asleep, saying it was by no means a "booty" call, but she was just reminding me we have only a few days before she leaves to visit her parents.

There's enough light for me to make out her high cheekbones and full lips. I watch her a few moments, the rise and fall of her bare chest, her thick mane spread across the pillow. Her skin silky, her curves so inviting, I don't know how I'll ever sleep alone again. *How could such an angel of a woman ever escape my attention? And* how the hell did I get so lucky to be with her now? My chest tightens and I draw in a deep breath. She's so still, so stunning in this moment that my desire surges. I skim my hand across her abdomen and down her hip and then her thigh. I want to wake her, pull her over me and watch her body rock on top of mine. Just imagining it has my pulse racing, pumping hot blood through my system. But then her head falls toward me, her face the picture of peace and beauty. I stroke her soft hair and kiss her forehead. And let her sleep. Before long, my lids grow heavy and take me over.

I don't know how much time passes before I hear my name in the darkness, a faraway whisper. I note my racing heart, my hands in tight fists, the feeling of panic in my chest.

"Logan, are you okay?"

My standard issue night terror graduates to something new with chaotic flashes of something horrific. Something I never wanted to see again. I open my eyes, hoping to kill the images of wreckage and smoke and fire…blood.

"Logan, what's wrong?"

I can hear the concern in her voice, feel her hand on my neck. "I didn't mean to scare you. I'm fine."

"I'm so sorry."

"It's okay."

There's a long pause before she speaks again. "It's not a great way to live, Logan. Something is chasing you and…maybe you should…"

"What? Stop running like a coward and face it?"

"No…but you said yourself it's getting worse. What if you stopped fighting so you can get past it?"

Anger swirls in my gut but I'm not mad at her. I've had the same thoughts, but I just can't. "I need to do this my own way. Please, you don't understand. Not until you've been there."

"I'm sorry—that doesn't help, I know. What can I do?"

"You don't have to nurse me. I'm good."

Mollie pushes herself up and reaches for the lamp with a sigh. "Hey, that's not what I meant."

I glance over to find her brow furrowed. I'm such an ass; she didn't deserve that. "Pretend I didn't say that. Guys can be dicks sometimes in case you didn't know."

She pulls the sheet up over her breasts, and I try to tell myself it doesn't mean anything. "Oh, I know," she says with playful sarcasm.

I run my hand down her arm to her wrist and then twine my fingers with hers. "You're not wearing your bracelets?" I hide my unexpected concern with a casual tone.

Her eyes flit from mine and pan to our joined hands. "No. It's still early. We should sleep more."

"Why?"

"Well I know I'm not ready to get up."

"No, I mean why aren't you wearing your bracelets?" It's not that I'm so hung up on her fashion choices, but I don't ever remember seeing her without them. Then I think back to last night and realize she didn't have them on then either. An unease settles over me as I wait for her answer and I can't figure out why. It makes no sense to me, yet somehow, I need to know.

"Guess I just forgot…"

The door swings open and Rocky waddles in and sits. Mollie slips out of bed and grabs a long sweatshirt off her dresser. "See if you can sleep. I'm going to let him out."

Heading out of the room, she tosses me a sweet smile. I roll over to my side, facing her nightstand, and pull the sheet higher. I take a few cleansing breaths with my eyes closed, afraid to sleep and return to my nightmare, but feeling drained from mentally running for so long. Knowing someday these nightmares—which are not really a nightmare considering it's my brain trying to remember—will eventually catch up to me.

When my eyes pop open once again, it feels as if no time has gone by, but the room is lighter. I can hear soft voices in the other room, but I'm not sure if Mollie is just talking to Rocky or someone else. I sit up and take a moment to look at her room. My focus is typically pretty direct when I'm in here but now, as I glance around, I'm reminded how impersonal it is. That makes me sad, though I'm not sure why. I suppose because it feels like the product of growing up without a lot of people in your life.

Feeling sluggish, I take my time "suiting up." I pull on each liner and by the time I secure my leg and get my pants on, the smell of coffee wafts into the room.

Just before I head out of the room, something on her dresser catches my eye. On the corner in a neat pile sits the three bracelets Mollie always wears. She said she forgot to put them on, but they'd have been the last thing she saw before leaving her room.

I step out into the hall and almost trip on Rocky. So, when I hear Mollie's voice again, I know she's talking to someone and not him. She must be whispering in case I was still sleeping. I hear Lou's voice and I smile. Of course, she probably wants the dish on me and Mollie. I'm glad Mollie has someone close by that feels like family.

I'm not confused about my feelings for Mollie. Every day we grow closer and she comes to mean more to me, but I'm not totally sure she feels as strongly as I do. It's not that horrible if I happen to hear her telling Lou how she feels about me, right? I stare into Rocky's sweet eyes, waiting for the answer to come. He just lowers his head to his paws. Okay.

Feeling like a jerk for trying to listen, I head toward the kitchen. A small photo album on the desk outside the hallway grabs my attention. There aren't many pictures in her place, so I'm dying to see something that reveals some of Mollie's history. I flip it open and grin. Mollie is smiling next to two other women wearing the same green scrubs she is. I was hoping this was a family album, but it's still nice to gain this insight. I turn each page over and there are similar pictures of her with the same woman along with others.

Behind me I can still hear Mollie and Lou talking. It's something about Rocky and whether Mollie wants Lou to come here or take him to her place.

I quickly realize this little album documents some sort of travel nursing, which is pretty damn cool. I remember her mentioning that a while back and realize I should have shown more enthusiasm at the time. I should know more about her life experiences.

I flip a few more pages when something Lou says catches my attention.

"Did you talk to that hunky doc about Logan?"

My heart jackhammers in my chest, and the skin on my face instantly heats. *What the hell?*

"Lou," she whispers. "We can't talk about this now."

"Well what are you going to do?"

Just then, Rocky starts scratching at the door. I hear footsteps in the kitchen, so I head to the door on instinct as the two women come around the corner. My heart beats so fast my expression must give me away.

"Logan, so nice to see you again," Lou says.

Mollie and I both stare at each other for a few seconds before she gives me an awkward smile. "Did Rocky wake you?" When I only shake my head, she walks over and touches his head. "Let me just take him out real quick." She glances at Lou as she opens the door.

"I should probably head out," Lou says and nods at me.

I try my best to give her a smile, but my entire body is on high alert, lit with anger for a reason I don't even know yet. *What the hell just happened?*

As the ladies exit, I head back to Mollie's room. I throw on my shirt and grab my wallet and keys. I have no idea what I'll say when I get outside, but my brain is spinning with too many scenarios right now. None of which are good and most of them end with my fist in said doctor's face. I pull in a few deep breaths because the last thing I want is to overreact. Yet as I pace back to the front door, I clench my fist at my side.

"Please don't leave yet," Mollie tells me as we almost collide outside the front door.

She lets Rocky in and closes the door behind him while I start heading to my car. I turn and lean against the hood, folding my arms. She stops a few feet away from me, like she's afraid to close the distance between us.

"So, you and the doc, huh?"

Her brows meet and she cocks her head. "What? No…Logan whatever you heard—"

"Why was Lou asking about him?"

She looks confused, like it's a tough question to answer. "He—He's my doctor." She takes a couple of steps toward me.

"Yeah? Until he had his tongue down your throat."

My words stop her and her jaw drops. "How could you throw that back in my face?"

The sheer pain in her eyes takes the form of a boulder and lands right in my gut. I don't know why I said that. "I'm sorry. I just can't stand that he's the one you turn to."

"As a doctor. That's all."

"That so?" I push off my car and close the distance between us, my heart racing. "Then why did I hear my name when you were talking about him. What could you possibly have to say to him about me? About us?" By the time I finish my voice is louder than I wanted, especially out front.

She looks so afraid I almost don't want to hear the answer. But there's no turning back now.

Her mouth is trembling as she opens it to speak. "Please, it's not what you think."

"Then, you didn't turn to him? You didn't confide in him instead of me? What was it, Mollie? What are you so afraid of that you couldn't talk to me about it?"

She's still quiet, but her eyes are welling with liquid. She reaches up to touch my face, and I don't respond. "Please, Logan, can you just trust me?"

"I'm supposed to trust you when you go behind my back and talk about me. To some guy you hooked up with? They're just dreams. Nightmares." I look away a moment because her sadness is cutting the anger I want to release. The frustration I want to get out so she can see what she's done. But then I see Rocky, watching us out the window like a scared child, and I know her kind heart would never intentionally hurt me. "You think I'm going to hurt you or something?" I say, turning to catch her gaze.

She leans toward me, touching my shoulder. "No! No, I know you would never hurt me."

"Then what?"

She shakes her head, drops her hand from my arm. "I —I'm sorry, Logan. I wish I could explain…"

But I'm already heading back to my car.

"Please, Logan. Will I see you before I leave?"

I don't answer and the last thing I hear before shutting the door is her faded words, "I never wanted to hurt you."

I don't even remember the drive home, but when I barrel into the house, I stop dead in my tracks. My dad is wearing a tie and helping Ryder fasten his around a stark white dress shirt. They turn to me and my dad raises his brows. "You're the last one I expected to be late today." I rack my brain for the answer I'm supposed to have and then it hits me. Today is Nina's birthday.

"Crap, sorry. Give me two minutes." With my head down, I pace back to my room to change, completely disarmed of my anger. This shifting of emotions has me feeling panicked. But this is no time for an attack. It's been so long since it's been full blown out of my control, and I pray this is not the day. I summon all my strength to push everything down. Not just about Mollie but Nina and this day. I look in the mirror as I change and choke back a sob threatening to come out. Then I suck in several deep breaths until I'm sure it's passed. I will make this day about Nina. She deserves it. My family deserves it.

I'm quiet on the ride over, but then so is everyone else. I do my best to keep my thoughts from Mollie and centered on Nina and by the time we arrive, a sense of peace and love has quelled the pain of what just happened. At least temporarily.

My brothers and I along with our father enjoy a breakfast out at Nina's favorite little hole in the wall, and then we head to the church where we all light a candle in her honor. Before I step out of the church, I say a silent prayer. My mind is so muddled, I don't even really know what to pray for, so I simply ask for strength. 253

2 3

LOGAN

Sweat runs like a river down my face, along my chest, and then settles into the grooves of my abs. I can't seem to pump enough weight to calm my frustration, to clear my head of the haze Mollie left me with. We haven't spoken in two days and the kids are asking me what's going on. Thankfully, I had her trip to point the finger at and told them she had a lot to do to get ready. She texted me when I got home that day, and instead of drilling her once again with questions, I asked her to give me some time. It just felt right. As much as I need answers—need her—I felt this gnawing at the back of my mind that I needed to work out some stuff on my end first. What the hell that is, I'm not sure yet.

"How's the course today?" Roger asks, pointing to me as he walks toward his office.

"Saw the changes, but I haven't tried it yet this morning." I manage some enthusiasm for Turner's dad when I thank him again. He doesn't show his face much during my pre-business workouts, but when he does, I owe him that much.

He stops at his door. "Justice told us about regionals. Pretty freaking awesome, man."

"Yeah." I nod and feel a pang of guilt for not giving him a bit more. At this point, everyone else seems more vested than I am.

He lets me off the hook, and I finish with the weights and then run the course a few times before heading home.

At the house, I notice a premade casserole in the fridge. I can see Gramps through the kitchen window in the backyard, digging up a rose bush. I stick my head out the side door. "Hey, Gramps. What are you doing?"

"I'm filming my DIY gardening show. Can't you see the cameras?"

I step outside and see his hat resting uselessly on the patio table. I toss it to him. "Come on, Gramps. It's not gonna protect you from those squamous cells on the table."

He points to the dark clouds over our heads and says, "See any sun?"

"Doc said all the time."

He puts it back on without a word and goes back to work. For some reason, I just lean against the stucco wall and watch. I don't know why he suddenly wants to rip out the bush, especially when Nina loved the roses.

After a few minutes, he stops and rests his arm on the shovel. "We let 'em die, kid. House full of able-bodied men and we let Nina's roses die."

I let out a breath and drop my head. What could I say?

"Got tired of seeing your dad look out the window at this dead bush. So, I'm replacing it with rhododendron."

"She liked those too?"

"Sure did. Guess I'll be responsible for them if no one else will."

"I'm sorry, Gramps. We'll take care of them."

"Maybe you oughta get your own life straight first?"

"Saw that casserole in the fridge. I was thinking—hoping—maybe Lou brought it."

"Nope. Mollie left here about ten minutes ago."

"What did she say?"

"Not much." Gramps lifts the new bush into the hole he dug and shovels dirt around. Then we both bend over and push the rest around the sides and pat it down. "Spent a few minutes with Belle and told her she couldn't go to the lunch at preschool."

"Damn. The casserole. I forgot. I'll take her."

We both stand and brush ourselves off of dirt. "Frank will take her…as he should."

"What about work?"

"He's taking off. That's what parents do."

I roll up the hose and then follow Gramps back to the garage. "Frank's been doing better, don't you think?"

"He has…but I don't think that's going to make you

feel any better about Mollie," he says as he leans the shovel against the wall and removes his gloves.

When he turns, I narrow my eyes at him like I don't understand exactly what he's just said.

"We all appreciate Mollie's help, but we haven't really needed her for quite a while."

"What are you saying?" My pulse quickens in defense, but I'm also confused.

"Don't get me wrong, Logan. I'm just saying Mollie's presence here hasn't been about need, it's been about want." He walks over and puts his hand on my shoulder, pinning me with a look I don't see often from him. "But I'm worried about her. I saw the pain, the hurt, in her eyes today. Gave me a hug that felt like goodbye."

I turn my attention from him. "I don't know what to tell you. I couldn't explain it if I tried." I break from his hold and head toward the kitchen door. "I know what you're thinking, Gramps, and I'm not the one who did something here. At least I don't think I did. I gotta take a shower."

"Sounds like you need to think on it more."

When I start down the hall, his voice catches me. "Logan. Can you take care of that old bush for me? Tomorrow is trash day."

I turn on my heel and nod before heading outside. I should have offered to handle this before he even asked. I wouldn't want Dad coming home to see Nina's bush uprooted and lying there. Gramps was right to get rid of it, though.

Once I get some gloves on and drag the can over, a

dull patch of clouds passes over. The rain that was predicted for today looks like it may be ready to show up. I'd have much rather spent a rainy day trailing kisses down Mollie's stomach, arm draped over her hip, as we listened to thunder roll in. Now, I don't even know when or if I'll touch her silky skin again.

I manage to stuff the bush in the receptacle as best I can and pull it out to the curb just as a light sprinkle falls from the sky. I stand at the trashcan a moment, unable to just walk away. I stare at the stupid rosebush, which now somehow feels like it's symbolic of my stepmother's life, and this wave of sorrow washes over me. I wipe at the rain drops on my cheeks and realize they are mixed with tears.

I'm weeping? I stay frozen a moment, dumbfounded by this emotional response that crept up on me. I can't even recall the last time I have actually shed tears. I didn't cry when I found out about my fallen brothers or even the loss of my leg. Maybe it was shock, waking up in the hospital feeling completely lost. I didn't cry at Nina's funeral either. I needed to be strong for the family. I've kept that wall up for so long it was bound to crack at some point.

But why now?

I scrub the tears angrily and run my fingers through my hair out of frustration. I can't help but wonder if part of this is feeling the loss of Mollie. Somehow, she does feel gone. And I don't even know how or why. I try to shut the lid over the bush but it won't stay down. I don't want this to be the first thing Dad sees when he pulls in so I yank on it, slamming it down a few times, hoping to smash it in there. "Goddammit!"

The rain is soaking my hair at this point, and when I finally get the dead bush covered, I'm heaving. I take a few cleansing breaths, but it's not working. Panic rises in my chest, which pisses me off to no end because I thought I was past all this. Except for my dreams, I had a pretty damn good handle on my emotions. Or so I thought.

Right now, I want to beat the hell out of something, but I can't take it out on the can which holds Nina's bush, so I pace to the house. I stop short before the door. I don't want anyone seeing me like this, especially the little ones. So, I go around the corner, lean against the garage door, and slide down until I'm resting my elbows on my bent knees and just breathe.

The rain is coming down harder now and I close my eyes, hoping it will lull me to a calmer place. I can still hear my pulse in my ears, seemingly pounding along with the beat of the rain. And then behind my eyes, I see the rain. But it's a different rain…coming from the dark desert sky. I see it but I can no longer hear it. The sound is being drowned out by the ringing in my ears. The muffled screams. The chaos surrounding me, swimming in and out of my vision. I try to open my eyes to escape the haunting vision, but I can't. I know exactly where I am and what's happening. Instead of opening, my eyes squeeze tighter when I hear a voice. It sounds like Jennings, only very far away, or weaker than I remember him.

Pain shoots through me, and I let out a strangled scream. I can't let my mind's eye continue down this path to its ultimate destination. *Breathe, dammit!* Just when I think my heart will explode out of my chest, I feel a soft hand on mine. It gently opens my clenched fists and places something in my grasp. I work my fingers over it, feeling instantly calmer. I breathe and focus on the sound of the rain, which slowly replaces the sounds of war until all I can see behind my eyes is black.

Moments later, I open my eyes and Belle's tiny body is nestled up against me, her hand in one of mine. My other hand is touching the soft woven bracelet she placed in my hand.

"Belle. What…"

"It's okay. I made you better."

I furrow my brow and try to get my brain to wrap around what happened. "Your bracelet makes me feel better?"

Belle bobs her head and beams, as if she's just gotten the answer right in class.

I run my finger along its ridges, close my eyes and focus on what I'm feeling. Another flash of memory takes hold of me and I draw in a quick breath. "How did you know?"

She lifts one shoulder and lets it fall. I can imagine it wouldn't be the easiest thing for her to explain at her age, but she's right. With both her and Mollie, there's been something about those bracelets that has calmed me when I was angry or upset, and at the same time gave me a sense of familiarity.

My head is still spinning, but I put my arm around her and give her a squeeze. "Thank you, Belly Bean. You're a special girl." I stand and take her hand. "I heard your dad is taking you to the luncheon today, so we better get you inside."

Surprisingly, I find Frank in the kitchen, getting things ready for the day. I hand Belle off to him and head to my room to get cleaned up. I play our conversation over and over again in my mind. The more I think about it, the more I know something is way off. I don't think Mollie is afraid of me. She knows I'd never hurt her, but dealing with my issues is another thing. I can't let this go, and there's only one way to get the confirmation I need.

I barrel out of the house and head to the hospital. Mollie's scheduled to work today, her last day before leaving for her parents. It is the worst possible time for her to leave, but at this point, I never want her to go.

Her floor is fairly quiet when I arrive, and I don't have the patience to wait around so I wander the halls looking for a familiar face to ask. Everyone is busy helping someone, so I head back to the station, intending to ask whoever shows up there to help me. Just as I round the corner, I stop, my jaw instantly clenching. Dr. Hall is opening the door to the office I saw him come out of with Mollie. I catch his eyes, and I can see his immediate reaction in them. He's definitely not happy to see me again.

I head toward him and he puts up a hand. "I've got an important call to make. Whatever it is—"

"Five minutes, Doc." I put my hand on the door preventing him from closing it.

He glances down the hall, his lips tight and something that resembles guilt in his eyes. "There's nothing I can help you with," he says in a low undertone.

I raise my brows and tick my head down. "You want to do this in the hall or in there?"

He sighs and opens the door, but I'm already pushing past him, my patience growing thinner by the second. "Where's Mollie?" I say as he shuts the door. I stand between a desk and a sofa with my arms crossed over my chest.

"Look..." He shakes his head and eyes me questioningly for two seconds before I realize this arrogant ass doesn't even know my name.

"Logan."

"Sure, Logan. I'm not just her doctor and her co-worker. I also consider her a friend..."

"Really? I'm not so sure she'd say the same."

"Maybe before... but now, it's different."

I run my hand over my jaw and try to decide if I want to deck this guy or attempt a conversation. Considering I'm practically in the dark, I check myself. "Hey, man, I'm sorry I powered my way in here but it's important." I grip the back of my neck. "I know Mollie's been talking about me. I get it. She's worried about me... about us, and now I know why."

He ticks his head to the side and goes behind his desk to sit as if that will provide a safe barrier.

"At least, I think I know," I say, turning to face him.

"I don't feel comfortable talking to you about this. I'm sure you realize, I actually can't." He leans back in his chair as if that ends the conversation.

His indifference, as justified as it is, only causes my pulse to quicken and some of my anger and frustration to creep back into my unsteady calm. I rest my palms on his desk. "If you're discussing me, don't I have a right to know?"

He raises his brows, seemingly unaffected.

"I had somewhat of a memory. A revelation really. I remembered being in the hospital, completely out of it, and a nurse was there for me. I think Mollie reminds me of her...of that time. Because ever since we've been together, my memories seem to be creeping back. She sees that. She knows I don't want to remember so she's backing off, right?"

The doc gets up and heads to the door. "I feel for your situation, Logan, but like I said, I can't help you. It wouldn't be right."

Before his hand turns the knob, I'm in his face. "Oh, and you're all about ethical, right?"

When he cringes and flattens himself back against the wall, my chest tightens. I can't do this no matter what I think of this guy. I grab the knob and pull the door open, Dr. Hall stepping out of the way just in time. "At least tell me where I can find her."

"I'm sorry, she left just before you got here. Said she was going early to her parents."

24

MOLLIE

My heart knocks around in my chest as I lean up against my car, watching Logan exit the hospital. He's a commanding force even as his face becomes clear and is awash with despair. My body misses his touch—the comfort of his arms as much as his skillfully sensual mouth. He doesn't notice me at first, but now his eyes have found mine and pin me with a cocktail of emotions.

His pace quickens until he reaches me. "I thought you'd gone already." And then he pulls me to him, and we are both silent, taking our moment, getting our fill while we can, the unknown lurking overhead.

Finally, I pull back, wanting to speak but suddenly unsure how to begin.

"It's okay, Mollie. I get it now."

"What do you mean?"

His arms are still at my waist. "I thought you were worried about my stability, the PTSD, all of it." His hands slide to my wrist where he brushes his fingers over my bracelet. My breath catches, but I fight the tears that spring to my eyes when his gaze meets mine. "But you're worried that you being a nurse will remind me of what happened to me." A tight smile masks his emotions. "And...your bracelets. I never realized how it takes me back there. When I was in the hospital...all that time, there was a nurse by my side. I was in and out of consciousness for days, but I knew she was there by her bracelet. I used to—"

"Logan, no," I say, my voice quivering. I shake my head. "You don't understand. I wanted to say something..."

He takes my face in his hands. "Look, I've been a coward, I know. And maybe I'm still not ready to remember, but if it's just the bracelet, we can—"

"No." I pull my face back, but his hands slide to my shoulders, unwilling to release me. "It's not just the bracelet, Logan. It's me."

He opens his mouth, his brows furrowed. "You can't help that you're a nurse. It's who you are and I—"

"I'm not just a nurse." She sighs. "I... I was that nurse."

His grip on me loosens and though my vision blurs over from tears, I can see the confusion, the pain spark to life in his eyes. "What did you say?"

"It was me, Logan. I'm the one who was there with you in Germany."

"I don't understand. Why— How?" He releases me completely and moves away. His mind is spinning, I can tell, trying to piece together a story he doesn't have all the parts for. He only gets two steps away when he turns back with recollection on his face. "You said you were a traveling nurse. The pictures at your place? Those were Germany."

"Among other places. Logan"—I reach for his hand but he doesn't move to take mine—"I wanted to say something. So many times…"

"Why didn't you?"

"Should I have? Because all I heard from you was that you would do whatever it took to not remember. And I kept seeing signs… It scared me. I didn't know what to do. I didn't want to be responsible for…"

He runs his fingers through his hair and stares at the ground as he paces in front of me. When he stops and looks up at me, he seems to be searching for what to say. "That day in the hospital, with Belle. You asked if I remembered you. You weren't talking about high school. And you seemed…"

My lungs struggle to push air through my system. "Hurt? I was a little." I wasn't sure he ever really saw my face with the bandages on his, let alone been conscious enough to recognize me. All I knew was that I couldn't leave his side. And when he didn't remember that, it hurt but I tried to convince myself he was just another patient. "I couldn't blame you for not knowing it was me. It's part of my job to give a patient whatever they need."

"How long?"

I knit my brows together.

"How long were you there…by my side?"

"Almost two weeks."

I see pity in his eyes then. "It had to mean more to you than basic patient needs. What you did—"

I was afraid to take myself back to the emotions I felt then so I cut him off. "I was more confused than hurt, though. So, I chose not to say anything at the hospital that day. And since I'd made that decision, it just got harder and harder to know what to do." No longer could I contain myself and I choke on a sob. "I'm sorry, Logan." I turn away and whisk my tears away, hating to make the situation worse. I cross my arms and mentally scold myself for crying when he's the one being ambushed.

The moment I feel the empty shell of loneliness settle over me, strong arms come around my arms and press me into Logan's firm chest. "Hey," he whispers softly against my hair. "Whatever you're thinking… whatever you're feeling, please know I'm not mad. How could I be? If anything, this is my fault."

All I can do is shake my head. If I had words, they would come out shaky, incoherent.

His hands rub my arms and then settle at my wrists. He runs his fingers over the one thing that marks our connected pasts. "I don't remember how long I laid there. In and out of consciousness, unable to speak, barely able to move, and bandages covering most of my face and part of my body." His body seems to relax around me, and he rests his chin on my head. "But the one thing I do remember is the comforting touch of a nurse who stood by side, held my hand, and whispered words of encouragement to me. I knew it was her—*you*—every time because of this," he said, touching my bracelet. Each time she held my hand and I felt this soft woven pattern, I didn't feel alone because of you…and somehow I knew I was going to make it."

He turns me to face him then, and I see his eyes glassy with liquid. "My only regret was that I never got a chance to thank her." Logan takes my face in his hands and places a gentle kiss on my lips. I taste a hint of salt on my tongue, and I don't know if the tears are mine or his.

"My angel," he whispers. "Thank you for saving me."

My heart swells and my chest heaves. The tears race down my cheeks, and I wrap my arms around Logan's waist. "I don't know what to say. I went there on a whim with some fellow nurses. Part of me was trying to prove something to myself but then I saw you." I pull back and look at him again. "I didn't know it was you at first, not until I saw your name, but I immediately felt drawn to you. And when I found out, I couldn't leave you."

"What happened?"

"The others went on without me. I had to stay until I knew you'd be okay. That's when I decided I was done traveling and settled back here."

"And you found me again." He gives me an endearing

grin that I can't return. Not when I'm dreading my next words.

"I have to go, Logan."

He takes in a deep breath and sighs it out. "God, I hate leaving you like this. I don't know how we'll get through these next couple of weeks but when you get back— What is it?"

"I'm sorry…"

"Mollie…"

I lower my eyes and turn away toward my car door. "I'm not just going for the holiday. I've applied for a position near my parents. I have an interview next week." I pull my keys out of my pocket, but he grabs my wrist before I can open the door.

"Wait, please…" His voice is desperate, pleading. "Why are you doing this? The truth is out now. How can you think we won't get past this?"

I want nothing more than to fall back into his arms and wait for the storm to pass, but I know life is not that simple. I pull my lips tight and look into his eyes so he knows what I'm about to say is something I've thought and fought over. "Logan, don't you see, your peace, your happiness, has slowly deteriorated since we've been together." He's already shaking his head but I push through. "The very thing you've been running from, will catch up to you because of me. If I'm not in your life—"

"I will likely still remember any way." He tightens his hold on me and pulls me to his side.

"Maybe. But I don't want to be the one who pushes you there before you're ready."

"What if I'm ready now?"

"I don't think you are." I touch his face, and the familiar feel of his beard brings another flood of tears to my eyes. "You started out as my somebody and somehow ended up my everything. But that doesn't mean this is the time for us. Or that we're both ready to fight the good fight."

Logan holds my gaze but doesn't speak. My heart breaks in two in that small span of time. Part of me thought he'd fight. Hoped he would. Try harder to convince me we could do this together. His hesitation tells me what I need to do. I kiss him gently on the lips, slide my hand down his chest and to his hand.

Logan brings our hands to his mouth and kisses my knuckles, my palm, and then my wrist. "I'm sorry I did this to us."

"None of this is your fault."

When he leans down and places a soft kiss on my dimple—claiming me just when I've gained the strength to leave—I almost lose it. But instead of asking him to fight for us I pull my hand away and open my door. My heart still feels nestled in his strong hands.

"No matter what, I'm still here for you, Mollie."

Words that should bring me comfort go down like poison. I nod and put on the brave face. "My somebody." Then I close the door and feel half my heart return to my hollow chest, aching to be whole again.

LOGAN

I swipe a hand across my forehead, surprised to find it damp.

"It's cool if you're nervous, bro," Justice says, sitting across from me at a small corner café in Los Angeles. We are the only ones out on the patio right now, everyone else preferring the cool air inside.

"Shut it. I'm not nervous. It's freaking hot out here. Winter in LA!"

Justice just shakes his head and laughs.

My tongue feels like sandpaper, but I refuse to admit this qualifier has me rattled. Where's that server? They haven't even come to the table or brought water, and we've been sitting here for at least five minutes. Mason and Ryder are parking the car and still not here.

"What's taking them so long?" Justice says, looking over his shoulder. "I could never live in L.A."

"I bet that Mercedes lot caught Ryder's eye."

"You're right. I'm going to text 'em and tell 'em to hurry the fuck up."

Though I know he's already tuned me out as he types, I still make the comment for my own sake. "Dude, language."

When he looks up, he rolls his eyes.

"What?"

"Bro, nothing. Stop. Save all that aggression for the course."

I turn my head to the side and can't help but laugh. "My aggression? What about yours?"

"Hey, I've learned to channel mine?"

"Since when?"

"Since my brother taught me."

Working on Justice's fear of being hit has helped us both and allowed us something we can do together. And his last game proved we really made progress.

Justice stands and shoves his phone into his pocket. "I'm going to take a piss and they'd better be here when I get back."

My brothers bug the hell out of me—most days, but not today. I'll admit—to myself—I might be a little nervous, but having my three brothers with me today gives me confidence and peace of mind. Mollie leaving gutted me. Especially when somewhere deep inside I know I could have stopped her. She said she left for me. I get that. At least I do now. So, I'm not going to fight to win her back until I can face her a whole man. And right now, I can't think of how to do that. It's been more than three weeks with little communication. It's like we rewound the clock to when we first became friends, probably because neither of us could stand to have a complete break.

Christmas was the toughest. I'd already bought her a gift, but it just didn't seem right to send it to her. We texted right before midnight Christmas night. She said she took a leave of absence from the hospital and would be taking a temporary position at a hospital near her parents. That prompted me to pick up the phone. I felt powerless on the other end of her explanation where she kept saying the word temporary as if that made it all right. Like we were college sweethearts trying to make a long-distance relationship work. She told me she'd always be my somebody but without seeing her beautiful lips say the words in person, they rolled to the pit of my stomach and sat there, a heavy reminder of what we lost.

Though her face was the last thing I saw when I went to sleep and the first thing to pop into my mind when I woke, my brothers wouldn't let me drag my ass around being depressed. These last few weeks could have been hell if not for my keeping my head directed at this qualifier. I just don't want to look like an idiot out there. Or worse, the pity case everyone claps for because I lost my leg fighting. Today means a lot to Ryder, so I sure as hell am going to try to get as far as I can, but part of me wonders if it's better if I don't make it to the next round.

I turn in my seat and scan the streets to see if they are coming. I can see the Mercedes lot from here. And, exactly as I'd predicted, the two of them walk out and are finally headed this way. I often wonder where Ryder's "need for speed" is going to take him when he gets older.

I continue to watch them and feel grateful Mason wanted to be here for this. Taking off from work is not something my big bro likes to do. A warmth settles in my chest when I see him put a hand on Ryder's shoulder.

The din of a busy work day surrounds me, and then something to my right catches my eye. I turn from my brothers. It's a family, mostly little kids but all boys like mine. A smile takes over my face as I watch them rough-house while the mom tries to settle them with a baby in her arms. My face falls, along with my stomach, when I spot one of the little guys behind the mom, heading for the street. Without hesitation, I pop from the chair and barely register it sliding back and hitting the ground.

I leap over the short brick wall that encircles the patio and take off at a run. I yell but my voice is lost among the street sounds. My heart beats radically in my chest and echoes in my head. I shout to the mother, to anyone who could get there before me.

The toddler wobbles off the curb and settles in between two parked cars. I'm sprinting now, dodging people in the street, pushing them out of my way. I risk a quick glance at the mother. She turns my way but narrows her eyes as if I'm coming to hurt her. To hurt her children. She cups the baby's head and turns in toward the two boys next to her.

The errant boy is now two steps farther into the street but still between the parked cars. Traffic is light but cars are coming north right toward him.

I don't know if the mother has figured out what's happening because I stay laser focused on the boy, not wanting to lose precious seconds. His hand is skating across the bumper of one car as he toddles along its front. I'm mere moments from him.

I've stopped breathing just as I reach the curb. I slide across the hood as the boy passes the front bumper and emerges in the street as the sound of cars roar in my ears. A rush of adrenaline I haven't felt in years shoots through my system as I slide off the car. I scoop the boy up, spin around, and fall back against the parked car just as another car beeps and swerves around us.

My chest is heaving and yet I feel suffocated. My ears must be plugged because every sound I heard moments ago is now muffled, and all I see is black. Light flashes behind my eyes, dizzying my head. I'm falling now, my arms still griped tightly around the boy's tiny body. Images I've never seen before take over my conscious-ness. Mo, Vin, Jennings, me. Laughing and smiling. In an instant, they're gone, replaced with smoke and fire, metal and debris...darkness. Where the hell are they? My hearing restores and screams ensue. Pleas for help.

Then I'm at Jennings side. I'm numb. My brain and my body feel non-existent and yet somehow, I know my leg is seriously fucked up. He's grabbing at my arms, yelling for something. "I'm gonna fucking die under here, man."

He's still grabbing at me, but I start yanking him too. I'm pulling but he won't budge. My heart is in my throat. I'm parched and can't find my voice so I tell him with my eyes. *I won't leave here without you.*

Someone is pulling at my arm, trying to get me away from Jennings. *No, stop.* I hold tighter. I can't let go. I won't—

"Logan…it's okay. Let go."

I shake my head at the voice. Light slowly replaces the dark and I open my eyes. Mason is leaning over me. Beyond him…the mother, with tears in her eyes. My arms hold the trembling boy, his arms wrapped tightly around my neck.

Mason grins at me and nods. The mother steps around him and kneels down next to me. I open my arms and the boy goes to her. She manages to take him into her arms while still holding her baby. "Thank you," she says over his shoulder. "You're a true hero." Then she turns to gather her other boys and simply walks away like it was all a dream.

A hand lands on my shoulder and I look up behind me. "You are a hero, Logan," Ryder says. "That was so freakin' awesome."

My big brother helps me up, and the three of us walk past a small crowd of people, who at some point had gathered around the commotion. I stay quiet, walking with Mason as Ryder runs ahead to tell Justice what happened. I'm sure he's going to revel in being witness to something Justice missed out on.

Before we reach the brick wall of the patio, Mason stops me. "Want to talk about what happened back there?"

I look past him, out to the street. "You saw, right?"

"You know what I mean. After?"

I can't put words to it just yet, especially not now, before I have to do this thing. On TV no less. "I appreciate it, Mase. But I have to stay focused or—"

He grips my shoulder to get my attention. "Your focus was just shot to shit, man."

I let out a sigh. "You're right. And I do need to acknowledge what happened. But not here. Let me do this thing and then if I need to talk, I'll hit you up." I turn to head back to our table and he slaps me on the back.

"Just know I'm here for you. You might not think I've been there in the past but we're brothers"—I pull out my chair and he grabs my wrist—"always, man."

I nod and tap my fist on his shoulder.

"So tender—can we freakin' eat now?" Justice flips a menu open, completely unaffected by anything that has happened. "I need a burger, like now."

"Hey," Ryder says as Mason and I finally sit. "Would you rather eat a burger with a roach in it or a cat turd?"

And, we're back.

By the time we reach the location of the qualifier, my mind is completely jacked. *So much for staying focused.* I thought about the boy and what would've happened if I hadn't seen him. I thought about the flashback I had and how I remembered some things I had never recalled before. My heart races just acknowledging that fact. The part that has me so confused is that I don't even remember talking to Jennings during any of it. All I know is that he was the only other survivor.

As we head to the registration table, all I can think about is how, for the first time ever, I feel like I need the whole story. How the hell am I supposed to tackle this course and try to qualify when my head is back in the desert?

"Dude, come on," Ryder says, yanking on my arm.

I hadn't realized I stopped short of the table. "Sorry, yeah."

Then my brother Mason is in front of my face, giving me the questioning eye. He turns his head to Ryder. "This isn't the only qualifier, Ry. Maybe after what happened—"

"No, I'm good." I smile at Ryder to reassure him. The disappointment on his face instantly fades.

"You sure?"

I nod at Ryder and tap Mason on the shoulder to step aside. Registration is a blur, but as we head to warm up, my head starts to clear. I'm here now so I need to push everything else aside until this day is over. Jennings has been after me for a long time, and I've been avoiding him. As soon as we're back home, I'm going to face him. Face my past. It's time to stop running. Oddly, I feel something stir in my gut. I'm no longer nervous about the course because whatever happens, I'll be good with it. But what I'm feeling build inside of me is hope. I almost don't recognize it, and though I don't know what it means right now, I like it.

"How are you feeling?" Ryder asks minutes before they are going to call my name.

"I'm good, Ry. But you know—"

"I know, I know. I don't even care." He wraps his arms around me and slams his damn head into my chest, and I choke back the speech I was ready to deliver. "Logan, I'm so proud of you. You're the champ no matter what. I just can't believe we're here."

I peel his arms away to look at him, thrown by how mature he's being about this when I'd thought he had all his hopes on me making it. When I lean back, he shoves his phone camera right into my face. "Logan Bridges, the next Ninja Warrior. What have you got to say?"

Before I can say anything, a middle finger comes between me and the camera. "You're next!" Justice shouts.

I've got three sets of hands patting me down as I walk toward this monster of a challenge and with every touch of my brothers' hands, I feel the energy surging through me. As they fall back and I continue toward the course, the cheering rolls over me like a thunderous crescendo. I didn't notice this much cheering for the other contestants. I slow my pace, confused by it all until it hits me. Man, I didn't want this to go down this way. The adrenaline I felt only moments ago is starting to seep from me.

"Why'd you stop?"

I turn and see Mason at my side. Suddenly, the crowd is chanting my name. "They're cheering for me."

"So?"

"So, I didn't want to be the charity case. They must know about my leg."

Mason laughs, his smile so wide I could drive a car through it. He shakes his head.

"What?"

"You dumb ass. They're not cheering because of that." He points to a giant screen above the field and there I am.

What the hell...

Someone must have taped what happened earlier when I saved that kid.

"They're chanting for a hero. You're a hero, Logan. Now go give 'em what they want."

26

LOGAN

The sun beams through the branches of the giant oak forty yards in front of me. Most of the leaves have turned brown and are still damp from the last three days of rain. The kids have been bouncing off the walls being stuck in the house, and though I was set to meet Jennings today, I couldn't say no when they asked me to take them to the park.

I glance at my phone, noting he's due any minute and I feel both excited and nervous. When I look up and see Colton making his way across the monkey bars with Justice spotting him, I can't help but feel pride. I had no problem making my way across the pipefitter during my course run but the block run almost took me out. My time wasn't the best, and I'd barely qualified for the next round, but the response from the crowd, from my family? It felt like I'd scaled that wall, hit the buzzer, and won the whole damn thing.

I check my phone again, but this time I'm looking for a response from Mollie. I haven't heard from her since she wished me good luck the morning of the qualifier. I called her after the competition. Not to share with her I'd made it to the next round, but to tell her what happened with the boy I saved. To tell her what I remembered. But I didn't want to text that, especially since I don't know what any of it means. The call had gone straight to voicemail, which means either her phone was off or she'd rejected my call. That thought settles heavy in my stomach, a foreboding throb I'm not ready to think about it yet. There must be a logical reason that doesn't involve breaking my heart into a million pieces.

A shadow moves across my phone and I look to find a man grinning down at me, arms across his chest. His hair is long enough to touch his shoulders and he's sporting a full beard and mustache. It takes me a moment before I catch his gaze and the piercing blue eyes I remember once belonged to my friend finally reveal the stranger in front of me.

"Shit, Jennings, is that you?" I hop up and we shake hands before he pulls me into a hug. "I was about to give you some spare change."

He slams my back a couple times with a large palm and it feels like home. "Yeah, well you look as pretty as a little girl. Like always," he says pulling back.

I take another look at his face and just shake my head. "Can't believe it's you, man."

"Yeah, well, maybe you'd have recognized me if you hadn't taken so damn long to see me." He puts a hand on my shoulder. "Why now?"

"I told you on the phone. Have a seat," I say, gesturing to the bench.

We both sit and I scramble for the words I prepared before he got here. When we spoke on the phone, I only told him I wanted to talk about that day. I rub my hands along my thighs and take a deep breath, ready to finally open the door that has been closed for so long.

"Look, Bridges," he says first. "I get this is tough. I'm just glad you're finally ready to talk. I thought you'd never forgive me."

My breathing comes to a screeching halt and I pass a glare over to him. "Forgive you? What the hell—"

Belle takes that moment to slide right up to us and stop in front of Jennings. "Who are you?"

"Well, I'm Prescott Jennings, little lady. Who might you be?"

"I'm Belle. You don't have any candy, do you?"

He smirks and leans on his knees. "Sorry, I don't have any."

"My cousin," I say, gently nudging Belle out of his personal space. "And that's not polite, Belly Bean."

She tilts her head and squints. "Well, I was just trying to help you. Justice says men with candy are bad."

"We'll talk about it later. Why don't you go back to the swings?"

"Okay." She shrugs and turns to go but then stops and spins back to us. "Hey, my friend Mollie can give you a braid."

I point to the swings with my stern face. Something this adorable should have had me holding back a grin, but just the mention of Mollie makes me ache. I pull in a lungful of air and focus on why I'm here.

"She's cute," Jennings says as Belle stomps away.

"She's also right. Geez, man, ever heard of a barber?"

"C'mon, you know I hated that high and tight bullshit."

I shift my body so my back presses into the corner of the bench and I stare at him, hoping some flash of memory will come to the surface.

"I didn't expect this," he says.

"What?"

"The way you're looking at me right now. So blank. Like we didn't go through hell and live to tell about it. Why is that?"

"Because, man…I don't remember."

A burst of air escapes him. He runs his hand over his hairy face and his eyes mist. "Shit," he whispers. "All this time…"

"I'm sorry." It's the only words I can spare when he looks like that.

We don't say anything for a couple minutes, him staring out into the playground, me watching him.

Finally, he turns to me. "You dumb motherfucker."

"What?"

"Why are we here if you don't remember? I almost gave up on you, man. So why did you finally answer after years of me texting and calling?"

Part of him must know some of my reasons. It's why there would be months that would pass before he tried again to reach me. Survivor's guilt is real. Yes, I was a coward and couldn't face what happened. I didn't want anything triggering my memory. But at the same time, I didn't want comfort either. I didn't want to share stories and talk about our feelings like some AA meeting. I just wanted it all behind me.

"I'm sorry. I just…couldn't. Honestly, I don't know how you could. At first, it was all about surviving, learning to live with my new leg." His gaze lowers when I mention my leg but I continue. "If I wanted to come back strong, I couldn't look anywhere but forward. And, I knew remembering would only make me feel worse because I survived. I couldn't do shit for our brothers. We were supposed to have each other's backs and I didn't—"

His hand lands hard against my chest. "The hell you didn't!"

I stare at him wide-eyed but don't say anything.

"Logan, I'm sitting here right now because of you, man." He seems almost angry as he leans his elbows on his knees and stares at his clasped hands. "You, pulled me out of that hunk of metal that used to be our Humvee. You, stayed right in my goddamn face the whole time, keeping me talking…" He swipes at his eye.

"And you, you dumbass, made them take me first." He turns his head, the pain in his glower slicing through me. "I'm probably the reason you lost your leg."

"No way." I shake my head, not even sure why I'm refuting him when I don't remember. And then, those piercing blue eyes send me back to that moment. Back to that horrible scene when his gaze gripped mine, pleading for me to do something. My leg was shot to hell. I knew that when I dragged my body half-way inside and pulled with everything I had to get Jennings out. At one point, the back of my knee snagged on some jagged metal or something and I cried out. I reach out and rub my knee, the pain of the past radiating as real as when it happened.

"You remember," Jennings says.

I place a hand on his shoulder. "My leg wasn't gonna make it either way."

"You don't know that. And the delay getting medical attention. Maybe—"

I wave his comments away with a hand and a determined expression. "No, man. No. I don't regret a damn thing. Hell, you know you'd have done the same for me." I smile because I know in my heart my words are true. All of them.

He returns a half smile, though he still looks hesitant. He's staring at me like he wants to believe me. Then his expression changes. "I don't know. Maybe I wouldn't have kept you awake the same way that you did for me."

I furrow my brow, reaching back and trying to recall

what he's referring to. I shake my head and when he starts to explain, I cut him off. "Wait!" I pause as the fuzzy memory comes into focus. "Did I… Were we doing De Niro quotes?" He just nods. "Holy crap, I remember that."

"'Someday a real rain will come…'" he starts.

"'…and wash all this scum off the streets,'" we both finish and laugh.

We're quiet for a few moments then. No matter what he's told me, I can't help but feel bad for all that came after. "I'm sorry I never checked on you… I mean when I was able."

"Hey, I get it."

"So, what was the final verdict for you?"

"You mean besides not dying? Damn sure that's what would have happened if it wasn't for you."

I give him a look to tell him to continue.

"Lost a few non-vital organs, a finger"—he holds up his right hand to show me where the pinkie finger is missing—"but that don't matter. I don't need any of that back. What I got back today means the most." He puts an arm around my shoulders and pulls me into a side hug. "I've been waiting three years to say this. Thank you, Logan."

"Like I said, you'd have done the same."

He releases me and places his arm casually across the back of the bench. "Missed you, man."

"Yeah, I missed you too." The moment feels like it was plucked from my past and dropped right into my current universe. Though it brings me comfort, it's laced with sadness, regret. I try not to latch on to the negative, especially after he's worked so hard to get us here. "So, what've you been up to?"

He reaches into his pocket and pulls out a ring box.

"Hey, I didn't miss you that much."

He shakes his head and his loose curls brush his shoulder. "I'm asking my girl to marry me."

"Stacy?" My surprised tone comes out before I can mask it.

"Nah. I was pretty messed up when I got back, plus she was kind of a bitch."

I raise my brows in silent agreement.

He smiles. "But Jessica…she's my angel. We have a little place in Fallbrook. Quiet, woodsy. Now I'm gonna make it official. He hits me across the chest. "And I expect your ass at the wedding."

"You get a haircut and I'm there." I chuckle.

"How about you? Anyone special in your life."

I pull in a hunk of breath. "That's a good question. There was— What?"

He's giving me that parental scowl as if he knows I've done something wrong. "It's been a long time. But I still think I know you, man. You need to make it right."

"Honestly, I wasn't sure how. I was just figuring it out and then…"

"Then what?"

"You. This." Suddenly I feel emotional and my eyes burn. I nod. "Thanks, Jennings."

"Besides being a pain in your ass, I didn't do much."

His wide grin projects more than happiness. In it I see hope and friendship. "But if it makes you feel better, we can call it even."

I dip my head and reach my hand for him to take. "Even."

27

LOGAN

I roll down the window when the hotel comes into view, the crisp coastal air dragging across my face. Oddly, it makes me think of Mollie even though she and I have never gone to the beach together. I'm sure it's because literally everything makes me think of her.

"Hotel Pacific seems a little upscale for us. What are we, on our honeymoon?"

"Relax. I'm writing it off," Mason, says, pulling into the lot.

"You're writing it off? Or your sugar momma is paying for it?"

"Screw you. Megan and I have a mutually beneficial relationship."

"Damn, that's so romantic."

He stops the car and glares at me. "You know what I mean. I really like her."

"That's powerful stuff, dude. Let me know when I should rent my tux."

"You're being a jack-ass, considering I just drove you almost three hundred miles."

I click out of my seatbelt, ready to jump out. "Sorry. I'm just so amped up right now."

The drive to Monterey took about four hours. I can't help but worry if I should have at least texted Mollie a heads up I was coming. But considering she didn't answer my last couple attempts to reach out, I was afraid of what she might say. Actions speak louder than words, and I know this is the only way to really get through to her. Plus, the thought of seeing her, touching her, catapulted me into action. When Mason found out where I was going, he offered to drive me, saying he'd been planning a trip this way to meet with some contacts he made through The Meyers Group.

This is the most time I've spent with my brother since we were both in school, and we spent most of the time reminiscing and sharing stories from our lives from when we were apart. Mason didn't even give me a guilt trip when we talked about the time I left to join the Army, and I was grateful to hear more about what he did for the family and the business, some of which I knew.

I really didn't have a plan when I set off on this trip so once we get check into our room, I sit on the edge of the bed and just stare at the closed door.

"You know I only reserved the room for one night,"

Mason says behind me. Knowing him, he's probably hanging the clothes he perfectly folded last night to bring with him.

"If all goes well, I won't be staying here so…"

"Maybe we'll both have good news."

It's a little selfish of me to not give a damn about his meeting. The opportunity sounds great, and yes, it's because of Megan, but I'm not digging her in my brother's life. She's too much like him and I'm not sure that's a good thing.

I stand and head to the door. "The hospital isn't far. I'm going to grab an Uber over there. If I'm not back before you go, good luck."

He gives me one head nod. "You too, Logan."

When I reach for the door, he comes around the bed. "Hold up." Placing a hand on my shoulder, he gives me the look of a father instead of a brother. "I don't know her that well, but Mollie's a lucky girl. And no matter what goes down today, I'm proud of you. You're a good brother. A good man, and if it doesn't go your way—"

"It will…but thanks, man. I appreciate it."

He backs away and I pull open the door. "And for the record, I'm proud of you too."

I walk out before we both get too sappy or one of us starts pretending we've got allergies.

The ride to the hospital passes in a blur and déjà vu hits me as the entrance doors slide open and deliver me into Mollie's world. My nerves turn to excitement as I follow the signs to the information desk. This hospital is much smaller than ours so when the woman behind the desk tells me she can't tell me which floor Mollie works on, I simply thank her and move on. I don't even have the patience to wait for the elevator and run up the stairs to the second floor.

No one seems to know her here, so I head up to the third of three floors, feeling trepidation creep into my enthusiasm. I head down a short corridor, glancing through open doorways as I pass each room. Someone at the end is clearly in pain, their screeching becoming louder as I approach. The pain seeps into my chest, bringing up a faint memory of visiting my mom in the hospital. I heard her crying out just like that when my father brought Mason and me to visit, but when we got in the room, it was as if our mere presence lifted the pain away. As I grew older, I became aware of her bravery and admired and appreciate how her love for us made her strong. I didn't live up to that with Mollie, but as I increase my steps down the hall, I know I will change all that. I stop in front of the nurses' desk but no one seems to be around.

"Can I help you?"

I turn to find a tall guy with broad shoulders you wouldn't expect to see in scrubs.

"I'm looking for a nurse. Mollie Fisher."

He's shaking his head before I even finish. Then he looks over my shoulder and bumps his chin up. "Sheila can probably help you. She knows everyone."

Sheila is pushing a cart in my direction and I meet

her halfway. The older woman with white hair greets me with a sweet smile as she walks around the side of her cart. "Did I hear you ask about Mollie?"

"Yes. Is she here today?" I find myself holding my breath when her expression tells me she's about to disappoint me.

"I'm sorry she's not." Her short haircut brushes her cheek as she shakes her head.

"Do you know when she works next?" I can see her hesitation and I don't blame her. She doesn't know me or why I'm there. "Please, I've come a long way and I really need to see her. I'm a...friend."

She glances over her shoulder nervously and then stares at me for a moment. "I'd say you're more than a friend, Logan."

I raise my brows and I don't know if it's embarrassment or surprise but I smile. "You know me?"

She gestures to a room with chairs and a TV and I follow her over. It's empty but the TV is on a home improvement show. We don't sit and she positions us so she can see the door. "Saw you on that warrior show. Mollie told me about you."

"Great." I brighten and fill my lungs with a relieved breath. "So, you know you can—"

"I'm sorry, Logan. Mollie's gone."

"What do you mean?"

"She was offered the full-time position here but she turned it down."

My relief short-lived, I try to process what she's

saying. "Do you know if she went back home? Is she with her parents or…"

She looks at me like I'm a patient and she's giving me bad test results. "I'm sorry. She took another job." She hesitates and I go closer, needing to hear what I don't want to hear. "She left the country. Took a traveling nurse position."

"No… When— Do you know where?"

"That's all I know."

I freeze for a second and Sheila touches my arm. I realize in that moment how long it's been since I had the comfort of a mother. "Is there anything I can do?"

This sweet woman would probably take me into her arms right now, but I steel the pain rushing to take hold and I step back. "No, thank you." I walk backward and try to give her some semblance of a grin. "I'm sorry I took so much of your time."

She raises her hand and opens her mouth to say something but seems to change her mind and just nods.

My brain whirls as I head to the exit. I take a seat on a bench just outside and notice a large gray metal statue of a woman with a child at her breast. I squint at it, wondering why I didn't notice it on the way in. I pull out my phone and press it awake, staring at the screen as if I don't know how to work it. Do I try calling her again? What would be the point? She's obviously given up on me. I tap open my photo album and swipe through some images of Mollie. Her doing a selfie on my bed. Her and Justice hanging upside down from the bars on the obstacle course at the gym. Mollie reading to Belle. That one she didn't know I was taking.

Suddenly the pain and confusion I feel inside burns into anger, and I slam the phone against the bench seat next to me. Dropping my face into my hands, I concentrate on my breathing, try to rein in my frustration. Because, damn it, I'm not angry at her. This all happened because of me. My eyes closed, I take slow deep breaths. After a moment, I look up and gaze at the statue again. It's the beginning of life for that baby. No heartache or war, mistakes or regrets. I'd love to start over like that.

A chuckle escapes me when I think of my meeting with Jennings and realize we all have the power to start over. Maybe not a completely clean slate but definitely a second chance. The opportunity to build anew. Even if we are building on the memories and lessons learned in the past.

And then my grin grows wider when I realize this little breakdown didn't pull me back to the devastation of war. It was simply about life. My life. Right now. I pick up my phone from beside me and scoff at the two cracks going diagonally across it.

Mollie might be gone for now. But everything in life is temporary and when she comes back, we can start over. I could walk up to her like in those movies and stick my hand out and say, "Hi, I'm Logan. Nice to me."

"Screw that," I say to no one. I don't know where that momentary lapse into La La Land came from but the moment I see Mollie again, I'm going to pull her into my arms and never let go.

But how long am I supposed to wait? What do I do now? I don't have a goddamn clue at this point. The only thing I know for sure is that I can't believe she didn't say goodbye.

2 8

———

LOGAN

The house is quiet when I walk in, and it feels strange I don't know the exact whereabouts of every member of my family. Dad and Gramps figured I wouldn't return until tomorrow at the earliest and assured me the schedule, the kids, would be taken care of. Still, I texted Gramps to let him know I was heading back.

I drop my bag at the door when I see the light coming from the living room, hoping Gramps is not asleep in his chair. My whole body is stiff and my leg and knee throb from sitting that long in the car in one day. I just couldn't bear the thought of staying there a minute longer, knowing Mollie was gone. Mason will stay an extra day and go back with Megan.

"You made good time," Gramps says, looking relaxed in his chair.

I notice the TV is off. "Where you waiting up for me? I told you not to."

"I wasn't waiting, but I'm glad you made it home okay. Long drive alone with your thoughts."

"Yeah, I guess you were wondering what happened."

"I've got an idea," he says, nodding. "But, Logan—"

"Gramps." I run a hand through my hair. "I know I've been sitting on my ass all day today, but I'm still exhausted. I thought I wanted to talk but now I'm thinking tomorrow?"

Gramps slowly eases out of his chair and comes to stand in front of me. He puts a hand on my shoulder and fixes a wise gaze on me I've seen countless times before. "You're a good man. You went to get your woman and it didn't quite work out the way you wanted. But, like I always tell you. These things happen the way they were meant to."

Anyone else said that to me and I'd pop off with a sarcastic comment. But something in the gleam of his eyes tells me to just nod at the old man and let him go off to bed. He lingers a moment longer and a smile materializes on his face. He appears confident and as he's always been able to do, he actually makes me feel better. "Thanks, Gramps. I appreciate you waiting up." I pat the hand he has on my shoulder before he slips it off and turns to walk away.

As he heads toward the hall, he says over his shoulder, "Told you, I wasn't waiting up." Then he passes the doorway to the kitchen, and my heart stops. My breathing stops. Time…stops. He was right, all that time alone with my thoughts messed with my head. I can't think of any other logical reason for what I'm seeing. Mollie is standing in the doorway. She squeezes gramps's hand and he continues on down the hall.

She slowly steps toward me and my mouth falls open. I will myself to take in a breath. "Mollie," I whisper as if I'm confirming her presence to myself. So many questions swim through my brain, but I push them all aside, close the distance between us, and do exactly what I told myself I would do. I take her into my arms, her soft, warm body so inviting. She melts into me like we'd perfected the move with endless practice.

"I missed you so much," she whispers into my neck.

I pull back because I need to see her face. I place both my hands on her cheeks and rub my right thumb over her dimple. She grins and closes her eyes.

"Tell me this is real," I say, putting my mouth against her lips. And before she can answer, I kiss her, slowly. Then I touch my lips to hers over and over, confirming just how real she is, the contact filling me with emotions I can't quite decipher. Confusion and relief. Excitement and anxiety. But most importantly—love.

When I feel her hand take hold of my wrists, I pull back from the kiss. "What happened? I thought you left the country."

Her soft gray eyes peer into mine, welcoming me

home, assuring me she's not only here but here for me. "I tried. I even went to the airport, intending to go but when they called my flight…" Those beautiful pearly eyes glass over in an instant, the pain evident. "I couldn't do it. No matter what was happening between us, I couldn't leave you. I just sat there. And then I started crying. I don't even know how long I sat there."

"I'm so sorry, Mollie. I should never have made you feel…" My hands slip to her arms and I look down. "I know this my fault. I didn't fight for you."

She gives me a small nod and it breaks my heart.

"Mollie, I didn't want to keep hurting you. I wanted to give you every piece of me, and I didn't feel like…a whole man."

"You know I don't care about your—"

"No." I shake my head. "I'm not talking about my leg." I release my hold on her. "I'm talking about here"—I point to my head—"and here"—I point to my heart, mimicking the actions of a wise old man.

"But I'm the one who made you feel like that. I should have been stronger, told you sooner."

"It wouldn't have mattered. You did what you thought was right. And I couldn't live my life running and wondering. What happened to me…it's part of who I am. And I'm done trying to keep the memories at bay."

Her hand takes mine and she laces our fingers together. "But you're already starting to remember, right?"

"Yes, some. I have so much to tell you about. So

much I was wrong about." I want to share what Jennings told me, but I also don't want to make this all about me. "And I promise to tell you everything, but right now, I just want to talk about us. There is an 'us' right? That's why you're here?"

"Yes." She beams with every feature on her face.

"But, I called and you didn't call me back. Last I heard from you— What?"

She laughs and rolls her eyes. "When I was checking in, they said my carryon was too big and made me check it. I totally forgot I had my phone in there. By the time I decided not to go, I couldn't get any of my luggage back. I had to wait for it to go there and back. And of course, they lost it along the way."

"You still don't have it."

"Nope. They said they're still trying to locate it."

"I'm sorry."

She shrugs like it's not even a big deal.

"Where were you going?"

"Guam."

My eyes widen because I'm kind of impressed. "Wow." I gesture with my head. "Come on. Let's sit down." I lead her by the hand over to the couch and when we sit, I wrap my arm around her shoulders.

"Yeah, I wanted to go where there was a big need for nurses."

My chest tightens at the thought of taking her from something so important. Being someone who has served the people and my country, I understand the need and want she feels.

She must have read my reaction in my expression. "Hey, it was my choice not to go, but someday I'd still like to do it." She puts her hand on my thigh. "Maybe we can do it together."

"I'd love that." I turn my body and wait for her eyes to meet mine. "Because I don't ever want to be apart again."

Her eyes say the same.

"Mollie, I know things are not going to just magically work out, but I believe we can do it. I have some work to do, but I will do it with you by my side."

"I'll be there every step of the way."

My gaze falls to her parted mouth as she speaks the words I need to hear. My heart thrums into a quick staccato and my body reacts, reminding how long it's been since we were together. I cover her mouth with mine, slide my tongue along with hers, tasting her sweet warmth. We spend a few moments reuniting our mouths and hands and bodies. Her moans are needy and it's all I can do not to satiate the longing we both feel and have felt for so long. Slowly, I rein myself in and pull back. "Mollie…"

"If all this is too soon…" she cuts in with an endearing smile.

"No, it's not that. I think it's fairly obvious it's not too soon for me." I'm still trying to slow my breathing and I let out a short laugh. "Hang on a minute." I jump up and run over to my bag that's still by the front door. I rummage through until I find what I need and then return to sit next to her. "I have your Christmas present."

Her eyes light up and she scoots herself up on the couch. "I have one at my place for you too," she says.

I hand her the small square box and she takes it giddily. "Is it a new phone?"

I cock my head and glare. "Not even close."

She rips the paper off and pulls the cardboard lid up and stares for a few seconds. "Logan, it's gorgeous."

I slide from the couch and kneel in front of her, reach in and take the silver charm bracelet from the box. She holds out her wrist so I can affix it. "This isn't to replace the others that jarred my memory. I'm not going to run from my past, Mollie, but I want to start making new memories with the woman I love."

She was watching me put the bracelet on but when I uttered my last words her head slowly rose. Her eyes fill with liquid and she licks her beautiful full lips. "The what?"

"The woman I love. I think I fell in love with you the moment you stepped out of my cousin's hospital room. I know I stumbled and fumbled all through our relationship. I tried to be your friend, your friend with benefits, and your somebody…and the truth is, Mollie, those were all accurate depictions. I want to be your everything and I hope you'll be mine too."

Mollie leans over and wraps her arms around my neck. "You are my everything, Logan. You have been for a long time. I was just waiting for you to see it. Accept it." She places a gentle kiss on my lips. "I love you, Logan. And thank you for the bracelet."

I kiss her dimple, the side of her mouth, her lips. "I love you, Mollie. Thank you…for loving me and making me whole again."

MOLLIE

The sound of laughter blooms through the open windows as Logan and I make our way to the backyard on a gorgeous spring day. I've been to dozens of these Saturday breakfasts, but today feels special because we're doing it out back.

We're greeted with boisterous hellos and I give big hugs to our chef, Bud, and his assistant, Lou. "Are you sure I can't do anything?" I ask as Logan wraps his arms around my waist from behind.

Lou gestures to the long picnic table set up on the patio. "It's all set. We were just waiting for you two love birds."

"Sorry," Logan says. "Mollie wouldn't let me out of bed."

My face flushes with warmth and I elbow Logan,

though he wasn't exactly lying. Since he moved in with me a few months ago, we've spent so much time in that bed it probably has permanent indentations.

Belle runs from the swing set and slips onto the bench right next to me as we all converge on the table. Since Lou joined the crew, she's been adding some unique dishes to their traditional eggs and bacon lineup. Today, it looks like she's made mini frittatas and home-made biscuits, and they smell divine.

Panning around the table, I notice so much change and so many happy faces, joy floods my body. I place my hand on Logan's thigh, feeling so lucky to be here and so proud of him all at once. He no longer talks about his experience coming home as a sacrifice. We both know what a blessing it was, and now his relation-ship with everyone at this table has grown into some-thing beautiful. I catch Ryder eyeing his big brother, and it warms me from the inside out. Though Logan didn't make the cut in the second qualifying round of the competition, Ryder still talks about his brother, the warrior.

"When are we having a sleepover, Mollie?" Belle asks.

Logan and I have been promising her she could spend the night, and she reminds me every time we see her. We wanted to move in together sooner, but he wanted to wait until Frank and the kids were settled into their own house, and the moment that happened, he packed his stuff and showed up at my doorstep. He's been working as a personal trainer at Roger's gym and still helps out with Belle and Colton some.

"How about this weekend? If it's okay with your dad…" I look across at Frank, who smiles and nods.

"Sounds good to me."

"What about me?" Colton says, dragging two pieces of bacon onto his plate.

Ryder steals his bacon and moves it to his own plate. "You can spend the night here if you want."

Colton brightens and grabs more bacon. "Awesome, yeah."

"No playing in my room, runts," Justice says, emerging from the sliding glass door.

"Guess it won't be your room much longer, college boy," Logan says, scooting to make room for his brother.

"You guys gonna miss me?" he says.

"No!" Ryder and Colton say in unison and everyone laughs.

Mason and their father sit at the other end and when my gaze travels that way, Ed stands. "Don't stop eating. I just wanted to say a few words without you all staring at me." He looks across the yard at the beautiful purple rhododendrons. "We lost two great women almost two years ago. They were everything to this family and we almost fell apart."

Uncharacteristically, none of the boys make comments.

"But I know in my heart they'd be proud of all of you." He sits quickly as if the moment might overtake him, but in the still-quiet wake of his words he speaks again. "And I also know they'd be as grateful as I am to Mollie for being a big part of how we got here." Ed looks right at me and I hold his stare, smiling and trying not to turn into a blubbering mess.

Thankfully, conversation continues, taking the spotlight off me, and we all happily gorge on our breakfast feast.

"This frittata is amazing," Gramps says and winks at Lou.

"I second that," I say, adding to her blush.

"Yeah, it's pretty dope," Justice says.

"Now stop, all of you. I'm just happy to be a part of this tradition. Thankful. Blessed, actually. Grateful, giddy—"

Just then Gramps leans over and plants a kiss on her cheek.

"Oh my," Lou says.

"So that's the trick," Logan whispers to me.

As the kids clear the table—a job Ed assigned them a few weeks back—I head to a lounge chair and enjoy the warmth of the sun on my skin, basking in not just the sun but the love of this great big family I somehow fell into.

I close my eyes and keep them that way even though I feel the weight of a body take up space on the edge of my lounger. His hand takes my wrist and he fingers the bracelet he bought me two Christmases ago when we found our way back to each other.

I feel his lips on mine and I open my eyes. Logan laces our fingers together and with his other hand touches the bracelet. "I think we need to add some more charms on here," he says with a gleam in his gorgeous eyes.

"I think you need to stop buying me presents."

"That's a tough request, but I'll try."

I shake my head and close my eyes again, feeling more relaxed than I ever have.

"After this one, though."

Confused, I pop my eyes open and see him holding a small square box. "What have you done, Logan?"

"It's not what I've done; it's what you've done. I don't know what I ever did to deserve you. First, you were my guardian angel, by my side at my lowest point in life. Then, you jumped into this crazy situation with me…" He smiles and I can't help but mirror it. "Smile bigger," he says, reaching his hand to my cheek. His thumb rubs one side as if I'm a magic lamp and my grin grows wider. "There is it." He breathes out what looks like a sigh of relief and then leans forward and kisses my dimple. "I think I decided this is my good luck charm," he whispers in my ear.

"What do you need luck for?"

"This." He pulls back and opens the box, revealing a crystal clear, princess cut diamond set in white gold.

I gasp and freeze, staring at the ring while I get my bearings. Slowly my gaze pans up to meet his. There's nothing but pure love in his eyes, as if he has no doubt about my answer. That's because he knows me better than anyone has ever known me.

"I could have taken you to some restaurant and hid this at the bottom of a champagne glass…but—"

I quickly lean forward and stop his words with my lips. "I wouldn't want it any other way. It's perfect. And the ring…it's, my God, it's gorgeous."

"It was my mother's."

My breath hitches and I wonder how much more my heart can take. I just breathe at this revelation, unable to find words.

He chuckles and takes the ring from its home. "An official response would probably be good here."

"Oh, yes. Yes!" I hold my hand out to him, noticing a slight tremble. My heart is racing but something pulls my gaze over his shoulder. Everyone is standing by the back door, staring at us with huge silly grins, and as soon as he slips the ring on my finger, they erupt into a ruckus of whoops and congratulations.

Logan and I embrace and I smile at them over his shoulder, a tear slipping down my cheek.

We stand and they all shuffle over in a clump of excitement, blurry faces attached to bodies with grabby arms, hugging and patting us.

"Guess you better get used to it," Logan says with a smile. "This is life in the Bridges family."

"I can't wait."

ABOUT THE AUTHOR

Lia Fairchild writes romance and women's fiction. Fans of her books praise her endearing, real characters that come to life in stories that will touch your heart.

Fairchild is addicted to the warmth of Southern California and holds a bachelor's degree in journalism and a multiple-subject teaching credential. She is a wife and mother of two.